THE DOGS OF PARADISE

THE DOGS OF PARADISE

ABEL POSSE

Translated from the Spanish by

MARGARET SAYERS PEDEN

ATHENEUM
New York 1989

•

Copyright © 1987 by Abel Posse

English translation copyright © 1989 by Macmillan Publishing Company, a division of Macmillan, Inc.

Atheneum
Macmillan Publishing Company
866 Third Avenue, New York, NY 10022

Library of Congress Cataloging-in-Publication Data
Posse, Abel.
    {Perros del paraíso. English}
    The dogs of paradise / Abel Posse ; translated from the Spanish by
Margaret Sayers Peden.
      p. cm.
    Translation of: Los perros del paraíso.
    ISBN 0-689-12091-5
    I. Title.
  PQ7798.26.O78P4713   1989
863—dc20   89-35292   CIP

10 9 8 7 6 5 4 3 2 1

Printed in the United States of America
Designed by Diane Stevenson SNAP·HAUS GRAPHICS

In memory of my son Ivan, with gratitude for having, with his joy, and before his leaving, given me the title of this work.

PRINCIPAL HISTORICAL CHARACTERS

Colón, Cristóbal, Cristoforo Colombo, Christovao, de Coloumb: Christopher Columbus (1451-1506)

Fernando: Ferdinand the Catholic (1479-1516), as Ferdinand V, King of Sicily and Naples; King of Aragón; with Isabella, the Catholic Sovereigns of Castile and León

Isabel Trastamara: Isabella the Catholic (1451-1504), Queen of Castile and León

Enrique IV: Henry IV the Impotent (1454-1474), King of Castile and León

Juan II: John II (1458-1479), King of Aragón, father of Ferdinand the Catholic

Juana la Beltraneja: Joanna (1462-1530), daughter of John II and Joanna of Portugal. Her parentage was often attributed to Beltrán de la Cueva.

Juana la Loca: Joanna the Mad (1479-1555), Spanish queen of Castile and León, daughter of Ferdinand II and Isabella I. Married to Philip I (the Handsome)

Tomás de Torquemada: Torquemada (1420-1498), Inquisitor General of Castile and Aragón

Rodrigo de Borja: Pope Alexander VI (1431?-1503), a Spaniard, he was called Borgia in Italian

*Beyond the tropic of Capricorn there is a habitable
land that is the highest and noblest place in the
world; it is the Earthly Paradise.*
—Pierre d'Ailly, Imago Mundi

*This is the Earthly Paradise, where no one may
enter except by divine will.*
—Letter from the admiral to the Catholic kings

*This is Paradise. Truly. These peoples love
their neighbor as they love themselves. I believe
what wise men and theological saints believed and
do believe, that these lands are those of the
Earthly Paradise.*
—Letter from Columbus to Pope Alexander VI

*He was sent in search of gold and daemons, and
he comes to us with angels' feathers!*
—Ferdinand of Aragón

*We hold as truth that the admiral reached the
center of the Earthly Paradise on August 4,
1498.*
—J. W. Kilkenny

I

air

CHRONOLOGY

1 4 6 1

Origins of the modern West: on the 12th of June, Isabel of Castile exposes the impotence of King Enrique IV, her half brother. Juana, La Beltraneja, probable daughter of Beltrán de la Cueva.

1 4 6 2

Cristóbal Colón steals an alphabet from the parish in Genoa. States he is to be a poet. Beatings; threats. "Nothing will save you from your fate as wool carder or tailor."

1 4 6 8

Belated, ambiguous, and purposeful circumcision of Cristóbal Colón.

2-House

Failure of Inca-Aztec negotiations in Tlatelolco. Decision against forming a fleet to invade the "cold lands of the Orient." Hot-air balloons of the Incas. Pampa of Nazca-Düsseldorf.

1 4 6 9

Landsknecht Ulrich Nietz, a German mercenary accused of bestiality for kissing a horse, arrives in Genoa from Turin. Land Wo die Zitronen blühen. Angst and the Judeo-Christian swindle. "God is dead."

1 4 6 9

In a climate of delicious adolescent lust, on November 18, Isabel and Fernando's concubinage recognized by the Church. Ever-loyal SS. The empire is born on which the sun will never set.

*T*HE *W O R L D* was gasping for breath, without air for life. Abuse of agony; satiety of death. All pendulums recalled being-toward-death. In Rothenburg, Tübingen, Avila, Urbino, Bordeaux, Paris, and Segovia.

Life was gasping for space. The Hebrew God, constipated with Guilt, had finally crushed his legion of fervent bipeds.

Flagellants lashed themselves. Then added brine to the wounds. Even athletes dreamed only of being nailed to a cross and bleeding slowly so they might die in holiness.

The Vale of tears at its apogee. *Totentanz:* a frenzied thread of young people, hand in hand, stringing tombs together. Black tights painted with skeletons. White lead for whitening skulls. And yet an air of nostalgia for life curled through the dancing line. A hint of desire. Smiles beneath black tulle; winks. A pelvic waggle corrupting the rhythm of the muted drums of the *Danse Macabre.*

Like an air, an aura, an eros. Like a warm breeze already blowing from the Caribbean.

It was not rare to see the guilt-ridden, exhausted from the dance, embraced between the flying buttresses of the church, or lying alongside tombs in the cemetery. Like rabid dogs, impenitent, bodies fled the robes of the Nazarenes and skulls of chalk.

It was an air. A zephyr at dusk perturbing young seminary students. A heavy sweet-and-bitter aroma, as if of a distant sea, a sleeping woman in the summer clouds.

But it was in Italy where the signs of that alarming air were most visible. Painting a Virgin commissioned by the friars of San Gerolamo, Pollaiuolo's brush slipped into a kind of hallucination of color, desire, and form, until upon the canvas appeared—magnificent! —Simonetta Vespucci, La Bella, her breasts exposed to that air. The brush—with guilt—tried to define the viper of evil, but the serpent coiled playfully around La Bella's neck until it was biting its own tail, transformed into a graceful necklace.

This was not a unique occurrence. In the second fortnight of April 1478, the young painter Sandro Botticelli found the space of his painting filled with delectable, half-naked adolescent girls dancing in the homage to the flowering of spring. The mustached nuns of the Sacred Frustration feared the end, and muttered in protest, crossing themselves: *Non c'é piú religione.*

A wild cat leaped from the goblet containing the host in the old gothic cathedral. It was clear.

The gasping of the Occident was becoming a death rattle. The powerful, alarmed, consulted among themselves. Prompt decisions were required.

The pressure from that caldron of mortality and chained desires could not find release in the south: the Muslims, men of a god as strong and broad as a scimitar, occupied all the Maghreb and the Al-Andalus of the merry kingdoms.

Nor could they spread beyond the boundaries of the primitive Christianity of Muscovy.

The Church had failed in its intent. By the score, missionaries were returning from Islam and Tartary with testicles and tongue, as desiccated as dried apricots, in a little pouch around their neck. Others, humiliated, lifted their much-traveled cassocks to the pope and showed him buttocks horribly embossed with verses from the Koran, or warnings of this tenor: "Allah is great. We, too, cultivate Guilt."

The fall of Constantinople into the hands of the Turks had been a decisive blow. Pope Sixtus IV announced it somberly to the princes of the Occident: "The Christian, Occidental world is threatened by a thick curtain of scimitars extending from the Caucasus to the south of our beloved Spain."

The multinationals were suffocating, reduced to intercity commerce. They protested with irate impatience.

The Berardis; Ibarras; Van der Dine, the dynamic Antwerp executive; the Negris; Cattaneos; Spinolas; the Buddenbrooks of Lübeck; the arms merchants of the Hanseatic League; Catalan weavers led by Puig—all rebelled against the impasse. They felt capable of much greater things. They accused sailors of cowardice, astronomers of ineptitude, kings of being sordid and slothful intriguers. Feudal nobility was reviled. "We want space! Precious woods! Markets! Spices and ivory from the Orient! Enough of things Turkish in Mare Nostrum!"

The Occident, gasping for breath, longed for its dead sun, its lost pulse, the buried fiesta. It groped in the darkness of the convent catacombs for the statue of the Greek goddess (which in fact someone had thrown into the sea). Empty men, with barely a shadow, sought their stature.

ABEL POSSE

The Occident, ancient Phoenix, gathered twigs of the azedarach tree for the bonfire of its last renascence.

Angels and supermen were needed. The sect of the seekers of Paradise, inexorably, was born.

•

June siesta. An air of invisible flames dissolving the mountains of Castile. Explosion of rocks split by the blast of the sun. A shepherd dozes among the brambles, eyes half closed like a lizard's. Sparrows sit like stones in the tree branches; they know that if they try to reach water they will drop to the ground, fried to a crisp.

And Isabel Trastamara:

"Come on, come on, this is a good time."

Childish mousescurrying in the sleeping Alcázar of Madrid. The guards, barefoot and barely awake, are playing cards in the shadow of the towers. They throw pails of water to settle the burning dust. They doze, dangling from their halberds.

La Beltraneja, who at five already had spies everywhere, understands that something important is afoot, something hostile. Her child-aunt, her enemy, Isabel Trastamara. The small Juana resists being put off, and tenaciously sticks with the group. She suffers the oppressive heat in royal trappings: a heavy green stole she found in a coffer; a cone-shaped headdress, like a fairy godmother's, with tulle drapery that falls to her cork-soled shoes, the tall cork clogs she stole from the boudoir of her frivolous mother, always aping the latest vogue. She yells at Isabel:

8

"I am *so* going. Don't get your hopes up. I'm not going to let you out of my sight." She lisps in her rage.

Isabel had summoned eight counts and hidalgos (the oldest is ten). But she could not keep the gathering secret. She is dressed in a torso-length top that does not (to the horror of ladies-in-waiting and nuns in her service) hide the tight panties edged with lace made by the Trinitarian nuns of St. Joseph of the Eternal Anxiety. A "baby doll," in fact, in her famous *jitoniscos*. Hair pulled into a ponytail. Freckled, blond, provocative.

Isabel often stands with legs slightly apart and head thrown back, and runs her hands through her hair. She likes to stick out her perfect bottom. A cause for the libertine court poet Álvarez Gato's having written in his secret book:

> *Her little ass* . . . . *culito*
> *like a cheese* . . . . *.quesito*
> *her little tits* . . . . *tetitas*
> *like oranges* . . . . *naranjitas*

The nuns would scold:

"Child! Child! Is that any way for a princess to walk?"

Now Isabel is in the lead. She carries a long smooth reed, one of the kind that grows beside the frog pond.

They thread through stone corridors. Everything in shadow. Everyone in Castile knows that light engenders heat.

They pad through the palace dining hall still smelling of the garlic of last night's lamb. Some take advantage of the mosaic tile to lie down and suck in the coolness. Others turn somersaults.

"Sssssh!" orders Isabel. And La Beltraneja:

"Who do you think you are to shush me! I am the princess!"

They pass before a modest panoply. More heritage than substance; the sword of the grandfather-king, crossbows with frayed strings, pale excuses for muskets. Moth-eaten heads of wild boar hunted more to sweeten the pot than imitate Burgundian or British niceties.

The throne: a chair of wood and tooled leather made sturdier, or easier, with the skin of an Ethiopian tiger. King Juan had used it until his death to prevail during after-dinner conversations. There he dreamed of extending Castile, crossing seas, snuffing out the faith of the merry Moorish kingdoms to the south.

These were the last remnants of an impoverished Spain, with a court where bones that remained after the banquet were stripped for the hash of the following noon, and wine left in the cups was collected for the jug of the second seating. A court that rejoiced when chicken was served. In those days, kings knew the art of estimating a year's crop with a simple glance at the olive grove or flock.

Now Enrique IV, the Impotent, had launched the kingdom into the luxury of inflation. The money exchange went from five to one hundred and fifty. Riches of jewels and stuffs, more than patrimony.

Beltrán de la Cueva, the favorite, wears sandals embroidered with precious stones and spangles like a stylish toreador.

Compared to him the king is a ragamuffin. He does not hide his admiration for his queen's lover. A cuckold courteous in the extreme, he orders the construction of a monastery to commemorate the place where Beltrán defeated other brazen pretenders.

Mournful pursuit of pleasure in that court of phantoms, from time immemorial menaced by madness. With princes who struggled against satanic monsters that emerged from mirrors; ghosts that left burns in Bible covers, blazoning the road to Hell; nuns who bled gently through the feasting, pierced by thorns from the crown of Christ; mystical ladies who levitated at dawn, until their maidservants seized their ankles and pulled them back to gravity and the weight of reality.

More than once the tiny Isabel had spied on the king, her impotent (relatively speaking) half brother, who was sinking—along with all the kingdom—into a marasmus of morbid melancholy. Isabel, peering through the skylight: Enrique (who was twenty-six years older than she) sprawled in his chair, his djellaba—a Moorish robe—stained with soup, his ever-present ruby and silver salver piled with the wild boar cracklings he accompanied with great swilling of cool water (he detested wine). The court whores with their incongruous voices and laughter, air upon air, capering like drunken nursemaids around a deaf and wealthy invalid. Two or three of them—like cats—climbing the large, lolling frame of the king, toying with his dispassionate sex. In one corner of the salon the cardinal and the notary reading embassy reports. They paused from time to time to cough, lungs congested with stinking smoke from the hairy Percheron hooves with which Enrique fed his fire (in summer the penetrating ungual odor of burned hoof was replaced with great trays of manure from the kennels and stables). The stench that enchants the king is so strong that the Marqués de Villena, at the suggestion of his enemy, the sophisticated Beltrán de la Cueva, always carries a sprig of fresh sweet basil in his pocket to crush and inhale deeply for relief.

Every time Isabel climbs down from the transom beam she is enraged. Revulsion for that brother in whom she senses the death of an epoch. She does not know why, but she runs until she reaches the patio of the Alcázar, out of breath. She hears the voice of her poor mother: "Never submit to madness. That is the worst, the only, abyss. Remember your father, your grandfathers. . . . Have no dialogue with the Devil; do not listen to him. Look at Enrique, he lives in fear of infernal beasts, a boar in heavy fog that appears beneath his bed, deformed wraiths he sees still blazing with hellfire, come to predict his miserable death. . . . Concentrate on what is real. Never listen to theologians. Celebrate your body. Surround yourself with animals and soldiers. Resist the temptation to talk to yourself. Despise peace! Look what peace is: a vacuum only demons will fill. Yes, you must die . . . die of life."

•

Behind the bossy Isabel, the children trooped to the audience hall. They met the chattering, fawning court prostitutes, irreverently escaping. Legs whitened with plaster dust, according to the mode. Faces black or violet, golden eyelids. Great Flemish swordsman's hats with yellow, blue, green plumes. They are on their way to the mule stables; they like to gallop wildly through the fields, scattering hens and unfortunate laborers.

Penumbra. A melancholic amanuensis contemplating the book of audiences. Apparently, none. But in one corner of the eternal return of such ceremonies, almost invisible, General Queipo de Llano—high boots with a high polish and breeches with razor-sharp creases—heads a committee of academics and magistrates (Díaz Plaja? Dr. Derisi? Battistesa? D'Ors?). They will ask the king for patronage and funds for the 1940 Congress of Hispanic Culture.

Penumbrous medieval Spain, smelling of past masses, of the last candle extinguished by the cough of a consumptive sacristan.

At last Isabel, the young counts, and the beleaguered Beltraneja burst into the corridor to the bedchamber of Enrique IV. There they find, according to plan, the venal *valet de chambre, don* Gregorio, who has distracted the guard.

An unforeseen obstacle (the old man babbles): a lion, grandson to King Juan's, is stretched across the threshold. With half-closed eyes he monitors the rhythmic royal rumbles. Eyes of boredom, not sleep. Full stomach, impervious to demogogy, how to deal with him? How to negotiate? There is about him the strong smell of a wild beast that has accepted peace but not subjection (only three years before he had devoured a Jew-turned-Catholic bishop, a *converso*).

La Beltraneja jeers. The old man attempts a gesture of authority, a tentative shove on the haunches that the beast ignores. Immovable yawn.

Then Isabel marches forward and yells:

"Go 'way!"

To no avail. She administers a determined punch to the nose. Infuriated, she digs her fingers in his mane and bites his ear. After a brief, menacing silence, the lion yields to the determination, not the puny strength, of the girl. He bares his eyeteeth, shakes his great head, and just as he is about to roar, receives an energetic kick in the chops. He opts to get up and lie beneath the window.

When the door is opened, *don* Gregorio, lacking sufficient bloodlines to see a monarch naked, is ordered to retire; La Beltraneja is the first to enter.

Isabel, wielding her reed, hooks the hem of the sleeping king's nightshirt, and works it up as far as the chest. The snoring resumes in the rhythms of one who sleeps.

Weak, white, hairy legs. Higher, the uncertain, shadowy zone. Eyes strained to glimpse the undefined. Brittle parchment came to mind. Or the peaches and apricots travelers dry in the sun for their journeys; or the immemorial, fragile sandal of the Roman legionnaire vanquished at the gates of Samarkand. (And again it is appropriate to quote the resentful Álvarez Gato:

> *. . . and your sealess mollusk phallacy*
> *unseen in mossy sea shadow . . .)*

Young Beltraneja pales. Isabel upholds her rod like a scepter. The young counts observe and judge.

It was true: not the slightest sign of turgescent life. In fact, an absence of any human sap. Beatriz de Bobadilla says she doesn't know why, but she is reminded of the stones of Soria. Juan de Vivero says no, it's more like the seashells that the Bay of Biscay returns as empty houses in its rolling waves. Isabel, defiant, forces the poor Beltraneja to look; she trembles and blurts out:

"I shall be queen. I shall! I *shall*! I hate you," and runs away, stumbling and tripping perilously in the too-large clogs.

And Isabel, smug, once they have returned:

"You have seen it. She cannot be his daughter. I shall be queen!"

The battle is joined between illegal legitimacy and ambition.

•

"He's blond and strong as an angel," Susana Fontanarrosa, his mother, always said. The boy had rejected the somber trade of tailoring. Neither did he want to be a carder, or a cheesemaker, or a tavernkeeper. The sensible, realistic possibilities.

Savage gods of the sea. To him they were alive. He believed, immodestly, that they had spoken to him in the harsh voice of winter, or, in that whisper only the initiate understands, in the soft summer dusk.

Now he is running along the beach, parallel to the surf. He breathes in the soft breeze of the moonlit night. He is nearly naked, his feet sheathed—as always, to protect his secret—in hose knitted by his mamma. He maintains the steady pace of the exalted; you might think him a running lama, one of those seen only in high Tibetan plateaus. He has no objective but to calm his anxiety, expend his energy, tame his wild blood.

Now he has passed the Torre del Mar. He knew that his Uncle Gianni, the guard, would communicate his where-abouts to his cousins, that envious pack of cheesemakers and tailors who already suspected in him the subversive presence of the mutant, the poet.

He ran the two leagues of the arc of the beach, his feet irritated by small shells and coarse sand. He maintained the tumtum-tumtum automatism of an aerobic workout. He ran higher up the shoal covered with colonies of mussels and from there dived into the surf with the serene purpose of an illuminato. He swam out to sea. He rolled onto his back and, once again demonstrating his abnormal buoyancy, let the tide carry him headfirst toward the shore until he ran aground on the sand. He lay there. Fascinated by the space of the cosmos. His eyes open and staring like those of the hake he had seen that morning in the market in Genoa.

Then, as before, he heard the scraping of the gentle waves the sands and tiny shells absorb. The last wave that collapses on itself and froths into foam the earth drinks.

The voice of the sea was whispering in verse. It was calling him. Beyond any doubt, it scanned:

"Co-o-lón.

"Co-o-o-lón."

It was not calling in Italian: Co-lom-bó. No. It clearly said, *in Spanish*: "Co-o-o-lón." the "lón" quick and abrupt—you might say, authoritative. The way the last word threatened by a sneeze is pronounced.

He felt that the dawn—the rosy-fingered one—was opening its way into night with the same caution Ariadne must have shown as she entered the Minotaur's lair.

The water was growing cold. In the distance he saw the still phosphorescent shirts of the gang of cousins approaching the beach along the shoal to the south.

He must flee their necessary and clumsy cruelty. He ran, forgetting the burning of mistreated feet. Higher. He gained the bastion of Genoa through cobbled alleyways beginning to stir to the sounds of milksellers and fishermen.

He understood he was trapped: a group led by Santiago Bavarello, married to his sister Blanquita, closed off the end of the narrow cul-de-sac of Vico de L'Olivella.

He gained nothing by beating on the heavy, bolted doors. The only response from the darkness of the stable was a whinny from the white colt.

He looked up toward the wooden balconies with their pots of geraniums and met the unwavering gaze of Susana Fontanarrosa, who was, with the first pink of dawn, already at her loom.

She understood that the rite that was about to take place was an essential test born of the hatred and resentment felt by the mediocre, and that it served to measure, fortify, and temper the virtue of the great.

She heard the heavy thuds of punches. Grunts of breath forced from the lungs. He lay flung against the heavy doors, bleeding from the nose. They worked over his sides and solar plexus until he was without breath. The boy already knew that fear as well as stored-up resentment tends to lend strength to the human arm. They beat him in silence. They sought the centers of pain almost professionally, as cold as torturers.

His brother-in-law, Bavarello, blind with rage, emerged from the depths of a tack room wearing a single hobnailed boot, one of a pair the family used long ago to climb the mountains of Quinto in search of she-goats in heat.

Two of them held him on his feet, legs spread. Two stout kicks to the crotch by Bavarello. A deep scream. The relief of unconsciousness, the blessing of the tortured.

They left him lying on the ground, and went off to breakfasts steaming on the fires of home.

They had taken revenge, once again; this time because he had ruined last Sunday's raviolifest by announcing his intention not to be a carder.

"I will be a sailor," he had said, without arrogance. But it was as if he had emptied a bag of spiders onto the placid, unsullied Sunday tablecloth.

The women on the balconies wept for him. His sister, his cousins, a youthful aunt. All platonic female accessories the Lustful One possessed metaphysically—together, separately, or taken apart in his imagination and recomposed, eliminating defects and harmonizing charms, in his laborious solipsistic love.

The whimpering women all looked toward Susana Fontanarrosa, but she, a woman of great breeding, kept her eyes on her weaving. She merely murmured between clenched teeth:

"It won't do them any good. He is of the race of giants. No one, no thing, can stop him."

•

Landsknecht Ulrich Nietz arrived in the Vico de l'Olivella, looking for a fountain where he could replenish his canteen.

Deserter from wars lost by fervent leaders. Wearied by the affliction of abstract thought and its perilous abysses. Threatened by theological reasoning and the tyrannies of Judeo-Christian monotheism with its bands of armed predicators.

Making his way southward, he had reached, finally, the sunny lands where the lemon tree blooms.

He longed to lie down in the vineyards, to steal pears, to sleep in the ruins of antiquity where his shadow would be enlivened with dancing. Afternoons of fawns but in bodies of Apollos.

He arrived with the aspect of a soldier who has survived fiery battles and pursuit by Vandals. He created an uproar as he passed by benches of fishermen. Tailors' scissors clanged like bells to announce a dangerous presence to the guild.

Nietz's mustaches were stiff as horsehair, inflexible; bristles of a wild boar whose mate had been slain in an infamous hunt. He had the eyes of a caged tiger; glints of yellow and chestnut striation. He reeked of the sweat of days without shelter, of military leather and rusted weapons abandoned to the rain.

He climbed toward the alley, to the sound of metal-reinforced boots and shabby scabbards. No one could have imagined that he had come from the duchy of Turin, pursued by the fearsome Guard of Savoy, accused of bestiality after having been found, *in fraganti*, embracing a horse, nuzzling its muzzle, sobbing, in the middle of the Piazza San Carlo.

He was fleeing a tomb of fog. Seeking the possibility of a life that would not transform him into a shadow of himself.

In Bern, that odious city of clockmakers, he had dared say that "man is a thing to be surmounted." Before the dawn, he was brutally beaten.

(Since that experience he jealously guarded a terrible secret that would be revealed only to the founders of an empire.)

Some misguided men like Giorgio Thibon thought that
he had come south in search of a post in the Vatican Guard.
But he had other, higher, ambitions. For the moment, he
was simply pretending to be as idle and brutal as his ancestors, who had galloped naked through the icy forests of
Germania, fleeing from public order and collective education.

"The sea air will sting my lungs, the burning sun
will bronze my skin." This was his most serious desertion, the one that no military tribunal of the epoch could
pardon.

The fact is that he did not find his fountain. He found a
blond youth lying unconscious in the *cortile*.

He moistened his temples and lips. He said, to console
him, in his atrocious German Italian:

"Courage, boy. What does not kill you more strong will
make you. . . ."

After delivering this grim teaching, he had to take to
his heels, because the small boys who had been chasing him
from the port were almost upon him. They were yelling.
They had already thrown the first stones. (In that time
Germans were still the Barbarians, filthy and lazy. As barbaric as Bulgarians or Gypsies.)

Young Cristoforo would remember those Teutonic mustaches. His vinegar water seemed sweet.

•

And the mast of the *Santa María*? It was then the trunk
of a great Pyrenean cedar rising from the sheer coast of
Santander.

During a January storm a lightning bolt had scorched its tip, just where the crow's nest would fit (at the end of the long gallop, the place Rodrigo de Triana would clutch as he cried, Land! Land!—believing he would be the one to collect the thousand maravedís the cunning Colón would swallow up for himself, saying he had already seen it as early as the previous evening).

The cedar's life had not been easy, facing the wild winds of the Bay of Biscay. It had grown on that slope of wolves' lairs, more stone than humus, since it was a slip of a tree, clinging to the cliff with roots like tiger claws.

Its happiness was the April breeze. When the wind stops whistling and changes quarter. Then it blows from the land, bringing a balmy aroma of horse dung, lowing from the stables, and voices of peasants calling to each other at dusk.

It was spotted from the sea by Galician fishermen (no human had ever been near it). They realized that the trunk was born to be a mainmast. It took a morning to reach it and an hour to fell it.

In the afternoon they stripped its branches. By nightfall it was stowed on deck, a flawless mast free of treacherous knots.

They sold it in the shipyards of La Coruña. There it was selected by the patron and builder of the *Gallega*, the *María Galante* that Colón would revirginize with the name of *Santa María*.

•

The childhood of the chosen one had passed harmoniously there in Genoa. Genoa of shopkeepers. Stoutly protected from culture and warlike duchies by its necklace of rugged mountains. Accustomed only to the sound of looms, discreet dealings in bills of exchange, the secure joys of commerce.

Delivered from Michelangelos and Dantes, a seamless ignorance favored community order and municipal progress. A free and easy Catholicism, tolerant of both converted *marrano* (filthy Jew swine though they were) and Moor, kept its youth safe from the mysticism and theology so injurious to the practical and concrete. They kept the Vatican at bay with semiannual shipments of serge for cassocks at an unrivaled price of two gold sequins.

Genoa: its three rows of mountains set like shark's teeth protected it from the century, from that time of profound mutations. By sea, they could not prevent raids by Turkish or Venetian ships. But if some rowboat managed to approach the steep cliffs, its crew met the ferocity of armed shop clerks. (There is no defense more cruel, or excessive, than that of one who believes himself weak, or just . . . or both.) Stray dogs loped down the beach to finish off the mangled bodies of such unwary pirates.

The childhood years of Cristoforo were the key to his strength. No plague, no victorious or imperial *duces*. The boy grew up in the bosom of apathetic family tradition and parochial—it would be inappropriate to speak of education—instruction.

Tenderly, he eased into the schema of his epoch's errors and terrors. Sweetly, it prepared him for dark and useful submission.

The priest, Father Frisson, after the *bagna cauda* or heavy *pesto* of a rainy, wintry midday meal, would launch into descriptions of the fire-eating dragons at the Gates of Hell, the incessant, unending, eternal tortures of the damned, or attempt a convincing depiction of the kindly nature of Christ, like someone boasting of a powerful, distant uncle, twice removed.

He taught the harsh piety of the century: kill the Moor, draw and quarter him, but never forget him in Sunday prayer (even prepare him a flameless niche in the limbo of the infidels).

But it should not be forgotten that it was the priest Frisson who infected Cristoforo with passion, pain, and nostalgia for Paradise. One rainy Friday (in the depths of winter) following a lunch accompanied by an entire bottle of Lacrimae Christi, the priest, before his astounded students, began to describe beaches of the whitest sand, palm trees rustling in soft breezes, the midday sun in a sky blue as porcelain, coconut milk and fruit of unimagined sweetness, naked bodies in clear, salty water, soft music. Bright colored birds. Warbling. Gentle wild beasts. The hummingbird sucking from the rose. A world of angels, perfect beings liberated from time. *That* is Paradise! And we were expelled from it by Adam and the Jews! Better now to die; better to forsake this vile, mournful flesh, the time we live in. Paradise, my boys, is supreme! The only thing worth living for.

The emotional priest, lachrymose. Profound sorrow and despair. Surely he had constructed that vision of Paradise from the illustrations in those depraved books—alleged travel chronicles—already being published in Venice, using a new apparatus called the printing press.

The boys went around in a daze. Cristoforo fell asleep weeping. He realized that mankind had been dealt a grave blow. Having had everything, we had lost everything. We had been deprived of true life!

•

A house dominated by white: fleece, sheepskins on all the chairs, woolen cloth, jugs of milk for making cheese, clouds of flour stirred up by the baker uncles. Susana Fontanarrosa, his mother, forever weaving white spinnings.

The fleece emerged from the carder warm, airy, more sugar than snow. Cristoforo chased after the tufts, puffing, lifting them high in the air.

Saturdays bright and early, at seven, his father, Domenico, began singing and drinking the wine of *le cinque terre*. Cheerful, by eight he ate (meat). By nine he was bellowing, with peasant jocundity:

> *No plague today! No plague today!*
> *Long live life!*
> *Death's far away!*
> *Death's far away!*

Then he would begin singing highly erotic songs like "Il Pellegrino," and Susana Fontanarrosa would place the boy in his bed of white sheep's wool and close the shutters facing the street.

Sound of an overturned glass. Laughter. Then a ponderous silence. Then more wine. Domenico singing alone. Giv-

ing praise to God. For the third time, counting his fort-
nightly wages.

Sometimes the boy spied from his white coverlet and
saw everything: his mother sweating, with tufts of sheep's
wool stuck to her body. Domenico, rosy-fleshed, like the
enormous turkey his grandmother plucked every Christmas.

They copulated with straightforward peasant resolution.
They were sustained in their feudal-Catholic order. They
slept, pleasured, serenely snoring.

They were liberal, proud of their mediocrity, indifferent
to the passions they glimpsed at the extremes of shame or
grandeur. They feared only one thing: a son better than they.
Poet, mystic, *condottiere.* The glory of warriors to them seemed
ephemeral; culture, threatening. To say nothing of heroes,
discoverers, or such.

The Colombos were prudently Catholic. They went to
mass on Sundays, ostentatiously, obedient, with the rather
constructive skepticism of the *petite bourgeoisie* before the
All-Powerful.

They were also known to have Hebrew blood. In the
tailors' branch, they could boast here and there of a hooked
nose, of a pointed ear or two.

At times they ate fowl they ostensibly bled in the alley;
this was for the benefit of the Berardis, managers of the house
of Spinola, the great multinational firm.

More than Genoese, they felt Italian. More than
Catholic, children of the most powerful God (they knew
that the most ruthless slaughter resulted from antagonist
gods).

They were skeptical, eclectic, syncretic, astute. They
sailed the seas of opportunistic polytheism.

•

At nine the boy gave them their first great disappointment. Showed his caste. It was after mass: a theophagist receiving communion with eyes half closed with devotion, like all the rest.

Then when the sacristan was not looking, Cristoforo stole the alphabet and the box containing the models of the letters. The letters of the alphabet were spelled out on two tablets that a designated priest kept under close guard, conscious of the dangers. (Only one or two children in each patrician family could delve into the four calculations, and the risky business of reading.)

For three nights, by candlelight, Cristoforo gagged on those dark, ubiquitous, dancing little insects. Forbidden grapes from the Tree of Knowledge. It was on the fourth—memorable—night that he composed his first word: *ROMA*. It seemed like witchcraft when he discovered its anagram: *AMOR*. Love. He was fascinated. The following week he was able to decipher the priest's precept: "The knife for the enemy of tolerance and faith in Christ our Lord."

He was discovered. They put a yellow hat on his head and he was spat on by his bootlicking schoolmates. He was given thirty blows of the ruler on the soles of his feet. He got off easy because no one could believe that he had learned to read or that he had made a perfect copy of the two strictly forbidden tablets.

He carefully hid the secret of his initiation.

•

Sometimes strange men, in oilskin boots and aprons flecked with bits of algae and minute shells, came down the alleyway of La Olica.

They smelled of salt, of the port, of crushed crustaceans. They seemed forever wet, even when it was not raining.

They were the men of the sea. They carried baskets of mechanical toys: sea urchins, spider crabs, crayfish, and lobsters they prodded until they slowly rotated their copper antennae.

From afar, the boy stared at those monsters, fearsome, but not repulsive like spiders, centipedes, and other land creepers.

The men of the sea spoke in loud voices. Laughed boisterously. The tailors, distrustful, leaned over the railings. They observed with rancor that the women, with implicit complicity, tolerated the heavy-handed banter laden with deliberate allusions to sizes and shapes as the blenny were being weighed or the redness of a hake's gills checked.

From time to time there was the sound of a solid smack on the buttocks, followed by a frenzied clicking of scissors: the tailors pretending to be busily at work.

They always offered them wine. It did not matter that it was not the best; it was obvious that salt had parched their throats.

They told tales of storms, unknown constellations, ships adrift without a crew, but with the running lights still blazing.

They told them obscenely. They gave kilos of smelt and small shellfish to poor widows, and to the cripples who followed them like sea gulls in the wake of a galley. They had other codes. It was clear. They lied massively: they told of roast meat eaten on the back of Saint Brendan's whale, stories of arms lost in encounters with the giant Octopus and murderous Killer Whale.

One, in Cristoforo's presence, told how the Maelstrom had dragged him down to the final abyss; he had lost consciousness, but he was saved when he was washed ashore on the beach of Bristol, and suckled by a freckled country lass.

Cristoforo stared at him in awe. The man of the sea reached out and stroked the blond boy's cheek. The caress was like a rasp. The man's fingers were tanned, cracked hide, crusted with salt. Dry lips. A few yellowed teeth the color of a narwhal tusk.

The boys followed the men, who now had the tailors' and carders' money, back to port. They were singing, and drinking hand over fist. Drunk, they passed out on the corpulent Syrian prostitutes: fat, lazy, polychrome. Flesh spilling over the opulence of cheap velvet. But then Cristoforo had to drop down from the high window, because there came lame Staffolani wielding the cudgel of municipal morality.

From that moment the boy knew that the sea was a different universe. He thought of it as a dyspeptic, wrathful, amoral god that from time to time rose up like Rizzo, the chief of the Palazzo Guard, when his daughter Ninfetta ran off to the mountains with the sacristan. The sea was roaring in the distance, and Susana Fontanarrosa adjusted the shutters. In the afternoon, the children of the cheesemakers and weavers were bundled up and led down to observe the awesome fury.

They watched the battering from the hill. An opaque, ever-renewed clamor. Saline seafoam scattered by the wind like the slaver of an honest man maddened in his chains. The sea tossed fish onto the beach, jellyfish, remains of ships. Even the tentacle of a gigantic squid.

To calm the furious god—when the fury lasted more than three days—they bought a hunchback from some neighboring village and threw him off the cliff, clad in a necklace of dried figs and a cape of chicken feathers to facilitate his sacrificial flight to the limbo of idiots.

The second or third day the giant would again grow calm, and the fishermen could safely go back to their fishing. Manta rays shattered against the rocks, planks, conch shells, were testimony to the tantrum. Once there was even a whale, shared by sharks and beggars.

•

A final solution to their solar problem was really all the Aztecs wanted. They were being crushed by the immoderation of their faith: they exaggerated the thirst of their gods, who drank only blood. They believed the time had come for the ultimate transfusion. A hecatomb that would fortify the anemic sun to the end of the cycle of time.

Huamán Collo, envoy of the Inca Túpac Yupanqui, put on his insignia in preparation for the last negotiations. Many moons in Tenochtitlán had slipped by, like grains of corn falling from the hands of a beautiful young tamale maker. He felt very far from the days when his reed raft had slowly followed the current north from Peru to the coast of the Aztec Confederation.

Difficult to negotiate with men already devoured by the senselessness of their gods.

They were too easily swayed by ominous signs. They did not understand the difference between symbol and reality. They were mobilizing, faithful to the prophecy of Quetzalcoatl when he had been expelled from the land: "I shall return in the year 1-Reed" (1519). What was the source of the idea that their sun was dying? On the ceremonial plaza in Cuzco, in Huacaypata, an eagle had also fallen from the heavens at the feet of the Inca. But unlike Moctezuma, the Inca had not confused an eagle struck by lightning with the end of an empire.

The Aztecs believed that the earth is a lizard dozing placidly in the mud. Naifs! They did not know the earth is a puma at the instant it leaps from shadow toward mist. Life . . .

It is not easy to negotiate when magic and imagination overwhelm the rational channels of science and numbers.

The emissary adjusted his *mascaypacha* and went out on the series of balconies that stretched along the side of the Imperial Palace facing the Market Plaza and the Great Pyramid. The movable feast of Mexico. Tenochtitlán. Tenochtitlán! Rich and metallic ringing of gongs struck by young boys with obsidian knives when the priests descended after the bloody sacrifice.

Happiness of a lengthening afternoon. Games, shouts. Streets teeming with people. An anthill where streams of honey have overflowed. Cries of haggling and hawking. Bargaining of buying and selling. Huamán recognized the sound: it was the dangerous bliss that only merchants can instill. They even had their own god, Yacatecutli. Why a merchant god in the sacred hierarchy? It was too much. His orthodox, loyalist, functionary's socialism was offended. Theirs was a different order of life (how could they deny the science of the *quipus,* the knotted strings!). These Aztecs were light-years away from sanctioning a law like the one Túpac Yupanqui issued recently in regard to miners: six hours per day and four months of labor per year. Six hours!

Frenzy of life. Muted song of warriors training in ritual ball games. From high atop the temple of Tlaloc, the somber rhythm of drums, and the single, profound, and futile howl of the sacrificed warrior whose heart the priests, sinister divine toilers, tore out to deposit in the hollowed bosom of the god Chac-Mool.

Vendors peddling flowers. Fluttering of caged toucans. Pirouetting monkeys in the dead tree limbs where they are displayed for sale. A penetrating odor of *salsa picante,* of tortillas stuffed with dogs' hearts. Tenochtitlán, the movable feast. The happy and festive life of great cities.

These Aztecs were open to grace and inexactitude. They tolerated free commerce and the lyric. The Incan world, in contrast, was geometrical, statistical, rational, two-dimensional, symmetrical. Socialist, in sum.

As she did every afternoon as the conch shells and trumpets blew to announce the coming of dusk, a delicious Tlazcalteca girl entered carrying a glass of foaming cocoa and a large goblet filled with feathers. Huamán did not disappoint her: he blew a handful toward the space of the open window. Floating iridescence. He felt the weight of official solemnity lift from his shoulders. He repeated the experience until the goblet was empty. The tiny colored feathers hovered in the air; some lifted and flirted in space like hour-old butterflies in torrid lands, like fluttering pieces of paper, confetti of the gods. An instant of joy and beauty before they disappeared.

"Is it worth the effort to invade the lands of the pale ones?" Huamán, skeptic, asked the *tecuhtli* of Tlatelolco.

"Those lands can be conquered, subdued," said the *tecuhtli,* as if he had not heard.

Huamán already knew that they wanted twenty or thirty thousand of the pale brutes to inaugurate, in the Aztec year 219, the temple of Huitzilipochtli, and plot the drama of the end of solar anemia. "The blood of the world, beasts, man, gods, is all one."

"Let us conquer them. Liberate them. Invade their coasts," the Aztec insisted. "You Incas know the secret of the rivers that flow in the sea. We could . . ."

Huamán Collo could not abandon the rational distrust of his lord Túpac Yupanqui. One assumed, of course, that the merchants of Tenochtitlán would want to clothe the pale ones in jaguar and bear skins, in feather capes. To accustom them to tobacco and coca; to pleasure them with stones of jade, and cocoa.

Bearded white faces, sturdy, and squat. More than once, in pursuit of tuna—indefatigable mercantile race—their ships had gone down in warm seas, or they had disembarked in the islands to take on water, gather fruit, then return to their cold seas.

The Aztecs, modest sailors, crossed their path repeatedly. Particularly on voyages of exploration made toward the point two weeks from Guanahani where the winds and currents meet. A motionless lake within the sea, with floating debris from both worlds: a ceremonial pipe; a fox terrier inflated like a wineskin; a chieftain's baton; several of those knotted intestines invented by Lord Condom, tossed by summertime lovers into the current of the Thames; a horse's head, surely sacrificed by the Saracens in ignoble revenge; a deerskin loincloth, its cords undulating on the waves; a rosary with wooden cross and beads, lost by some Galician priest on the day of the Virgin of the Rivers.

They knew this scarcely captivating world of the white faces through minute deductive analysis of these objects, and by the incomprehensible signs left by the insignificant island sailors who were being seen less frequently than in previous centuries. But there could be little doubt that they were not as experienced in these matters as the Incas.

Huamán solemnly spoke of transatlantic flights. With modesty he informed the *tecuhtli* that they had already overflown the Smoking Islands (the Canaries) and the tip of the Jaguar's Snout (Iberia). With true humility, not to offend competitive Aztec pride, Huamán reported:

"One of our balloons reached Düsseldorf. Men there are pale, and seem unhappy," he said with remote indifference.

The balloons were constructed of fine Paracas cloth and outfitted with small reed baskets. They rose up in the warm air of Nazca, or from the Yucatán, and took advantage of the difficult science of the warm winds. "The other sea, the sea of the sky."

The *tecuhtli* realized that it would be difficult to overcome the indifference of the Tawantinsuyu toward the white faces. They would not be embroiled in an imperial adventure to conquer the cold lands. The negotiations had failed.

Huamán's skepticism was substantial. He knew that men are a joke of the gods, sent to mortify the animals. They emerge from the continuum, from the origins, but they retain their wretched nostalgia or lamentable hope. Bipeds, like macaques they lurch as they walk, and never totally adapt to reality, until they return to the Open, to the place without shadows. Why expend energy in greater adventures, in new conquests?

Ceremoniously, they strolled toward the banquet in the Imperial Palace. They entered that pantheon of light and color depicted in the *Codex Vaticanus C,* part three, forever lost in the burning of Aztec documents ordered by the brutal Bishop Zumárraga.

They entered the *Codex* with slow and solemn step. "Solemn as kings in a deck of cards," on their way to the last banquet. Greeted from both sides by youths waving fans of colored feathers. The ideograms do not record the last attempt of the *tecuhtli,* expert practical politician that he was, to convince Huamán:

"My lord, it would be best if we ate the white-faces for lunch, before they have us for supper."

•

It was a cold, foggy morning, a gray balloon beginning to be punctured by rays of sunlight. Autumn winds against the walls of the palace.

Entrance of the hunters. Thudding hooves, horns focusing the excited pack. Halberdiers, children, and scullions milling around looking at the quarry still swathed in the vapors of life.

High in the belltower (no one knew how she climbed there) stood La Beltraneja, draped in a disreputable boa of ibis feathers she had surely stolen from one of the prostitutes. She had daubed her face with the colors in fashion—violet, yellow, carmine—but without benefit of mirror. The result was rather like a wash drawing. The wind was challenging her perennial fairy godmother hat; its tulle wrapped around the posts of the belfrey.

A little lower down, but still with a view of the trough where the horses were slaking their thirst, ensconced on the merlons of the watchtower, Isabel and her friends. Her cousin Fernando below, he of Aragón: stripped of princely trappings, disguising his rank, in order to prevent this brief stop from turning into a boring—and unwanted—official visit.

Dressed like a well-off goatherd. Young, he displayed the spirit of his race of highland men: light chestnut hair, flat, broad face, eyes curiously almond-shaped. A sturdy youth with the bearing of a king. He walked back and forth among the mules, keeping a check on any potential excess or carelessness.

"We leave for Zaragoza before midday," he ordered.

Someone handed him a leather wine *bota*; he drank gratefully. As he tipped his head back, his eyes located what really interested him in that somber palace.

His boots resounded with a military ring upon the dark granite stones of the courtyard: a man's tread, nearly as grave as that of his grandfather king. He counted the rewards of the hunt: rabbits and hares torn asunder by dogs not schooled in the English fashion; a musk deer, clubbed to death; two boars, their blood still flowing slowly and thickly, smoking on the paving stones.

The foot soldiers cleaned bronzes misted with fog. Put away daggers, swords, crossbows. The preferred weapon of

those unrefined valiants was the cudgel. They were particularly skillful: they could even bring down a wild bull. (The
Aragonese got their exercise hunting Catalans, that constructive community with the manifest destiny of protecting all
the Spains.)

Again, Fernando's voice rang out. He had brought before
him the dog that had quailed before the third boar. He asked
for a long bow and, despite the protest of a soldier who was fond
of the dog, shot an arrow that skewered it from chest to tail.

A man, it was plain to see. He did not hesitate a
moment to sacrifice an expensive dog on the altar of justice.
The halberdiers of the guard watched with nostalgia (righteous cruelty is always a source of fascination in Spain).

No one believed that he was merely killing a dog. That
arrow carried the weight of decisiveness. (Might Atahualpa
have felt a pang in his liver?)

Isabel, in her short smock and ingenue's ponytail, swung
her bare legs outside the wall, clinging to the rough stone of
the merlon. Fernando pretended to adjust his mule's girth,
enabling him to repeat his towerward gaze. A steely gaze,
implacable, the eyes of the killer whale, that climbed the
granite wall, melted as it reached thighs, and came to final
rest on that disturbing shadow. Fernando heard a buzzing,
felt unexpectedly faint. He had to gasp for air, lifting his
head like a stag shoulder-deep in a swamp, like a warrior
blindsided by the two-handed blow of a sword. That warm
shadow, that valley. The tail of the vixen that at dawn had
flashed into the brambles.

Isabel stared at the nape of the youth's neck. It was the
neck of a bull in rut, a knot of power, the knee of a Roman
gladiator.

The girl-princess felt her legs part sweetly, felt that she was floating in the gray air above the neck of her cousin, El Aragonés. A pale, delicate butterfly circling around a flame; but when Fernando, sweating, reached up to trap her in his hands, she fluttered just out of his reach on beating, fragile wings, playing the foolish virgin.

Juanita La Beltraneja understood perfectly what was taking place at that moment.

She could not choke back a frantic sob. She yelped several times, like a small animal threatened by high water.

"That's no way for cousins to look at each other!"

She hung from the bell rope and angrily clanged the clapper. Her scrawny feather boa tangled in the cords. More than the sound of bells, a rain of shattered glass.

The girl slid down the rope (a bit of blue tulle left floating in the shadow of the bell tower). She raced to the confessional of the good Torquemada (confessor of princesses). From that funereal armoire, where the monk spent the day in expectation of inflaming confidences, emanated a strange and penetrating odor, like that of a pissoir.

The priest listened to her news, but La Beltraneja gave him no time to react; she was already running, desperate, toward the throne of her father, the king, to inform him that Isabel was no longer a virgin, that she had vulgarly given herself to her cousin Fernando de Aragón, the incognito goatherd.

"Now she can never wear the crown of Castile!"

Meanwhile, the Aragonese executioners were laying out the quarry on crimson paving stones. They kept the deer for themselves, to be roasted in camp on their return home.

The prize of the hunt, a boar caked with blood and clots of dung and clay, with a broken arrow protruding from one

eye, was not destined for King Enrique, as the halberdiers might have believed.

It was in fact a present, a true *billet-doux,* intended for
La Trastamara:

> *For Isabel, princess of Castile,*
> *This vanquished but tender boar . . .*
> *An unknown admirer.*

There could be little doubt that the simplicity of the text
veiled darker intentions. Isabel was ecstatic over that bit of
parchment stained with black blood. She ran and hid it in
her missal.

Five weeks later, an anonymous emissary arrived at the
Castle of Zaragoza bearing as a gift for Fernando, also King
of Sicily, a fragile sugar boar, with bristles fine as pins,
pierced with a purple-and-yellow-painted pick, bearing no card.

Isabel, without the knowledge of La Beltraneja, or
Torquemada, or other court spies, had confected that patient
and silent affirmation.

•

A rabbinical bobbing, an ambiguous circumcision, that
was what Domenico thought indispensable for Cristoforo. It
was time for him to make his way in the world.

Father and son went to the ghetto. As he saw the sea
from the hill, Domenico said with gloomy resignation:

"And that is what you want? But you will be disappointed; you will come to miss the carding brush, the secu-

rity. The delights of a monotonous afternoon that ends with dinner-table conversation and a good night's sleep. My boy, God—Yahweh—punishes us with ambition; if He desires our ruin, all He has to do is grant us what we imagine."

They entered the cavelike quarters of the dubious rabbi Ibn-Solomon. Antique claptrap, cabalistic trinkets. Stuffed birds and fish. Books on mysticism. Talismans of Isis that the ancient obviously sold at wholesale.

He was an independent rabbi, bothered neither by orthodoxy nor by authorities of the Diaspora. His forte was the interpretation of dreams, which he performed in the market for the price of one gold sequin. He did not know he was a pioneer of a regrettable discipline, psychoanalysis. When he saw Cristoforo, he said, sarcastically:

"Another youth preparing for the true faith!"

He spread out his utensils: small knives disinfected in a mixture of vinegar and cheap brandy; flannel gauze; a whetstone; a pot filled with spiderwebs, considered highly efficacious for healing wounds.

Cristoforo, impressed, looked at the wall: a geometric Tree of Life with thirty-two limbs. From the branches hung little papers with dates of payment (the rabbi practiced a reliable and not very costly usury). A bronze Star of David, articulated so that faster than a wink it could be transformed into the Holy Cross. The ancient was expert in the matter of pogroms.

While he sharpened the knife, he said:

"All magic derives from Seth, the son of Cain, who was initiated outside the walls of Paradise. But, boy, the first magic is rebellion and despair; the second, obedience. You must command reason, and obey your instincts. Whosoever modifies this law of Yahweh will not die in his own bed. Of this you may be sure."

Domenico had arranged for the rabbi to perform a pragmatic circumcision, with the goal of the boy's being able, without prejudice, to earn a post with some multinational enterprise. Ibn-Solomon suggested his specialty: a medium cut that would serve both propositions. A circumcision with multiconfessional uses, which, although not entirely homologous in the synagogue, would be acceptable to bankers, armsmakers, and moneylenders. Yet would not expose the youth to the growing anti-Zionist animosity of emerging empires. (It was a time of mutation. From the four corners of the civilized world was arriving news of Jews burned or enthusiastically stoned.)

Ibn-Solomon passed the small knife several times through the flame of a green candle, the same candle he used to read the future during consultations, when he cast the cat bones. Finally, he dipped the blade in the ash of incense. Then, crudely and sarcastically:

"Have no fear, boy. I paid for my studies by castrating lambs in Lebanon."

Then, presto, he was holding the prepuce in his fingers while Cristoforo was still wondering whether or not it would hurt.

"We are the only race that is finished by hand!" said the ancient. "You'll be running around in no time, if you wash yourself twice daily with boric acid. If it bleeds, apply a shrew. If it burns, pork lard will do. For every grief, green brings relief! Remember: many a bird's been betrayed by his pecker. With this wisdom you can be one of the chosen on Saturdays, and on Sundays, one of the goyim."

He tossed the foreskin into a pasteboard box containing others already dry and dark as raisins. He rattled the box with professional pride: the sound of leather coins, like those the Persian camel drivers used for their transactions.

Ibn-Solomon charged the agreed price: two wheels of *pecorino* cheese, and a length of midseason-weight serge.

"We have modified the design of Jehovah, boy! Now you are, as the French say, a *demi*. But woe unto you if you make a mistake when you show your documents!"

Cristoforo covered himself with a delicately crocheted cover-penis his sister Blanquita had woven from the best wool that had been washed with rainwater and purified in the sun.

•

Two weeks later they tested the water in the great houses: Doria, Pinelli, the aforementioned Berardi (with headquarters in Florence, also the capital of the Medici).

In the end, it was the great financial house Centurione that expressed interest in him.

As he was on his way to the interview, Domenico said to his heir:

"I can't understand the person who being well off wants even more! Pure madness: you will have black days; the world is filled with assassins, princes, and adventurers. What is it you want? Only idiots believe it is better to be an eagle than an ox. But it's your life."

Nicolò Spinola, manager of Centurione, demanded excellent Castilian and supervisory bookkeeping skills (addition and subtraction and knowledge of how to keep track of dispatching and receiving).

"You will be working in the merchant marine, boy. All Castilian and bookkeeping. That's what's needed in these times. . . ."

•

The Impotent plotted international romances to keep his half sister Isabel far from the dangerous Fernando and the throne of Castile. He looked for ambitious princes, erotomaniac caballeros, suitable nobles. But Isabel dreamed only of the nape of El Aragonés. She raged at the mere mention of any other possibility.

Craftily, Enrique resorted to the widely known lechery of the Maestre de Calatrava. An aged sensualist who quickly learned through obliging spies the details of the physical attributes of the sixteen-year-old princess. (While she was sleeping, false nuns took the measurements of breast, waist, hips, and thighs. The Maestre had a plush doll sewn to those dimensions, in order to have an approximate but realistic idea of the beauty being offered him by interests of state.)

The gouty old lecher thought that God was rewarding his services in his lifetime. He set out from Almagro toward the gratification awaiting in Madrid. (He knew about the *jitoniscos*, the long straight hair, the delicate ankles hidden beneath high-buttoned boots.)

He organized an opulent entourage of eight carriages. In two of them, with fingers bleeding from needle pricks caused by the potholed road, traveled two groups of seamstresses, stitching and gaily singing.

They were preparing the trousseau, the ooh-la-la lingerie that welled from the imagination of the entranced Maestre, who, in his own carriage, filled leaf after leaf with charcoal-drawing designs. He contrived silk underdrawers with deliciously secret slits, brightly colored ruffles that would flicker like butterflies in the shadow of the bedclothes; he added unexpected buttons, flounces, hemstitching, ribbons. Nervous arrows pointed to "the best China silk," "finest linen," "embroidery," "embellishment directly above Venusberg."

In fact, the aged Maestre was not original; he was inspired by distorted memories of libertine visits to the brothels of Venice and Paris.

But it was difficult to concentrate with so much jolting. He threw his head back, abandoning himself to the swaying of the carriage, and dreamed inflamed dreams of nuptial half-light. Once married in the eyes of God, no one could separate them nor stand in the way of his rights. When they were back in Almagro Castle, he would tie the princess, completely naked, onto the great oak dining table and sniff her sex, hour after hour, day after day. His savage, perverted, profound, sincere love would demand the girl's eternal virginity.

All during this time, Isabel was pacing through the palace, agitated by the long march of the libidinous Maestre. She had precise information on every detail, and on what was being sewn in those two carriages of singing seamstresses.

Her confidante, her great friend, Beatriz de Moya, cried out:

"No! God will never permit it. Better death!"

They had to prize the knife from her hand. Beatriz and Isabel threw their arms about each other, and sobbed together all night long. One could see the fine hand of the Impotent. While the Maestre de Calatrava advanced toward the court, he, to put an end once and for all to his sister's ambitions, organized a campaign to establish highly visible proof of his virility, with a view toward refuting suspicions about the questioned paternity of young Beltraneja.

He succeeded in having the archbishop issue this statement:

Examined by me personally were four prostitutes of Segovia, BE IT KNOWN that His Highness had congress and knowledge of each of them as man to woman, and that he had a virile and firm penis, which issued its yield and virile seed like any other potent male's, and like other powerful men.

(This document is cited by Gregorio Marañón, for anyone who wishes to pursue the subject.)

Enrique had the statement duly notarized, and circulated it to every member of the skeptical court, which realized that the general principle did not really clarify the specific case of La Beltraneja.

It all seemed rather more like the propaganda of a discredited Italian gigolo.

Those were tense times. But the great plan failed in the embryonic stage. When the aged Maestre reached the posthouse in Villarrubia, he suffered an attack of "sudden malign fevers," which his menservants first interpreted as a common and normal masturbatory crisis.

The next morning he was found dead, with the Star of David clutched in one fist (his God at the hour of truth) and with virgin underdrawers from the trousseau pressed to his right cheek.

In those days of desperation, Isabel and Beatriz, who were never apart for a moment, had sent a swift horseman to Zaragoza with a gift for Fernando: a tiny pastry dove badly pecked by a coarse and ugly bird of burnt sugar.

Hours after the arrival of the news of the sudden demise in Villarrubia, Isabel received a genteel reply, worthy of a Sicilian bridegroom, from Fernando—who was not King of Sicily for nothing:

> *It seems that your intended groom,*
> *He of Calatrava, in the vicinity*
> *of Villarrubia, unexpectedly fell ill.*
> *In another nuptial bed—infinity?—*
> *awaited him a different divinity.*
> *A friend . . .*

•

The flesh of the girl-princess was tumid with the imminence of love. Heady, turbulent days. Winds, in her presence, were transformed into warm breezes. Not even the gusts of September, already beginning to blow, could cool her.

She tried to find relief by galloping wildly over the rocky terrain. She winded three horses in ten days' time.

The chronicle records that she began to exude the strong—but not, of course, repulsive—odor of a large cat in heat.

In the late afternoons it was difficult to contain her: to help her through the hour of the rosary, her ladies-in-waiting applied compresses of cool brine, and made her sniff ammonia.

For the young Beltraneja these were days of savage suffering. She understood everything: she was in the presence of that caravan of lions, true love; of desire that must inevitably explode.

She harassed her father to stir himself from his indolence and take measures:

"Another Maestre de Calatrava, another French prince . . . but someone, for God's sake. Someone!"

Hysterical, she sniveled and threatened. She tried to move the somber Torquemada. She accused his aunt of being a Jewess. Everywhere she turned, she thought she discovered the lovers' emissaries. She had the halberdiers double the guard around Isabel's quarters.

She issued orders to lash and rack several innocent goatherds unfortunate enough to wander in from the east. Clenching her tiny hands, quivering in the platform-soled shoes of a precocious little whore, she pawed through merchants' saddlebags, looking for sugar boars, small painted arrows, or anonymous letters. In every itinerant trader she saw a messenger of love.

Isabel was aware that the circle was closing. The climate of repression and distrust was growing intolerable. As the last straw, her breasts swelled and stood as erect and hard as acorn squashes. She feared that at any moment they might open like the roses of April, releasing a steady flow of milk.

At times, while trying to pray, she heard the hiss and then the fatal r-r-rip of the seam of her dress, opening from waist to ankle. She had the precise and disturbing sensation of being about to burst open like a ripe pomegranate in the heat of the June sun; yes, like a garnet grenade, in Granada, no less!

The signs began to spread. Isabel's (aforementioned) scent of a tigress in heat drew rabid packs of envious desire. Males converged on the court from the fields of Segovia, Ávila, and Salamanca. They could be seen from afar, an infernal presence, a single raging monster threatening travelers from behind every hill. No one could sleep at night because of that ocean of fury, of barking, of howls aggravated by frenzy, by savage erotic combat.

Scouting parties were organized and armed with axes and clubs to keep them from storming the walls.

(Thence was born a custom that would become a tradition in Spain: to prevent their heads from being splashed with the dogs' blood, the cudgelers of the Brotherhood began to wear outlandish improvised headcoverings of washable, flexible, waterproof cloth.)

Autumn was unpardonable. The days grew short. Nights, permeated with frustrated nuptiality, became unbearable. At three in the morning, Isabel and Beatriz, who slept in each other's arms, got out of bed to pass the time however they could until the liberating light of dawn. They prayed. They attempted artistic embroidery. But in vain: the girl-princess felt as if she was drowning, and had to stand by the window and breathe in the icy, damp air of darkest night.

Decisions had to be made. In stealth, taking advantage of the absence of her Cerberus, the Marqués de Villena, faithful servant of King Enrique, Isabel fled from Ocaña to the monastery of Madrigal, where tall towers evoked memories of childhood. Weeping, she kissed the nuns who had nursed her. She spoke with her poor mother, who, after listening for several hours, said only, before returning to the inviolable silence to which she was accustomed:

"My daughter, however you can, slay the beast of desire. Desire is the essence of Evil. Live. One repents only of what one has not done. Kill, before they kill you in life. Fear only madness."

But soon, even in her own palace, Isabel was threatened, betrayed. She must cross her Rubicon, burn her ships. She preferred danger to the tepid protection of her hearth.

"Valladolid! On to Valladolid!"

That day, with that cry, wars were begun that would last for twenty years. Dressed in leather garments, she rode out, followed by her faithful. She believed leather was not only best for the hard days ahead, but also the only clothing that could contain that ever-present threat of bursting. (Isabel was nineteen and, as all the chroniclers affirm, she was blessed with "ample and perfect hips." More than a teenager's, her body was that of a thirtyish rumba dancer. Very much, in fact, like Blanquita Amaro's at her peak.)

She hid her river of blond hair, the color of old gold, beneath a large, wide-brimmed felt captain's hat. Enchanting!

She realized she had to transform sexual compulsion into a national and popular crusade. Freudianly, she sought an ideology to channel such desire into an adequate superstructure.

"I must attempt the impossible," she said. "High shall my banner fly, bright shall my emblem blaze!"

She spoke of a world without pederasts, moneylenders, or destructive *comuneros*. She promised a war against inflation. She said that Spain should rise from its knees, rather than continue to drag itself in the dirt. She spoke of bread, work, greatness. She was properly demagogic: the people, like serving girls, in exchange for a promise, will give themselves without a regret.

The chroniclers do not record the text of that proclamation; as always, they jot down only what is easily understood.

Then Isabel set off for Valladolid, followed by her retinue. For almost two leagues the cavalcade rode to the rhythm and beat of the Isabeline harangue.

Then they had to take cover in a poplar grove to hide from an enraged band of the Marqués de Villena's men under the command of La Beltraneja, who rode past sobbing with frenzy when she realized she had lost her aunt's trail in the dust of the road.

Triumphantly, Isabel reached Valladolid, which thenceforth would be her bastion.

•

He would never forget the smell of that first ship, the enormous carrack belonging to Centurione and bound for Chios.

Susana Fontanarossa had outfitted him with a duffel on which she had embroidered a guardian angel (which would be a source of unmerciful ribbing by his fellow seamen in the hold). Into the bottom she slipped a packet of homemade candies, a talisman of Isis, and a small bag of camphor to ward off the many contagions of shipboard life. She did not fail to include a rosary blessed by Don Abbondio, whom everyone believed slated for certain sainthood.

Early on the morning of the departure, his mother cooked him bacon and six fried eggs, and, for the first time,

Domenico gave him wine to drink instead of the breakfast milk. Afterward, the three of them, solemn as death—and without waking his sister Blanquita, who would have shed maudlin tears—walked down to the *molo vecchio*.

Stevedores, deckhands, water carriers. In the pale light of dawn the heavy canvas sails of fortune were being unfurled. Bow anchor and kedge anchors being weighed. All to the sound of exasperated cries.

Threads of porter-ants swarmed from dock to bilge. Casks of chestnuts in heavy syrup. Raisins in brandy; boxes of tortoiseshell combs; Frascati wines in jugs like Roman amphoras. Casks of olive oil, permeated with the aroma of the grove. Summer-weight cloth. Embroidered Voghera silks fit for the undergarments and blouses of a sultan and his harem. Basket after basket of Neapolitan and Florentine religious trumpery, Catholic kitsch hoping to find a market in the Venetian expansion toward the Aegean. Collapsible altars that could be enlarged at will, embellished with candelabra, little gilt angles, and mass-produced paintings of Calvary.

What would they bring back from Chios, center of trade with the dominions of the Great Turk? Their famous resin for marine caulk and varnish, their waterproof mastic, all indispensable in those years of nautical exploration. Turkish ornaments and Oriental brocades. Heavy Egyptian perfumes.

When the bosun came to "Colombo!" as he called the roll, Cristoforo leaped on board. So excited he was not even aware of his parents' tears. And for the rest of his life he would see them from a distance, standing among the bitts on the dock with their arms around each other.

Pungent odors of hardwood, pickled foodstuffs, fresh varnish, India hemp hawsers, and various oils filled his nostrils, but, above all else, the hard and noble wood of the deck planking. For a lifetime he would be seduced by that smell of a floating emporium, of sweat in the hold, of sour wine. That enveloping effluvium tempered by the tang of sea salt and iodine.

Standing on the deck of the *Mariella,* he watched as the mizzen of the foresail and the great mainsail began to fill amid the perfectly arrhythmic chants of the crewmen straining at the halyards.

Enormous, benevolent udders swelled against the dawn. Feminine power, the *ying,* of sail. Inhaled breath, pregnancy, invisible wind transformed into power and direction. Angels trapped in a white pillowcase. Benign god indulging the naive cleverness of humankind.

Hard, precise, curt commands:

"Heave! Heave! Heave! Steady on! Hee-yuv!"

The galley was underway. Cristoforo watched the Sant'Andrea tower and the Genoa lighthouse grow steadily smaller.

He felt the stirring of wild freedom. He climbed to the forecastle to feel the air cleft by the prow.

A grave and ponderous hand was impelling the galleon toward the Aegean sea. What science was this? How could he master it? How could he ally himself with those invisible powers?

He would have to learn the art of enduring the sea with the ease of the gulls, of the Galicians.

He felt that surely it was a matter, as in anything else, of instinct and courage.

He would have to give himself to it, surrender himself. Throw caution to the winds to find his salvation.

If he risked everything, death itself would be disarmed.

As it disappeared into the fog of the Sant'Andrea tower, he realized that the world of cheesemakers, carders, and tailors, with their petty disappointments and joys, was behind him.

Cristoforo felt he had passed from mere existence to life. The time had come to take risks, to emerge from his protected world of walls, shelter, the Christomancy of sabbatical catechism, the parochial Virginalia.

The joy of setting sail! The joy of the sea! The newness of this morning like no other. The dangers. The pure air.

For one decisive second not recorded by historians or correspondents, he felt the *satori* of the freedom known only to one who owns nothing and owes nothing. The freedom of one who delivers himself unto the great god of chance, into the hands of the gods of the four winds. And the one who will seek eternal alliance with them.

•

It was learned that Fernando would arrive disguised as a goatherd. His trip was top secret. In the Castle of Valladolid the tension mounted to the breaking point.

Isabel, Beatriz, and the ladies-in-waiting knelt without interruption before the princess's portable altar. Feeling increasing asphyxia. At moments, Isabel's was as severe as an asthma attack. Quickly, the women would surround her and stir the air with their fans. It was like blowing on glowing coals. The girl's chaste sex emitted a delicate but uncontainable whistling sound that her four petticoats and woolen skirt could not muffle. First the whistling was barely audible, then clear, filling the brief intervals of silence during the recitation of the rosary. The ivory Christ was vibrating strangely. Frightened, Isabel placed her hands before her eyes, then looked again. In vain; He was vibrating so violently she feared He might fly off His sandalwood cross.

In the stables, stallions and studs whinnied and kicked wildly at their stall doors.

No one said a word, but everyone understood.

The hours passed, slowly. They feared the worst, because the king's search parties were watching all the roads to Valladolid.

To the entrenched powers it was very clear that the union of those forces, compelled by a cosmic eroticism, would result in an unprecedented political, economic, and social mutation. The synarchy, with no strong desire to support the ominous reign of Enrique IV, was nevertheless aware of the dangers that threatened all the Occidental world and, in particular, its central bastion: the Church. If they were unable to prevent that conjunction of the angelical and savage adolescents, the entire world would be forced to prepare for the horrors of a Renaissance. The larval lethargy, the guarantee of terrified underdevelopment, that had protected Europe from heroic action for at least six centuries now—since Charlemagne—would be lost.

It was the clear knowledge of the synarchy that in the adolescent prince and princess, who seemingly, and with due modesty, meant only to "defer death with kisses," was concentrated a transcendent power of incalculable force.

A heroic messenger, run through by three arrows shot from crossbows, reached the guards just before dying, and succeeded in transmitting his comforting message of confirmation: Fernando had started out on the 5th of October, traveling at night and at great risk.

It would be difficult to identify those travelers among the many groups of humble strangers entering the city.

At eleven o'clock on the night of October 14, a group of six goatherds, heads bowed by their travels and the inclement weather, stopped to water their donkeys at the fountain. They did not realize it, but they were unrecognizable beneath layers of mud and yellow dust hardened into masks by the fog.

It was Gutiérrez de Cárdenas who, pointing to the shortest goatherd, raised the cry:

"That's him! That's him! That's him!"

Chacón and Alonso de Palencia ran toward the youth, who—now in safe hands—collapsed from the six nights without sleep.

Everyone congratulated Cárdenas: had he not recognized him, Fernando and his men, somnambulized by the cruel march and constant pretense, would have continued on their way, believing that Isabel, hotly pursued, had gone on to León. That very night, Isabel granted the faithful Cárdenas the privilege of using the sign "SS" on his noble escutcheon. Thus was born that brotherhood of men and women faithful to the royal couple: Beatriz de Bobadilla, Alonso, Chacón, Fernando Núñez, Admiral Enríquez, Carillo, the Archbishop of Toledo, and other initiates.[1]

---

[1]Author's note: About the birth of the sect of the SS, see Prescott's *History {of Ferdinand and Isabella}* and the work of the Ballesteros Gaibrois, among others. It is no secret, according to authors such as Pauwels, Sánchez Dragó, Bergier, and others, that Hitler expressed his unconditional admiration for Isabella of Castile to Göring and his adherents. Austrian, and common to the end, the Führer wore a scapular of yellow plush that guarded a sprig of wheat from La Mancha, and a portrait of Isabella.

The bathing of the exhausted, slumbering prince lasted until six in the morning. Chacón, the archbishop, and Cárdenas himself went at it unstintingly with long brushes of boar bristles. The youth, following Aragonese orthodoxy, had reached the age of eighteen innocent of any total ablution other than his warm and inaugural immersion at birth.

A good anthropologist, a Lévi-Strauss, would have found in the dregs of that washbasin the structuralist signs not only of a life, but of an entire culture: dried leaves and piñon nuts from the various forests stalked by the inveterate huntsman; drowned creatures that had dwelt happily in the tangles of his hair and other hirsute habitats, organisms that thus had never known any but their normal Aragonese environment: sweat of each of his summers, in (eighteen) successive parchmentlike layers exact as the annual addition of rings in a tree trunk and an oxidized arrowhead, fallen surely from his umbilicus, his prepuce, or auricular circumvallations.

At six in the morning they dressed the prince in a robe of raw linen worthy of his imminent nuptial initiation. And left him fast asleep on a cot until the following dawn.

It was on that night that Isabel, defying the enemy siege, rode from the castle in a mad flight toward the north. Beatriz Bobadilla de Moya and the ladies of Isabel's train hurried after her, following her trail with hunting hounds.

It was understandable. It was vertigo before the proximity, the imminence of the macho. Penis horror. Her powerful desire was not crushed but transformed into kinetic action. Her irrational attitude was that of the defiant torero who yields, at the moment of truth, before the bull's charge. Essentially, it was a matter of the manifestation of the "Mary syndrome," as it is called by psychoanalysts. Was Isabel, proud she-male, seeking self-deflowering? Neither Gregorio Marañón nor López Ibor has been able to clarify this matter.

Desire, however, to return to the sexual epicenter quickly diffused the impulse of the Amazonian flight into Valladolidian wilds. It was a dialectical reaction: desire-denial-return. In truth, no one overtook her: her desire, like a traitorous janissary, stayed her horse's hooves.

By dawn she was drowsing, still breathing heavily, in her (now) closely guarded bed.

What followed, during those four days and nights prior to the civil ceremony, is not to be found in the chronicles. Sworn witnesses, the SS, did not disclose the slightest hint.

It *is* known that at some moment in the middle of the night, the prince and princess, like sleepwalkers, met in one of the stone corridors of the palace and headed directly for rooms abandoned for years.

Based on their conduct during the official wedding, entered on October 20 in the official register by notaries of the court, we can deduce some part of what occurred.

Isabel would have held sway over Fernando like male to female, without noting the mimetic and cynical lizardlike motionlessness of El Aragonés.

Her Trastamara pride, her reputed mannishness, made submissiveness anathema to her.

Probably she was possessed as she possessed him, and her maidenhead simply ripped, like the strong fine silk of the tent of the Great Turk surprised in his encampment by a summer storm. Rupture through internal convex pressure, not external concavizing action.

In sum: at some moment during the tilling and toil of the night of October 15 and 16, the turgid gland of the

Aragonese prince confronted—"man to man"—the aggressive Isabeline hymen.

Following the first couplings, as uncomplicated and bucolic as the dawn, Fernando revealed a tendency toward perversion that Isabel found fascinating. He harbored unspecified grudges which he expressed phallically. The sadism of a vindictive peon. A sadism consisting of delayed execution, or of barbaric, not always vaginal, invasion.

They hid during that rutting, like any fine, noble young animals. Protected from human approach by the legend of ghosts and apparitions in that wing of the palace.

They opened chambers that had been closed since the century of the founding kings. They supped on cheese and crusts of bread, and sipped wine from a *bota*, like the shepherds of Arcadia (Fernando, clever fellow, had prepared for almost everything.)

No one must have witnessed the bellowing, the thick prefatory silences, the flights and scufflings in the darkness, that dislodged pyramids of helmets and tiers of dusty lances belonging to long forgotten armies.

They must have returned to the inhabited corridors guided by the pervasive aroma of garlic in the guards' stew, unaware that with their contusions, scrapes, and bruises, they were practically unrecognizable. Angels, they were oblivious to the state of their filthy, ruined woolen robes.

They remained isolated in the bell jar of mutual desire. They heard the voices of their friends and subjects as if through glass, or above a gale. They took advantage of the extreme idealism of their century: reality was neither apparent nor evident, so that they could copulate in full view of everyone, without being seen or believed. The court was still planning the wedding; captains were outlining their defense strategy against the feared attack from Madrid. The unruly metaphysics of the era made it possible for them to plunge beneath the tablecloth in the midst of an official banquet and madly fornicate until the dogs and the dwarfs of the court sniffed them out.

But the purity of the bride and groom was never in doubt. Isabel's virginity was dogma.

From six in the evening on, they took refuge in their quarters, "to continue planning for the royal wedding and for the future concerns of the kingdom," as the good Fernando del Pulgar duly notes.

One of those nights, at about three in the morning, they thought they heard the lament of a lost wolf. From the rocky hills the harsh October wind carried a wild cry, a howl that rose above the blasts of the wind. They rushed to the window just in time to catch a glimpse of the white mare— Isabel knew it well—of young Beltraneja. A true soul in pain. Ruled by spite and hatred. The lovers, compassionate in their way, promised each other to liberate her as soon as possible from that nonlife.

After the initial eroticism—feverish lust—that had stolen their tongues and frozen their faces in the grave masks of notaries or hangmen, came the first dialogues, spoken during sleepless moments or in that fatigued lassitude of lovers without skills of execution.

"An end to the sinful merriment of the Moors in the lands of Al-Andalus!"

"One empire, one people, one leader!"

"And terror? How to achieve unity without terror?"

"And money?"

"The Jews have money. Since they lend money, why not take their capital from them in the name of the true religion? Is it not true that a Jew without suffering is as vulgar as any Christian?"

"So much to be done! The world! Life! We must conquer France, Portugal, Italy, Flanders! Draw and quarter the Moors! And take the seas! The seas!"

"And the Holy Sepulcher!"

"We shall not forget that."

Until they were silenced in a kiss, which was primary, and again melted into one another.

With a papal dispensation falsified by Fernando and the Cardinal of Toledo, which established that even though they were cousins they were not committing incest, they were wed in a civil ceremony on the 18th of October. By the Church, in white, and with royal pageantry, on the 20th.

The secret rituals of Castile were observed: Cardinal Cisneros, with pastoral humility, washed the princes's genitals with the holy water of April rains.

The Church, conscious of its moral dominions, thus tried to bring beneath its feeble wing Fernando's precocious, perverse, and excessive sexuality.

The official nuptials took place in a great room warmed by four braziers burning eucalyptus and incense. (That pharmaceutical odor did not cool their spirits.)

The famous motto the royal couple had adopted as their device, *Tanto monta, monta tanto, Isabel como Fernando*—"One is as good as the other"—was reinterpreted by wags: "She rides high, as high as he."

The people kept watch. At dawn, the SS came out on the

wide esplanade of the palace, exultantly displaying a sheet with the traditional red circle—suspiciously perfect—in the center.

Fernando—ever astute—had found in the bottom drawer of the bureau that had belonged to Juan II the flag of an ancient embassy of the mikado.

•

Huamán Collo and the *tecuhtli* of Tlatelolco tiptoed on sandaled feet across the delicately painted paper of the *Codex Vaticanus C* that narrates Huamán's farewell banquet in incomparable Tenochtitlán.

In the upper margin, officials in their best robes bowing reverentially. Stupendous women with heavy black braids. Incense burners of copal.

Jaguar and eagle warriors. Tambours with drumheads of barbarians' skin. Heron-bone flutes. Light from torches and oil lamps. *Le dernier cri.*

A curious orchestra composed of dwarfs and surgically deformed freaks, with perfectly arrhythmic singers. They are dressed in toucan-feather capes and bird-of-paradise headdresses. Two partially deboned contortionists are twisted into unbelievable positions.

Young girls in brief *huipiles* approach and offer canapé-sized tortillas to be spread with caviar of aquatic larvae: delicious *axayacatl.*

(The emperor had by now retired to his rooms in order not to inhibit the guests with his divine presence.)

Flawless Toltec slaves awaiting the privilege of sacrificial death surrounded the dignitaries with their trays. ("Why slaves? Why not all of them workers of the empire, as with the Incas?" Huamán asked himself.)

Hot or mild tamales wrapped in corn husks or banana leaves, boiled or steamed. Turkeys, wild pheasants, doves, spiced baby monkey. An infinite, almost Incan, variety from the imperial kitchens. Huamán had to admit it.

Huamán is seated at a private table and provided with two washbasins. The offerings file by. Roasted peppers and tomatoes. Snails with squash-blossom sauce, frogs cooked with chili, the ubiquitous *axolotl,* grilled hare, peccary stuffed with pungent herbs.

Politely, the *tecuhtli* indicates the best dishes.

With a certain flourish, an iron spit is borne in on the shoulders of two gigantic Olmecs. In a row, pierced from butt to snout, chasing each other down the shaft of the white-hot spit, a dozen hairless dogs, done to a crisp; they look like boys from the provinces who had risked an evening with the Marquis de Sade. A chef has ceremoniously used a stubby feather brush to baste them with honey and chili. In the *Codex,* the little dogs shine as if they had been varnished.

These treats are immediately followed by large trays of fruit, dewy with cool water and accompanied by trained birds that do not fear the human hand: when the chirimoya is chosen, they alight on the papaya.

Fruitful tropics. Warm lands, the Yucatán, palm trees, coastal valleys.

The space of the *Codex* is filled with tiny brushstrokes drawn with hummingbird feathers, portraying branches of fruit, grape clusters, bulging guayaba, military-plumed pine-apple, regimental ranks of bananas. The small bananas, not the large tasteless ones intended for the Tlazcaltecs, Chichimecs,

and other vassals of the empire who, because the fruit is large
and of uniform size, think it is better (as if it were a matter
of women, or obsidian knives).

New washbasins, and linen towels for the guests' hands
and mouth.

Now they distribute the first pipes and tobacco, and the
musicians, who until then have remained at the margins of
the *Codex,* approach the center of the scroll.

Ritual dancers glide among the guests. Impressive baroque costumes: they represent stars, divinities, sweet and
harsh moments of life.

Huamán believed he saw in the ballet the obsession of
the times: solar anemia, the danger of the final extinction of
warmth and light.

Impossible to remember the names and vicissitudes of so
many gods (generally discontented and bad-humored). Difficult now to understand the symbology and depictions of the
Codex. The signs and colors are consciously multiplied, to
obfuscate the human lucidity that removes all possibility of
understanding the mystery, the mist, of the gods.

When that ceremony was ended, the conch shells sounded
to announce the last diversion of the long Mexican night.

The stunningly handsome adolescent serving boys and
girls reappeared (no one could imagine that after 1519 they
would be sold as servants to the syphilitic Galician halberd-
ier, or to the scrofulous parish clerk, meat for the new race
that would be born of violation, rape, and indecent violence
wrought on domestic servants). (How could anyone imagine
that those adolescents and solemn princesses with large full
lips like the goddesses of Cambodian iconography would one
day be dishwashers and waitresses in the Nebraska Cafeteria,

"only fifty meters from the Plaza de las Tres Culturas. Reserved parking"?) Now the youths were offering trays of hallucinogens of various types and effects. It was the hour to erase rational thought, to peer into the realm of the Origen.

Passing strange are the images on the *Vaticanus C* scroll that was burned by the brutal priest Zumárraga. (He and Bishop Landa did as much harm as all the treacherous flames that destroyed the Library of Alexandria.)

The drawings and ideograms show small men with wide, staring eyes; dignitaries on their knees weeping for lost Unity; courtesans swimming on dry land, trying desperately to return to the maternal womb; eagle captains who believe they are flying, bearing the sun in its flight.

Some had ingested *peyotl*; most, *teonanacatl*.

Thus they had washed away the ego, visited their opposite being: hatred, desire, love, fear.

Some were weeping; some were laughing; others were overwhelmed with fear or delight.

The lord of Tlatelolco, to the surprise of Huamán, who had stayed with his *chicha,* huddled beneath the table, and wept heartrendingly.

After that mass exorcism, the goddess of love, Tlazelteotl, appeared in all her might. Young girls, young men, dignitaries removed themselves to the most discreet areas of the margins of the *Codex.*

They believed that with their bodies they also pleased and regaled the gods.

Finally came the announcement of dawn: fluttering in the ornamental bird cages.

Then many voices were raised in a hymn and, newly, as if resurrected, the sound of tambours and timbrals.

With eyes irritated from the labor of the fiesta, almost everyone went to the window to greet the sun.

The god had not died. Happiness for another day. Renewed hope.

They sang a dissonant but eloquent ode composed by their beloved poet-king Nezahualcoyotl:

> *Oh, may he never die!*
>   *Oh, may he never perish!*
> *There, where there is no death,*
>   *There, where he dwells in triumph,*
> *There go I.*
> *Oh, may he never die.*
>   *Oh, may he never perish.*

II

fire

CHRONOLOGY

1 4 7 6

Colón in Portugal. Marriage. His last plan for fleeing uniqueness. Sect and passion of Paradise.

1 4 8 5 – 1 4 9 2

Spain. Colón scrambles to enter the swastika of power. Years of civil war. Consolidation of the empire. Dangerously angelic nature of Fernando and Isabel. Torquemada and his condemnation machine. A Roman Catholic empire.

4-Calli

Conference in Tenochtitlán. The high priest, speaking to the eagle-men, predicts the goodness and purity of the Christian doctrine held by the bearded men who will come from the sea.

1 4 8 7

On the 27th of February, in a secret ceremony, Rodrigo de Borja, the future Pope Alexander VI, anoints himself with the consecrated semen of Fernando and Isabel. Vatican rescued from pietist sybaritism. Renaissance.

1 4 8 8

April 9. Colón's panorgasm. Accord of the highly secret sect of Paradise sealed with Isabel of Castile.

T H E   T A V E R N of the New Phalanx of Macedonia: unaffiliated halberdiers, prostitutes, cardsharks and craps players, defrocked preachers, free-lancing adventurers. The rain was coming down more heavily, splashing mud on his yellow shoes.

Cristóbal—the Cristovao of his time in Portugal left behind— knew that he was on the absolute fringe, in one of the driest and most remote branches of the structure of Power, which in those times was not vertical (like Vance Packard's famous pyramid) but a horizontal dextrogyratory galaxy; a swastika that as it whirled left destruction in its path, its arms converging toward that difficultly achieved and eagerly sought after epicenter where, dressed in an Antwerp brocade gown of the royal green, sat Isabel of Castile, plucking her eyebrows.

How to approach her? The usual thing was to cash in the chips of success. Join some group and set up what was then called *una picada*—an early entrepreneurial association.

The usual entrées were the arts, medicine, fabulous philters, variations on religion, spiritism, sports. It helped to be an astrologer or pederast. For women, as always, prostitute or lover.

It was not unusual to see setting off for the palace on the same morning assorted *picadas* of the great unwashed; one of stargazers capable of predicting the death of Boabdil and the miraculous destiny of Prince Juan; or Italian acrobats in skin-tight spangled tights, with their towers, ropes, and trapezes.

By nightfall, or some days later, you would see them again, dismissed, ruined, once again excreted to the dark reaches of the galaxy, pulverized in the fierce competition. Clubbed, perhaps, by the men of the Holy Brotherhood; raped by Bulgarians and floating in a ditch; murdered because of the careless oversight of not carrying something to give the assailants.

The terrible reactive force that emanates from all Power.

"If you want to get to heaven, it'll cost you seven," murmured a sour prostitute from Toledo, while eating her custard. (Her eyelids painted with a filigree of gold and azure blue.)

Cruel, gray afternoon. Boredom, desolation. He took off the yellow shoes he had bought from a dying man from Milano and began removing the mud. They had not been a purchase so much as a true investment. Not only did they have long pointed toes, as the French mode demanded, but the point continued and curled in three spiral turns to encircle a gay little bronze bell.

With the patience of the hopeless, he wiped them with a damp cloth until, in all its triumph, the canary-yellow color—his favorite—reappeared.

He heard coarse hoots from some of the tables. They threw him a bone or two, already gnawed, of course, by the dogs.

The unspeakable rabble that smelled, in Spain, their possibility of greatness. Mercenaries (like Ulrich Nietz) who did not cherish the opportunities offered them in the burgeoning burgs—more crowd control than soldiering. Men of action and imagination, both malefactors and honest men, fleeing the cities of the Hanseatic League, where the privileged were the notaries, lucky haberdashers, and the scientificartesan Jewry that was beginning to populate the canvases of German and Fleming regionalists (the Arnolfinis and the solemn, broad-beamed apothecaries puffing their pipes in Holbein's canvases). Spain was the land of all possibilities. Adventurers converged upon it from Flanders, Burgundy, and Franche-Comté.

Spain offered a landscape with nooks for first-class evil and crannies for cynicism and adventure.

The terrible, Catholic—in the narrow sense of the word—princely couple, Fernando and Isabel, guaranteed the destruction of everything that threatened manhood.

But what exhaustion! What long afternoons of doubt! What a gray afternoon!

And Colón, yellow shoes in hand like two Aeolian harps awaiting the fingers of the breeze, is empty, stupefied, dejectedly watching a blind guitarist who, on the edge of the impossible, is trying to change a broken string.

"What *mishiadura!*" Colón, wretchedly exclaimed![1]

[1]Author's note: Colón, like many Argentines, was an Italian who had learned Spanish. His language was necessarily bastardized, macerated, dulcified, and explicatory—like the language common to the literature of the Río de la Plata. Colón said *piba* instead of *niño, bacán* for *bon vivant, mishiadura* instead of *miseria,* and *susheta* instead of *mujer,* words heard today only in tangos and the slang of *lunfardo* poetry. During his relationship with Beatriz de Arana, in Córdoba, he had picked up the infamous all-purpose *ché.* (See Nahum Bromberg, *Semiología y Estructuralismo,* 4, "El idioma de Cristóforo Colon" [Manila: 1974]).

•

A great, unified, and powerful Spain was being forged, and both Isabel and Fernando knew that nothing could be accomplished without the violence that accompanies any birth.

They must move a quiescent, timid people toward empire! Shake them from the evils of a peaceful life. They knew that the people were infected with the profound hatred of life immanent in medieval Judeo-Christianity, infected with organized fear, with suppression of the body and dread of instinct. A rational Christianity of priests protected by the walls of the monastery, the pallor of the nuns, and the deep circles beneath the eyes of the seminarians. The peace of resigned and sick men. The virtue of impotence. At dusk, the whisper of litanies. At night, the prowling of devils. One slept by the light of a trembling candle flame. One fornicated wearing a thick woolen nightgown.

A true king is nothing more than a response to the deep intuition of a race, of a people. And Fernando and Isabel believed that by burning the Hebrew they were cauterizing *in noce* the never-healed Christian wound.

There was nothing to stop them from racing headlong toward Roman Catholicism. *Condottieri* with pliant penises converged on Spain. And men who felt threatened by equality and by the mediocrity of a bourgeois Europe that aspired to nothing greater than being a multinationalist mercantile community that offered only two choices: wholesale trade or a life of common crime.

The young monarchs realized that they could not overtake that cruel pagan fiesta without passing through the door of established superstition. Before the people, they assumed a pontifical attitude. They challenged bishops to exhausting tourneys of prayer (Isabel raged if some monk in the choir, asleep on his feet, blurted a wrong note during the *Kyrie Eleison*).

More than one sincere but embarrassingly pious priest went to the stake, accused of judaizing.

The kingdom was consolidating, gradually. Meanwhile, a secret, personal war was being waged parallel to the external one recorded by historians (history records only the grandiloquent, the visible, acts whose results are cathedrals and processions; that is why history composed for official consumption is so banal).

The fact is that there was a struggle of enormous transcendency going on between Fernando and Isabel. A war of bodies and sexes that was the true foundation of the contemporary Western world, and its subsequent horrors.

Everything began with Isabel's coronation. An immediate, surprising, and independent event that took place on the day following the death of Enrique IV. December 13, 1474: a true *Putsch*. Fernando was wounded in the most delicate region of his machismo. He was in Zaragoza, and was not consulted. Isabel failed to grant him the primacy of his sex.

Today we may believe that Isabel was at the palace of Segovia expecting—or eagerly anticipating—Enrique's death. We know that she was exhorting the seamstresses to complete their work on her tight-fitting silk gown and sumptuous, pearl-embroidered ermine cape.

The minute the news of a natural death was confirmed, the princess came down to dine in rigorous mourning. But on the morning of the 13th, stunning in white, she appeared at the head of the archiepiscopal and military procession. She walked directly behind the sword of Castilian justice. No female had ever dared claim as her own the instrument that united and decided life and death.

Upon an aged pony of proven protocolary tranquillity came, resting on a scarlet cushion, the crown of Castile.

Musket and harquebus fire. Shouting and weeping in the crowd, spellbound by that convergence of power and opulence. Beggars, matrons, and lepers wallowing in lachrymose tenderness. Rumbling shelling filling the air. Whinnying. The horses of officialdom pawing the ground (those of the troops merely brushing away flies with their tail). Bewildered pigeons on the Municipal Palace take flight.

She had caught the world off guard; she was queen before either the synarchy or her husband learned of it. As for young Beltraneja, she thought she would go mad; she paced around and around Enrique IV's coffin, and when she heard of Isabel's coronation, she rolled in the palace pigsties and covered herself with the ashes of the horses' hooves burned on the hearth of her alleged father.

That very night Isabel dispatched a messenger to Zaragoza:

"Death, that never-expected duenna, has come to claim the soul of our inattentive but God-fearing king. The Sword of Justice, which preceded me this morning, was but a metaphor. You, majesty, are the center of consecration."

From that moment, Fernando would subject her to the aggravated libido of the vindictive, and the deceived. With great ostentation, he surrounded himself with other women, because Isabel had humiliated him. (She had not put the horns on him through sex, but by seizing the short, hard sword of Power. Unacceptable behavior in that age of adamant phallocracy.)

On that very Friday, a day of fasting, Fernando reviewed the troops of the guard, accompanied by Aldonza Iborra de Alamán (Isabel spitefully called her "La Alamana, that *German*!"); her riding habit was copied from the suit of a French swordsman, and she wore high boots that came halfway up her thighs.

Isabel fell into the trap, and thenceforth the path of her love wound across the rocky terrain of jealousy.

At night, she would lay Fernando on the bed, on his back, and naked. Anxiously, she would begin to sniff his skin. She smelled his entire body, and then his clothing— hat, boots, weapons—until at some instant she detected a suspicion of enemy female odor.

Isabel sniffs and snuffs the elbow of the shirt that in the shadowy room becomes a puppet of an anemic monk. Is it Egyptian perfume, or the sweat of La Bobadilla or La Alamana, or of that dreadful young French whore "Monkey's Tail"? These are moments of deep pain, when the deceived wife has in her hands almost definite proof, but is clinging to a last hope she may be wrong. (Mightn't it be the sweat of the sick mare Fernando was riding yesterday?)

Desolate, naked, dependent, and breathless, she has no recourse now but to immolate herself in the Buddhist extinction offered by the crimson Fernandian flame.

Both Isabel and Fernando, deeply spiritual, ruled by the theology of catechistic Thomism, tried not to attach impor-

tance to such absurdities as body and desire. They treated
their own with a certain indulgence, the casual attention one
devotes to household pets. Bodies, mischievous animals that
they are, get out of control. They must be given their head to
run themselves out. Like runaway horses.

Indecent, uncontrollable, and also *untranscendent*.

The murky caverns of the human instincts, therefore,
had no place in the elevated categories of reality.

Everything was "ideal." Plato, from the depths of
his cave of time, governed the delirium organized by
heaven's professionals, who brazenly derided the geometries
of Aristotelian thought.

The eroticism that joined the young monarchs was total,
and they learned—intuitively—to liberate it from the exclusive genitality of the age.

It was this truly holy impulse that caused them to
refuse, from the first day of their wedding, the ritual and
gothic *sarcophages d'amour*: twin coffins lined in quilted silk,
whose thin wooden partition was fitted with a hole just large
enough to allow the passage of the male *lingam*.

When a couple was enclosed in the dual casket—which
was *de rigueur* between Easter and Pentecost—four candles
were lighted to facilitate the reading of the *De Mortalitate*
and canticles for the dead. In this way the noble wedded pair
bowed to the demands of the flesh, recognizing the vanity of
pleasure, the ephemerality of life, and evidence of the
Heideggerian *Sein zum Tod* (being-toward-death).

With almost surgical rigor, coupling was crudely confined to the genital. (*Arañar el mamparo*—to claw at the
partition—is the consciously pornographic saying, curiously
unrecorded by Casares, that survives today in some villages of

Castile, and is not unlike the French *faire mordre l'oreiller*—to make bite the pillowcase.)

Thus foreplay was effectively eliminated, the mingling of moistnesses and tongues, manual stimulation, oral caresses, the spur of nudity, and other "demoniac adjunctions," to use the language of the spiritual advisers of the time.

The two sexes were like two bastard children wandering in a desert. Cut off from all emotional ties and all eroticism, they mated with short-lived frenzy in the *sarcophages d'amour*. Soon they wilted like unwatered parsley, lacking that basic protoplasm of affection and excitation in which they would have found the strength to be renewed.

Fernando and Isabel, living the adventure of their infinite passion and their implacable war, are remanded from Heaven to Earth; they fall from a ludicrous metaphysics into the mystery of reality.

They are creatures of the Renaissance and, at the same time, its source. The passion of their embrace corresponds—directly—to the damsels of Botticelli and Titian, and to the sacramental bodies of Michelangelo.

In the giddy fornication of those sublime adolescents, the Middle Ages gasped its last breath.

Fernando and Isabel erupt in an age of exhaustion. Their potency is strictly angelic. They do not seem to be, they *are* angels: beautiful, violent to the point of extermination, dazzling, and free of cavities. The obtuse and generally parochial historians who obscured their glory nevertheless had to qualify them with words that correspond to a rigorous angelology.

No moral problem could distract them from their purpose. "Morality" is a proposition of the fallen, of the human, of the degraded. Of beings who must create and justify themselves.

Fernando and Isabel were, naturally, exempt from this human abberration, as well as from any other redemptive tourney.[2]

•

He meditated on his existential situation. He nourished the modest orphism of the apprehensive: he ordered another

[2]Author's note: In Muslim angelology, there is a clear reference to the category of angels that come to Earth, in germinative return, consigned by the anger of a God harassed by the indiscreet, cognitive passion of humankind.

The *angelus* is substantially the messenger (see Henri Corbin). Proclus also refers to them (*Theologia Platonica, Book I*): in their least sophisticated and most "human" form, they assume the character of *daimons* and heros. For Saint Thomas and the Scholastics, Fernando and Isabel would be included in the third hierarchy (that closest to human nature). Almost unanimously, angelologists agree as to the awesomeness and insolence of these beings that dwell on the margin of the Christian code: they do not need *salvation*. They do not need faith or hope; they do not know charity. Probably they are repulsed by piety. Their only concerns are the laws of their mission.

Their remoteness, their essential aristocracy, is centered in their lack of guilt or of any notion of original sin.

One must remember that when on January 8, 1912, Rainer Maria Rilke stood on the terrace of Duino Castle, he was assaulted by the descent—or passage—of these splendid and insolent beings.

This exquisite poet was terrified in the face of such power, and sought refuge in the first "Duino Elegy," in which he recounts his hazardous experience.

In spite of the opinion of Salvador de Madariaga, the case of Cristóbal Colón was different; he was a superman, not an angel, an impassioned creator—like a Gonzalo de Córdoba or the Marqués de Cádiz, or Botticelli or Michelangelo—of something new.

jug of wine. The muddled and inconsequential noise of the tavern was the very silence he needed for cloaking himself in angst. He searched his soul. Imprudently, he made the journey inward through the corridors of the past. He did not suppress nostalgia or self-pity: in the process, he conceived a prototype for the tango.

He looked back on his twenty long years as a sailor and castaway, as a self-made cartographer and husband-for-gain. He pondered the days of resigned, womanless erotomania. The months at sea, the commercial piracy, the ports of brilliant sun or hyperborean fog.

What had he done in his life? Almost nothing that could satisfy the ambition of a man who—in all modesty— knew himself to be a direct descendant of the prophet Isaiah.

Up to then, nothing. Alone, without a country, an outsider, a widower without a legacy, destitute, and burdened with a terrible esoteric knowledge that no one seemed to appreciate.

In any case, the research that had consumed him for years was not lost. His intuitions had jelled. He knew, beyond the shadow of a doubt: he had been chosen for the Mission.

Long years of gathering information. Searching for clues in veiled remarks. Stealing insect-riddled maps from bureau drawers while the seduced widows of sailors less fortunate than he slept the exhausted sleep of pleasure and guilt.

There was also the time when—relentless—he kept slapping the dying shipwrecked sailor on a beach in Madeira.

"Come on, don't die on me now. Talk!"

"We saw pale copper-colored men with straight black hair. Must have been the men of the Great Khan. A way off in the distance, a raft was breaking up; it had the kind of palm roof, and a big yellow fiber sail of some kind, and on the sail was this dumb, grinning face of a god . . . like the big masks . . . they wear . . . when they have the fire festivals . . . in Valen . . . cia . . ."

The sailor died in his arms, and Colón was unable to continue questioning him in the name of science.

In Rok, a city in Ultima Thule (Iceland), he had tortured a Viking, and made him describe with his handful of Latin words the coast of Vinland where Bishop Gnuppron had landed during a pastoral mission.

He felt the choking sensation of knowing himself bursting with knowledge that had not been received as it should. How to approach *Her*?

Twenty years of voyaging, and danger, and yet here he sat, in the bowels of a tavern, powerless.

It was difficult for him to accept the incredible scheme of things. He had to keep in mind that if he started to run toward the royal tent, shouting his revelations, he would be torn apart by guard dogs.

Essential knowledge would disappear with him: the dichotomy of all creation; the fact that all beings are either aerial or amphibian—since at the time of Genesis there was only water or air (or, if you wish, mist, which is the combination of the two). Underneath it all, we are all fish or birds! What is human hair but the remnants of a magnificent plumage that has faded from lack of flight? Though the human being has no memory of flight, only envy. And, above all, there was his secret knowledge of an Earthly Paradise.

But he would not waste time before the monarchs in describing these great discoveries. He would go right to the point: he would explain something that undoubtedly had great geopolitical consequences (a phrase not in usage in those days). He would explain to them how, contrary to generally held belief, the earth is flat. How one can sail to the end of the Ocean Sea, to the rim of the last land on earth, which, like a quarry, contains the waters of the sea.

Years before, after listening to many sailors, Colón had reached the conclusion that mariners are afraid to sail far out to sea because they know they will be sailing, at their peril, around a sphere—that of the curvature of the earth. They know that since they do not have gum on the soles of their feet, and nothing to hold their ships in the water, they will inevitably fall into the Stellar Void once they have passed the tolerable limits of the curvature they attribute—wrongly—to the planet.

Colón had ruminated on this problem for years, and could defend it before the learned men of Salamanca: when the humble little ant makes its circuit of the melon, it does not plunge into space, because its gummy little feet and weightless body allow it to counter the Negative Force (that is what Cristóbal called it) that drags everything and everybody toward primordial Chaos, the indefinite, silence. (In this, he concurred with Anaximander.) Man, in contrast, physically cursed—and progressively worse off—lacks the advantages of the modest and unpresuming little ant. The annoyance of sweaty feet, the part of the body that perspires most heavily, is the vestige of a lost aptitude.

Only a man who knows that the earth is flat—even though the *world* is round—has the courage to sail toward the Indies! The king and queen must be so informed! He almost shouted it out, but contained himself. Once it had been

tailors who persecuted him; now it was the Holy Brotherhood, the men wearing the sign of the arrow!

He knew the frustration of the scientist who faces the
impenetrable wall of ignorance.

That was absolutely one of the worst afternoons of his
life. Gloomily, he thought back to his missed opportunity for
order and happiness: his marriage to Felipa Moñiz Perestrello,
in a Lisbon that would remain forever behind him.

•

She lived like a prisoner in a strictly run school, and was
allowed out only on Sundays. She came to mass on her
grandmother's arm, elegant, dazzling in her youth and grace,
and Christovao greeted her with his best smile, which she
returned with a genteel nod. Those bronze voices, summoning
the faithful to eleven-o'clock mass!

The brilliant light of Lisbon, on the steps of the Convento
dos Santos.

Christovao was twenty-eight. Without a ship, burning
with ambition, dissatisfied more because of restlessness and
ideologies than driven to "find a profession"; a halfhearted
employee of Genoese multinationals which, like the same
companies today, operated in two spheres: commerce and
piracy.

He could not believe that light, those girls on their way
to church in the long summer skirts that protected them
from visual rape. But just as Felipa Moñiz Perestrello was
entering, a breeze rose from the Tagus, blew—at a velocity of
about six to eight knots, ENE—along the avenue that led

from the Marine Arsenal to the Royal Palace, and belled out Felipa's skirts. He felt as if he had been poleaxed; his knees buckled; he was abnormally flushed. He saw a dimple in a cheek, a nose with nostrils like butterfly wings, a fuzz from just south of an ear to the plane of a cheek: a ripe peach.

Like Dante when he saw Bice Portinari (already well developed at nine), he felt that "within me, my heart was all atremble."

It was April in Portugal; to be exact, April 14, 1477. It is a well-known fact that in the northern hemisphere this is the month that causes the lilacs of the heart to burst forth from a barren earth eager to escape winter.

For him, left without a ship in an unfortunate piratical venture, a seller of maps and nautical books, poor, and not even honest, the vision of that *jeune fille* of good family was truly cataclysmic.

Christovao realized that his ambition lay in that dimple.

On August 13, 1476, half naked, floating on his back like a cork, paddling with one hand—the other clutching a broken oar—he had reached the rocky Portuguese coast. So many men had drowned! What had saved him was his unflagging sense of mission, and his intuition of the benefits of his amphibian heritage (in spite of the rough seas, he had struggled free from his hose but once on shore immediately had the luck to find something to cover his feet, his secret).

He was washed ashore on a shoal between treacherous reefs: the sandy palms of a God who, after mauling him about considerably, was now taking him in His hands. He felt safe. *Confirmed.* He knew that his pirating days, from which he had received so much satisfaction and knowledge, were something that belonged to the past.

Ragged, disoriented, followed from the beach by a mangy dog, he introduced himself at the offices of Spinola, a branch of a Genoese company, and they promoted him to the respectability of employment as a copyist and dealer in nautical books. It was they who suggested the advantages of a good marriage.

"Who is she?" he asked on the steps of the Convento dos Santos.

"Felipa Moñiz Perestrello, with her widowed mother."

After eight eleven-o'clock masses, he won the favor of her glance. Five Sundays later, the first, barely perceptible bow: "to the gentleman from Genoa—like your dear departed father—an employee of Spinola."

Three weeks later, wearing a dress suit that the Berardis rented for weddings or accepting a public appointment, he was received in the Perestrello home. Shamelessly, he praised men who plied the seas, staring at a portrait of the dead man who had earned renown as a sailor. It is known that he was charming.

"Ah, Portugal! Ah, what balmy weather!" For a partner's share, the Berardis had created a fictitious family for him: one Susan Fontanarossa, the solemn wife of one Domenique Coulomb, a French admiral; two snobbish sisters; an aged nana, who called him "lad"; and even a feisty little dog, fat from a diet of *marron glacé.*

The wedding festivities were low-key, in order not to offend the unarguable lack of appetite of the departed Moñiz Perestrello. They threw the traditional rice, and then left them alone in the family mansion. Señora Perestrello, sobbing, took her valise and went to the home of her brother, the Archbishop of Lisbon.

So there was Felipa Moñiz in her embroidered gown. And Colón, toweling off the sweat streaming down a plebeian neck that strongly resembled an Assyrian wrestler's. Incredible agitation. Vertigo of reality.

For two hours, sobbing with panicky gratitude, he clung to the thigh of the girl who was staring at him in absorbed silence; she was torn between terror at the unconditional surrender of her body to a proprietor anointed by the Will of God, and the intoxication of an unknown and powerful desire that recalled the symptoms of a bad case of influenza she had suffered two years earlier: muscular spasms, the threat of diahrrea, and a strange warmth that made her skin throb.

They were immobilized for hours, considering the incredible treasure house of unwholesome possibilities before them. (Possibility can be paralyzing, Sartre would say, with pathos and publicity, four hundred and fifty years later.)

He opened a trunk that smelled of lavender, and fished out fine underdrawers, bright red garters from long-ago noble weddings, and stockings knitted with the perversity of the Alentejo nuns.

Several times he dressed and undressed his inflatable doll—now in the maniacal hands of a man who had all the time in the world. He felt as if he had come into possession of that marvelous upper-class girl through a happy but grievous error for which sooner or later he would pay dearly. (Colón was constantly threatened by the knowledge that he was a fraud, an auxiliary form of guilt.)

A strange odor began to invade the house. Felipa was afraid they were being engulfed by an unusually high surf. In the large, handsome library, Christovao found the beam he needed. He rigged a tackle, and prepared a slip knot. He strung Felipa up by her ankle, like the twelfth tarot card (Le Pendu), which a gypsy had turned up for him in the port of Marseilles.

She hung there, slack, disjointed, her hair almost touching the floor. Now Christovao could confront the evidence of her flesh, study it, smell it, stroke her limbs, observe her most adorable and secret regions. He labored with serene perturbation, interrupted from time to time by postorgasmic lethargy.

The thrill of possession! It was beyond his understanding that through some legal-religious hocus-pocus the delicious body of Felipa had become chattel, his exclusive property.

As the night advanced, so, too, did he advance across the most secret valleys of her person. Her fabled, mythic flesh was revealed in all its majesty and awesome power.

He marveled: "Now nothing and no one can sunder our union or stand between us. God has joined us together." His eyes filled with tears of libidinous gratitude.

For the first time, he had known a consecrated woman.

Finally, at twenty-eight, he had passed from metaphysics to reality.

He nibbled her fleshy parts. He studied the secretion and nature of her moistnesses. His tongue explored the expanse of that well-bred skin. He tasted, dumbstruck, the faintly salty savor that confirmed—scientist to the end!—his theory on man's, even woman's, amphibian past. Salt remained in the pores, remnants of a mythic life in the sea.

Since Felipa found the rope painful, he searched through a bureau and found a piece of soft woolen cloth to relieve her discomfort.

In the same drawer, in the back right corner, he found the famous secret chart the Florentine geographer and cosmographer Paolo Toscanelli had sent to the departed Perestrello with a clear X-marks-the-spot over the Antilles and Cipango, not far off the coast of Portugal. (In spite of his sexual excitement, he immediately registered the importance of his find, which he would study in the weeks to come. This was a decisive moment in his destiny: ignorant of that erotic geography, which to him seemed fantastic, he thought he had discovered the map of the Earthly Paradise.)

Their bliss continued until dawn. Only with the first stirring of the birds in the trees was Christovao emboldened to venture inward. Two days later, in the sacred seclusion of the newly wed, he reached the hymen.

They received no one for six months. Worried, the widow of Perestrello knocked at a door and shuttered windows that were bolted as securely as if the cautious occupants had left for the summer. She had to be content to communicate by means of a basket lowered from an upper balcony, in which the worried mother placed food, and physiotheological instructions for Felipa.

After several weeks, they left for Porto Santo, in Madeira, the family seat of the Perestrellos, where Colón was intended to revive the business of raising rabbits, an enterprise in which the dead patriarch had truly shone.

Christovao had to learn the science of conies: their reproduction and their diseases. Those were happy days. Little Diego was born. They made their first shipments of rodents' pelts and salted meat for the slaves of Lisbon.

But Porto Santo, a small Atlantic island in the Madeira group, was no place for Christovao to establish himself as a good bourgeois, or to forget his descent from Isaiah, a bloodline he himself humbly recalled among friends.

Felipa was becoming impatient with his wanderings along the white sand beaches, the long nights spent staring at the sea, his inattention to the rabbits, which multiplied into an omnivorous mass that devoured all the vegetation in the garden, and even clothing of the vigorous colonists drawn from Porto to Porto by dreams of wealth.

Three months after the birth of Diego, the routine lost its charm. Colón, changing the baby's diaper, broke into a cold sweat, and felt the pangs of angina; he realized he was betraying his Mission.

Lunch was at twelve, dinner at six. But he might stumble in, oblivious, at three in the afternoon, carrying pieces of wood or reeds he had found on the rocks, signs, he was convinced, of the unknown continent he sensed was so near.

Once, returning home after midnight, he told a sobbing Felipa:

"I couldn't come any sooner. I was standing out on Ponta da Agulha, sniffing the air. It carried the perfume of strange flowers, flowers from another world. . . ."

Felipa began to decline. She neglected her doves, and the rabbits took over the dovecote. She lost her happiness, her peace of mind, her small pleasures. She began to waste away in silence, in the manner of sensitive persons affected by a disappointment over which they have no control. She took refuge in embroidery and prayer.

She realized that her husband, a titan with an eye out for his chance in life, would not be lingering in the season of love. She felt this was irreversible, and a great tragedy.

By March of 1484, she weighed thirty-eight kilos. Followed by the tiny Diego, Christovao would carry her outside

in his arms to take the sun. If it was a warm day, he carried
her to the fountain, and tenderly subjected her to ablutions
he presumed to be curative.

"You must build up your blood," he told her. "Eat
rabbit stew with lots of garlic, and raw carrots. . . ."

But she could not swallow a mouthful. She vomited
every time she saw a family of rabbits.

He lay awake, night after night, annoyed because the
sound of the conies munching the wood of the house prevented him from hearing the rhythm of the waves. By candlelight, he read and reread the book written by Cardinal
d'Ailly.

His conviction grew. First: one could return to the
Earthly Paradise, as the cardinal said: "There is there a
fountain that waters the Garden of Delights and which forks
into four rivers." Second: "The Earthly Paradise is a pleasant
land situated to the east, at a great distance from our world."
Colón noted in the margin: "Beyond the Tropic of Capricorn
is found the most beautiful of all dwelling places, for it is the
finest and most noble spot in the world, the Earthly Paradise." Third: he knew there was nothing there that was not
jewels or gold. Therefore, he could bring back enough to
invest in a Genoese business and buy the majority of the
stock. And, oh yes, he would recover the Holy Sepulcher and
reopen the route to the East now under the control of ferocious Tartars and their "iron scimitar curtain." Fourth: he
had shaped an esoteric knowledge he could not write down,
but confined to memory.

His exultation during that time knew no limit. His
megalomaniac solipsism distanced him from reality. He went
around in a daze, kicking aside the hordes of rabbits. Calmly,

gratefully, modestly, he recognized that, in him, genius had surpassed human bounds.

Insofar as his marital life was concerned, tenderness—like weeds or the rabbits—had ineradicably replaced eroticism. Conjugal eroticide had been committed.

Tenderness but not love (maybe there had never been love). The fact is that Felipa looked more and more like a faded paper doll. Before his eyes, she grew increasingly bidimensional: first it was her breasts, then her thighs, then the curve of her face. She flattened out like a thin layer of veneer. So thin, that to Christovao any possibility of penetrating her carnally seemed madness, something that might do her irreparable harm.

By the end of that year 1484, it was over: she had no *relevance*. She was a portrait, a memory, which he must frame and hang above the carving board in the dining hall. By now the children of the colonists had finished off the rabbits, and then, as the last straw, the King of Portugal had vigorously and contemptuously rejected Christovao's proposal to sail to Cipango and the Antilles. No one took him seriously.

Historians cannot agree: once they were back in Lisbon, did he kill her (that is, in more precise idiomatic terms, put her out of her misery) or, with the generosity of a true Discépolo, to spare her the shame of living with someone who had hung her in the dining hall above the aforementioned carving board, did he sell her to Moorish white slavers, who then auctioned her off to the highest bidder in the market in Casablanca?

No one ever knew. The fact is that no one ever found the tomb of this person who from birth had been reserved a vault in the most fashionable cemetery in Lisbon.

It was about that time that Christovao and young Diego traveled, hastily and inconspicuously, to Andalusia—without bringing their good furniture and with very little money— where they sought shelter in the Convent of La Rábida, a little beyond Punta Umbría.

And while Padre Torres, assured by the presence of the boy, was looking for the master key, little Diego asked his father: "Papa, where is my *mamita?*"

Colón was visibly distressed. He pretended to have to urinate, to hide his tear-filled eyes from the boy. When someone disappears—whether or not by our own doing—the pain we feel is the sorrow of those who are left behind, of those who suffer the loved one's absence, the void. To us, the dead person seems liberated. We suffer for the emptiness *we* feel. (That is why the Chinese, wiser than we, celebrate and laugh when facing the reality of death. They are thinking of the person who died, not themselves.)

•

Caonabó, Anacaona, Siboney, then Belbor, Guaironex, the *cacique* Cubais. The delicious and frivolous Bimbú. All of them, standing high on the beach, observing the young initiates on their journey toward the Open. They had drunk the necessary potions, and already some were staggering like cormorants trying to get off the ground. The changing color of the iris of their eyes gave them a strange glaucous gaze that focused on something beyond their surroundings.

Some were stretched out on the sand, howling. That was the first, the wholesome, horror when they realized they

were dissolving in Space, and tried to cling to "reality."
Some seized tufts of grass, or the root of a palm tree, but in
vain: they were being dragged away by a hurricane-force
wind (although the blithe palms were not stirring). They were
dissolving; that is why they were howling. They were visiting
the House of Nonbeing, which no one should forget during his
brief sojourn in Being. Because although both Being and
Nonbeing are Being, the human being, endowed with painful
reason, cannot resist pride in his ephemeral incarnation—
definitive, yes, but unsubstantial and untranscendent.

"Pity them," commented the beautiful Princess Anacaona.
"How they are suffering."

The *tecuhtli* of Tlatelolco, an occasional visitor in the
islands, was also observing the voyage toward Totality of an
entire generation of youths.

He was there to offer the protection of the Aztec
Confederation to those happy island people, constantly harassed
by the excessive (a fact that must be recognized) religious zeal
of the cannibal Caribs: theophagists, they believed that they
could eat the beauty and courage of the gods. By feasting on
handsome Tainos, they would eliminate ugliness and ferocity
from their race.

The great Taino chieftain Guaironex, perhaps feeling
nostalgic about his own initiation, ran down to the beach and
performed several dance steps among the drugged young men.

Sound of tambours and bones. The deep moan of huge
conch shells. It was a warm evening on the royal lowlands of
Guanahani, October 12, 1491 (for these Lucayas people, who
possessed a magical calendar, it was the year 16-Star).

With that voyage to Totality, they averted the danger of
being subsumed in the immediate and ordinary; two funda-

mental dangers—one spatial, the other temporal. The howling youths were dissolving, terrified, in primordial Space; they were falling from human time into eternity. They were visiting the All Great.

Only after three days would they begin the return.

The young females, led by Siboney and Anacaona, danced gentle *areitos* to the monochord note of the tambours. Wearing only their ritual *naguas,* the short transparent skirts that merely veiled the shadow of the mound of Venus.

Summoned by purest desire, the disoriented youths began their return from Space. As their faculties returned, they reclaimed mobility, sight, objects, familiar faces. They were returning from an immeasurable altitude.

Some were beginning to enter the rhythm of the dance. The girls took them by the hand, led their steps. One youth lay among the dunes with his welcomer; woman was the best port of arrival.

One of them, only one, a visionary, said that on the sea, to the east, he had seen the shadows of the *tzitzimins,* the invading devils, the furies, who had the ability to remove men from the sacred continuum of the Origin. But no one believed him.

They put too much faith in metaphor.

•

"Death must be swift; this affords the soul of the condemned person the maximum opportunity for salvation. Yea, verily: be hospitable and charitable with the wayfarer."

Isabel was reading the *Instructions* for the Holy Brotherhood. She signed with a decisive flourish. She knew that the soul that dwells in the body of a sinner is corrupted. The Orientals are very careful in this regard (Torquemada had told her about the Bardothodol). The soul: an ethereal essence that falls like the gentle dew.

There was need for the most rigorous Public Order.

Years of civil war. Years of being on the march to impose the crown. No time to linger on the pitiable—*le pitoyable*. Better one day as a lion than one hundred years as a sheep! Ride! March!

> *Ride, Fernando,*
> monta tanto, tanto monta,
> *and, equally well,*
> *ride, Isabel!*

And the cavalry! And lancers! Infantrymen, halberdiers, crossbowmen! Since we must die, better to die in battle! And fire, fire and more fire, until unity is imposed and tolerance reigns! Death to intolerance!

The royal grooms, embarrassed, eyes to the ground, held her stirrup as she mounted Apollo—astride.

"Our objective: Christendom! Our motto: Humanism!"

She was splendid. Tight-fitting long elkskin breeches, glossy boots. Jubilant, she sits her horse (two nuns cross themselves to see feminine fragility placed in such danger of being crushed upon a saddle tree). Red waistcoat with gold frogs. A short military jacket buttoned beneath a stiff collar and, over that, a short riding cape, a tabard of black velvet with a silver chain (an F with the sign of the arrow on the hook, and on the eye, a graceful Y). A beaver hat with a green pheasant feather from the marshlands of the Pripet. And her marvelous red-blond hair flowing in the wind as she galloped.

Raze Madrigalejo! She was off to the fiesta of war. Feverish days. The fury and joy of battle. Time that was measured in winded horses: Madrigal, down with a leg broken in the foxholes of Ávila; Apollo, winded in Despeñaperros; then Baturro, sunstruck beneath the blazing sun of La Mancha.

Nights galloping through the mists of Galicia. Afternoons in the burning dust of Castile. Which way? Has the tower been sighted? Farther south! Ever southward!

Hoofbeats on the arid drum of Spain. Battle against wavering counts, and barons inclined toward the flimsy legitimacy of La Beltraneja.

Dawns beside icy watercourses. The bone-chilling cold of January, and the melancholy songs of the troops around the green fire of a sacrificed poplar.

Merciless, they demolish the fortifications of Madrigalejo. Rebels with slashed throats hang from its steaming walls. Good artillery work with the polished white marble balls quarried in Carrara (opening the vein where Michelangelo will find the impeccable block for the *Pietà*).

Isabel is exhausted (and to top it all, her campaign tent is swarming with campaign mosquitoes). She lies awake and writes Fernando:

My king, my lord. I and Madrigal still deafened by the blast of the canons singing with cannonballs, balls from Carrara. Have you purified Zaragoza? Let not your hand tremble. At least, offer an Occident in decline a way out of the last four or five hundred years. And, by the way, have you come across the blond knave the gypsy witch saw in your cards? The dark knight, I have no doubt of it, has turned up: his name is Gonzalo, and he is from Córdoba. But to more practical matters. The new regiment of Galicians is a marvel; imagine, they bleed only when hit in an artery; you would think they were solid flesh. In cooperation with the Duke of Cádiz, we have installed a breeding pen for Nepalese gurkhas. They reproduce just like humans, every nine months; they are small but muscular: perfect for scaling towers.

I, the Queen

The following day, dressed in brocade, wearing her ermine mantle and the crown she had learned to wear without its tilting, she entered Trujillo, preceded by her handsome but defiant heralds. The people, stupid, obedient, as always, in awe of bejeweled royalty:

Aragón's flowers
bloom in Castile.

But "March!" "March!" That same night, taking advantage of the cool air, she rode at the head of a troop of cavalry, on toward Cáceres. Two thousand lancers at the trot, chewing on olives stolen from the moonlit olive groves of Extremadura.

The New Order was solidifying. The black-robed figures of the Inquisition were now in every city. Innocent children and servant girls flocked with smiling curiosity around the mournful horsemen as they arrived with mule trains laden with a kind of mobile workshop: ropes and pulleys, wheels and cranks, braziers; leather trunks crammed with scissors, Neapolitan boots, nail pincers, trained rats, bronze eyeball prods; Moroccan scorpions, delicate nerve tweezers, and crucifixes.

It was Isabel who had convinced Torquemada. "You, a monk; how can you live in the quiet world of the court! You must go out and seek sin in the streets, in bodies! You must save yourself saving others!"

They knew that the Occident could be reborn only in reaffirming its Greco-Roman roots.

For the masses: renunciation and rosary. For the lords: the fiesta of courage and power.

Men-dogs in their places: plants, fish, public employees.

The cult of the Virgin Mary was sinfully close to paganism. Processions multiplied. For every saint an altar, not a candle. Christomania left no room for thought. Regiments of nuns and priests were forming, devoid of even the most elementary good sense.

Fasting three times a week. Asceticism of hard bread and well water. Forced confession. Flagellation.

Isabel held them captive in their own absurdity, and in their scorn and fear of the body.

Every priest's heels were raw from repeated processions to the rocky Mount Carmels found in every locality. Tales of levitation began to proliferate, mystical visions, sacred apparitions, souls returned from the dead with horrifying descriptions of desired purgatorial fire and despair and suffering in the caldrons of Hell. Children, as they left church, were trembling and pale.

With the vision of inspired politicians, Fernando and Isabel realized that they needed a papacy cut to the measure of their empire. A Vatican salvaged from the ruin of pietist lethargy.

The mission of the Valencian Cardinal Rodrigo de Borja, justly praised by historians, was their opportunity to define an imperial, cruel, and renascent Catholicism. A Catholic Church that would not fear the *man* in mankind, and not affix plaster fig leafs to Phidias's wrestlers.

Rodrigo de Borja would be the pope they required. In turn, that Renaissance pope would arise from the strength of the angelic adolescents. Borja was forty-two when he arrived in Spain from Rome. He had black eyes and an athletic build: "a dominating and majestic figure." He was versed in the ways of the world, capable of exercising power with innate violence.

On October 20, 1472, he was greeted in Valencia with the news of the massive slaughter of Jews and *conversos* in Córdoba. He was preceded by black-uniformed drummers and an entourage of chamber musicians. He hosted a meal with thirty-two dishes and wines served in golden chalices to honor Pedro González de Mendoza, whose ambition was to be cardinal and who would be a key player in consolidating the power of the terrible adolescents.

But the historically decisive understanding between Borja (the future Pope Alexander VI) and Fernando and Isabel required consecration.

This occurred near Alcalá on February 27, 1473.

It was a mild dawn, Fernando and Isabel stood on a hilltop. Fernando had enveloped his body and hers in a large, full-length felt cape. From a distance, it looked as if the rocky hillock were crowned by a kind of rigid cone, a Druid monument.

Cardinal Borja, unaccompanied (he had traveled in the greatest secrecy), was climbing the hill on foot. As he came nearer, he could see the heads of Fernando and Isabel emerging from the cone of felt: the glow of red hair in the blue-gray mist was unmistakable.

Fernando was standing behind Isabel, holding her tightly to him, possessing her with serene concentration. The cape was their shelter; a chamber for their tense, interlocked bodies. Her slightly bent knees compensated for the shorter stature of the monarch-incubus.

The scene had ineffable ritual power.

They achieved orgasm—barely a shiver of delight—just as the prelate came within a few steps of the erotic mandala.

This was the supreme consecration, the holy hymeneal, the engendering of a new synarchy.

The empire was born, as well as a Catholic-Imperial Church that would jettison the ballast of a grim, beatified Christianity. For an instant, Rodrigo de Borja stood before the embraced and motionless adolescents, who, eyes still half closed, were descending from the velvety lassitude of satisfied lovers who have soared to the highest heights—true communicants. Then he slipped his right, ringed, hand with the enormous seal of nobility inside the felt cone, and from the warm thigh of the princess wiped away a drop of that precious sperm born of the purest and most powerful love, and with it anointed his brow.[3]

Fernando let the cape fall, and all three knelt upon the cool, dew-covered grass. They joined hands, and, with

---

[3]Author's note: The site of the scene just described has been authenticated. It is a few miles form Alcalá (where Isabel then resided), between Lëches, today Loeches, and Torrejón de Ardor, a little to the north of Torrejón del Rey. Today a rubber and vulcanizing plant stands on the spot.

quiet devotion, Fernando and Isabel, following the cardinal's rich baritone, recited three Our Fathers and three Ave Marías.

·

The body of Giménez Gordo, a powerful businessman who had not read the antibourgeois and antiliberal signals of the new imperial order, was still swaying gently to and fro.

Fernando was pacifying Zaragoza.

He had invited his influential opponent to dine, and, at a sign during dessert, the guards had hanged him. For rebellion.

To and fro. The oval belly in a Flemish silk waistcoat reminded Fernando of the pendulum of the great clock in the cathedral of Berne.

He continued peeling his orange. When he had finished, he asked for his writing case, blew away the breadcrumbs from his meal, and wrote to Isabel—so far away and diligent in waging her civil war in the fields of Castile:

. . . *naturally, I allowed him to finish his custard. He had a sweet tooth and spicy conversation.*

Have you found the knave with the sea-green eyes? They tell me that on Aragonese playing cards all the knaves have dark eyes. Only knights, and two of the four kings, have blue. But you must persist: every empire is founded on one admiral and one grand marshal.

Pacifying Zaragoza is a nightmare. I find my sole pleasure in hunting parties with the Archbishop of Zaragoza; he is ten now,

*and happily innocent of catechism and Vatican cunning. You know,
he even resembles me slightly."*[4]

*Our diversion in these dark days is riding through the rocky
hills with Beatriz de Bobadilla—the Marquesa de Moya's niece. I
ride slightly behind this slender Amazon and the archbishop. How
refreshing their laughter on the trail of the fox! What fresh and
perverse innocence!*

*My smaller falcon—Copete, you remember?—was harassed
all this morning by a young swallow. He was never able to make a
kill. He returned to my shoulder mortified, without prey, and with
his heart pounding from the fruitless hunt. I had to spit brandy
beneath his wings, the way cockfighters do. But I am sure that
tomorrow, or the day after, my clever Copete will have his way with
the little swallow. Even as I write these lines I hear him flexing his
wings, restless in his iron cage.*

Fernando

Isabel felt herself slipping into her worst anguish: jealousy. Her old and unconquerable enemy. The black cloud
that darkened her peace of mind. That hussy! Little swallow,
indeed!

The prostration of the afternoon was followed by the
terrible ravages of passion. It was a night of wild she-wolves.
The campaign tent was alive with shadows and desperately
nuptial sighs. The wind moaned like a damsel yielding to love.

---

[4]Author's note: Fernando, with great hypocrisy, was referring to
Alfonso de Aragón, his natural son by the Viscountess of Eboli. Alfonso
had a brilliant career: archbishop at six, cardinal at eight. He was never
bothered either by mysticism or an excess of faith.

Padre Talavera and the Conde de Benavente—one calling upon faith and decency, the other upon reasons of state—tried to calm her.

They gave her soothing teas. From time to time she fell asleep, but immediately awakened with a terrible cry (a lioness giving birth), so drenched in cold sweat that her teeth were chattering.

Such fierce excitement infected the lancers, who began to wander about the campsite. Without knowing why, they began scuffling and trading punches. They were at loose ends, and aggressive. Military discipline was dangerously weakened.

At dawn, facing the untenability and intensity of the crisis, a solution was proposed: a messenger was sent to Fernando, ordering him to a secret meeting at a point midway between them: the Convent of Almagro.

That Bobadilla, playing the cunning child. Isabel knew through the girl's aunt, the marquesa, Isabel's best friend, that the girl, abnormally advanced for her years, was not ideal company for a young bastard archbishop.

She had astonished the court with her artful eccentricities. Especially her appetite for dressing in metal: no one else wore bronze thigh guards. These *toneletes,* once in style during the time of the scandalous Burgundian court, had the effect of lifting and accentuating the profile of firm buttocks (in the case of the exciting Beatriz) clad in tight black corduroy. Since the time of the mythic Joan of Arc, the fetishism of the "Amazonian armored virgin" had excited the imagination of adolescent princelings.

There was also talk of her intimate gold armor, worked by the renowned Stanislav Mahler (who decades later would be famous for smithing the armor of John of Austria, today displayed in the Escorial). His chastity belts were legendary (Beatriz wore them autonomously), embellished with cameos of hunting scenes, or coats of armor crafted by artisans from Toledo.

In court circles, gossips had it that on summer nights Beatriz ran tauntingly among the halberdiers and guards wearing only that medieval garb. Laughing like a madwoman, she took pleasure in watching furious captains fighting among themselves, or trying key after key in her lock. She hid the true key in her bedchamber, beneath a statue of the Virgin of Carmen, to whom she prayed. (It was also rumored that it was the meticulous tracker Fernando who found the correct key.)

Isabel raged when she received the letter: it was like pouring oil on an already burning passion.

For his part, Fernando relied on the revenge mechanism of sex to offset Isabeline superiority: her Latin, which he never learned; her family grace; her Petrarchan poetry; her calligraphy. We must not forget that he was short, stocky, uncouth, and short on imagination. Isabel had slender ankles, and—and this is an essential bit of information—in her instep one could see a delicate network of blue veins and tendons tense as a Norman filly's. The similar tendons at the nape of her neck were notorious: they bounded a valley of finest fuzz that betrayed the Lancaster line of the Trastamaras, blood she received through John of Gaunt.

In contrast, Fernando's feet, very simply, were socially unacceptable, scaly, with cuticles like those of some of the lower lizards.

None of this is without importance, it matters.

These sociosexual differences were manifested in their nocturnal clash of desires, in their wars of passion. Fernando's penis emitted a grave, unwavering buzzing, something like the humming of an affable shopkeeper stocking his shelves. The Isabeline *yoni,* on the other hand, whistled ever so sweetly, like the barely audible call of Colombian orchids in heat.

Isabel rode from her camp at breakneck speed—today the site of the town of Venta del Prado (on Highway 630).

"Faster. Faster! Spur your horses!"

Whirlwind pace. She was obsessed by the image of the insolent Beatriz, trotting before Fernando and the boy archbishop in her provocative *toneletes.* This ghost, made painfully more beautiful by jealousy, appeared and reappeared in the dust of the road.

In the warm light of dawn, villagers watched the spectacle of a horse being ridden into the ground by a dusty, intense Carmelite nun; from all appearances, the horsemen who were eating her dust were enraged because they could not catch her.

Botijas. Villamasías, Orellana la Vieja, and then, the town of Don Rodrigo, with its bitter water and swollen-bellied children watching a wild-eyed nun flash past, a nun—oddly enough—with a dagger at her waist.

From a different direction, an enigmatic Franciscan—his profile lacking the benignity and humility one expects from that order—was entering the province of La Mancha from Teruel; his horse's hooves were chipped and jagged from the rocky terrain of Aragón, and he was eager for the relief of the marshland of Pantano de Alarcón.

In both riders, the internal level of passion was rising; it was worse than what could be perceived externally.

They converged upon the convent in Almagro within an hour or two of each other, blown for two days and two nights on the winds of desire.

The Franciscan claimed to be a teacher of Latin. The Carmelite gave assurances that she was carrying instructions from her order for the convent in Balbastro.

It was almost two centuries later, in Venice in 1687, that the account of an abbot-voyeur was published in the titillating collection entitled *Picaresca Castellana*. We must allow for the pornographic tastes of the time, but infer that, after al fresco ablutions, they met in a cell for penitents. The abbot writes: "Her habit dropped to her alabaster feet and her marvelous naked body shone in the moonlight. She was still wearing—dizzying proof of her religious state—the starched wimple white as the wings of the marble angel guarding the tomb of Lorenzo de' Medici in Florence. When she removed that, her hair fell loose in blond torrents, molten gold flowing down the slopes of a volcano. She sprang forward like a leopard someone had unwisely tied in a sack."

The night of the penitents was long and intense.

The next morning in the refectory, following matins, the abbot heard evidence that by a surprising coincidence all the dreams of the seminarians had been of zoological nature. One said that in his dreams he had seen an ass braying hoarsely in its death throes, another that a green hyena had been snarling beneath the arches of the sanctuary; a young student from Asturias told a nightmare about a circle of howling wolves that formed into a blazing ring that melted the snow as it rolled.

The abbot, who evidently had not slept well and was in a foul temper, imposed silence and ordered "The Martyrdom of Santa Lucía" to be read from the lectern.

As they left the hall, Padre Azcona observed:

"Is it not curious that the Franciscan and the Carmelite who arrived yesterday left without breaking fast and without hearing mass? Did anyone see them in the chapel?"

And the abbot:

"What about the horse that died at dawn by the water trough? Have you ordered it to be butchered? That may have been the source of the whinnying."

(The noble Madrigal, foundered from too rapidly slaking the thirst of burning roads beneath the spur of the Carmelite, was quartered and salted down for convent use. The head, tail, and hocks were distributed to the poor.)

•

The celebration for the Conde de Cabra lasted seven days and seven nights. Nothing like it had ever been seen in Castile. From the epicenter to the outermost shock waves, the dextrorotatory spiral was roiling and rumbling. The conde was entering the intimate, the ultimate, sphere of the king and queen: he was consecrated SS.

Isabel exercised her exclusive privilege for the occasion: the color green, in a silk gown with ballooning sleeves. She was dazzling in her famous ruby necklace and a wide belt encrusted with lapis lazuli. Her wire-framed conical hennin was three feet tall, and from its tip fell a fifteen-foot length of cloudlike tulle that floated at the whim of the breeze.

She wore a carmine farthingale trimmed in cloth of gold, and, for when it grew cold, a stole of golden red furs, a gift of her German relatives, inveterate huntsmen.

Imposing. Her face colored with powders from Alexandria. Her perfume, essence of orange blossoms.

Fernando was beside her. Black breeches and high boots; a black beaver hat with a black ostrich plume. Upon his chest, in silvery paint, five enormous tears symbolizing his chagrin that any Moor remained on Iberian soil.

Behind them came the Conde and Condesa de Cabra. In pristine white—the color for sacrifice or homage—their faces painted yellow, except for her eyelids in iridescent mauve.

Then the Marqués and Marquesa de Moya costumed as vanquished Moorish royalty (perhaps Boabdil and his mother).

Torquemada, properly without a partner. Barefoot, and wearing a mended habit. Walking gingerly, because with every step his belt of thorns pressed upon his kidneys.

Beatriz Bobadilla, always bizarre, in bluish steel armor and helmet with lowered visor, but with a disturbing inset of red velvet at the crotch. Since she could not walk, she was drawn in a small cart pulled by two ridiculous Hungarian dwarfs dressed like toy sailors.

Fernando and Isabel solemnly advanced toward the place of honor. They were to begin the dancing. A double row of heralds straight out of Carpaccio announced them with more enthusiasm than unison. Fifes. Drums. Shepherd's flutes.

Isabel, annoyed by all the protocol, grumbled:

"Enough of civil wars. A waste of time. What we need is a *holy* war!"

And Fernando, prudently:

"Not yet. It is not yet time, my lady. Better first to find the knave with blue eyes, and enlist the dark knight."

The Portuguese, inept but ambitious, had entered Extremadura.

They were captained by young Beltraneja, drunk with legitimacy, followed by King Alfonso, her brand-new and untested husband (they had begun their tragic campaign—as it will be seen—before consummating the union). An obese and dreadful military man who rather than a honeymoon was being treated to the bile of Mars. (La Beltraneja, riding furiously, seemed to be saying: "You see, Isabel? I snared a man, too. A king!")

When the dancing began, Isabel, very serious and pretentious in her entangling tulle, asked *doña* Leonor de Luján to be her partner.

Fernando chose Aldonza Alamán, a ploy to defuse suspicion with overt action. (Sometimes brazenness is better than dissembling.)

The dancing was merely an appetizer. After a half hour, they moved on to tables arranged in a meadow; aping Burgundian artifice, all the boulders had been painted gold.

As they were served light wines and tidbits, an astounding horological display was presented, especially organized for the honored guests. A dozen mechanical goats (*cabras* for the Cabras) of finely wrought tin, complete with fleece and ringlets and curls, whirled upon three geared disks moved by a wheel turned by two mules encased—to maintain the mechanical illusion—in rectangular metal plates.

As they passed before the head table, the kids blurted a piercing, scarcely metallic baa-a-a-a-a.

The Condesa de Cabra could not contain an emotional tear, shed for the refinement and prodigality of the sovereigns.[5]

•

The New Phalanx Tavern was a place where impromptu *picadas* were hatched. An anthill of ambitious men. Colón felt that the moment had come to make his move.

People were saying that the vogue for science, poetry, and music was fading. Inventors and theoreticians were getting short shrift. Whereas anyone dealing in erotica or in novelties in armor fared slightly better.

Ulrich Nietz was among the losers. He had presented himself as a preacher. An independent visionary in a time when all aberrations were orthodox!

He was brought into the tavern, badly wounded, after a beating at the hands of a patrol of the Holy Brotherhood.

Chance, the twists and turns of life! A fate that might have been invented by a novice novelist would have it that twenty years after he first saw him, Cristoforo, now Cristóbal, should be the one to minister to Ulrich Nietz, to place vinegar compresses on his bruises and give him well water to drink.

During his few moments of lucidity, the retired Landsknecht told how with stealth, and under cover of darkness, he had penetrated the intimate sphere of power. How

[5]Author's note: This gadgetry is described by J. Huizinga in his *Waning of the Middle Ages.*

he had given a eunuch in Isabel's service a desperate philosophical message that was mistaken for a *billet doux* from a sex
maniac. Actually, what it said was: "Forward! Man is a thing
to be surmounted! We are in the midnight that precedes the
glorious dawn of the superman. Forward! We must not be
halted by a morality that is the refuge of the aged and infirm:
of those who deny life."

They had given him a severe drubbing. They took him
for dead and threw him into a ditch. Where his Teuton
mustaches sopped up the mud. Luckily, the local dog packs
had already eaten, and chose instead to stretch out for a long
siesta.

"Now speak your piece, and be on your way!" The
lieutenant of the Brotherhood jeered as he discharged his
responsibility.

Doggedly German, the Landsknecht had not understood
that gods and supermen simply *are,* and that they detest
rhetoric.

When they are described or named, they rage as if the
namer were stealing their fire, and as if it might be extinguished among the icy pages of the *logos.*

Once again Ulrich Nietz had been rejected by the community. Pure instinct, which could not sustain any rational-
ization or "theory of instinct," had turned on him. In the
long run, it was a good thing. The Chariot of Power had
begun to roll. Isabel and Fernando were on their way to
finding their heroes, their supermen (Gonzalo de Córdoba;
the swineherd Pizzaro; an unscrupulous Genoese; the adventurer Cortés. Supermen innocent of the least theory of
supermanhood. Lacking piety or visible greatness. For Spain,
they would find the appropriate cardinal, Cisneros, who

would say: "I find the smell of gunpowder far sweeter than all the perfumes of Arabia.")

Ulrich recognized Cristóbal:

"I think once I told you that what does not kill us more strong will make us. . . ."

Cristóbal, too, had failed in his ambition to reach the epicenter. Desperate from having waited in vain, from not being recognized, from not being found by those who were looking for him and had not sensed his greatness, he joined a *picada* sponsored by the Orange Growers' Association. It was an opportunistic and pointless venture.

They had constructed a large allegorical float featuring the goddess Ceres and three giant orange spheres filled with marmalade. It took six teams to pull it.

Colón and five youths were submersed in the jelly. As they passed in front of the monarchs' box, they were to leap up like gnomes from the fruit and sing ditties touting price supports and trade barriers to protect the orange growers.

They were naive to think that anyone might find that interesting. So they were not allowed to pass before the royal pavilion, and while they were still at the entrance, their cargo was scooped clean by Gypsies from the rice fields. Two acrobats drowned in the gelatinous orange nectar.

Two days later Colón seized another opportunity, which he thought might offer him a forum for communicating his message.

This float was a mechanical allegory prepared by unfathomable German technicians, an ambitious representation of the solar system: large red balls revolving around tall poles. Suspended from a trapezelike affair, Colón, in golden armor, orbited the sun as the omnipotent god of cosmic order, Apollo, averting the ever-present threat of stellar chaos.

To his misfortune, his ellipse soon became erratic; the blind Moors turning the wheel that controlled his orbit were divided between followers of Allah and partisans of political integration. The gilded cardboard of his armor began to tear apart. His golden glory ended in disaster. He was barely able to shout his message as he fell victim to entropy: "The earth is flat! We can sail east without fear of falling into the void. It is *flat*! We can reach the Indies and monopolize the spice trade!"

Aldonza Alamán, sitting beside Fernando, said teasingly:

"Would you like me to add a little pepper to your majesty's wine?"

Through the slits in her steely visor, Beatriz Bobadilla had followed the flight of Apollo closely, with special attention for his out-of-luck athlete's body.

Isabel did not even look up: she was discussing the exorbitant cost of the banquet with her chief steward. Then she embroiled Torquemada (Torquemada embroiled would be only fair, considering the unfortunates he had sent to the stake) in a long account of predictions made by tormented *revenants* back from the tomb. The monk, no doubt about it, had what the Italians call *fascino* (today we would call it charisma). He was a child of darkness and mist. From time to time as he was listening, a drop of blood rolled from beneath his hairshirt and down his icy thighs to tickle his ankle.

So passed the first week of the celebration. Besides the amazing mechanical goats, the technical extravaganza bound by onomastic motif to the subjects of the homage, the best entertainment must have been the three Neapolitan prestidigitators who turned three large truffled turkeys into three fried sparrows that were revealed, tiny feet in the air, when the lids from three silver platters were removed.

A gourmandizing chronicler noted, in addition to lamb, and the aforementioned turkeys, the following details of the Homeric menu (dinner [I] and *souper* [II]):

I   SALMAGUNDI OF SAUSAGES AND PARTRIDGES
     GOOSE IN QUINCE JAM
     CALF DRESSED WITH CATERPILLAR SAUCE
     ROAST SONGBIRDS ON TOAST
     FRIED TROUT LACED WITH LEAN BACON
     CREAM PASTRIES
II STEWS
     PORK PIES
     RINGDOVES WITH BLACK GRAVY
     VOL-AU-VENT (*PETS DE NONNE*)
     BLANCMANGE

And assorted fruits, conserves, breads, wafers, and pastries, along with long lists of local wines and wines imported from Franche-Comté.

•

One day during those perilous times a squad of the Holy Brotherhood terrorized The New Phalanx Tavern. Expressionless, leathery faces. Glassy gamblers' eyes, empty of any gleam of humanity.

They were demanding proof of Christianity. Colón sensed

the end was near. Deep in his heart, he was relieved. State terrorism leads to an insane dialectic of self-preservation and flight versus surrender and the urge to confront the worst once and for all. He was so nervous that he had to cut one of the knotted strings of the velvet codpiece the exact color of his breeches. This defensive toggery was common to the age. It is a fact that the only male in the animal kingdom capable of attacking his enemy's testicles is man.

The leader of the patrol was observing the operation with professional suspicion. A puny Andalusian subaltern counseled his chief:

"Slightly snub, but he'll pass. Next!"

Colón, like many of his fellows, tucked away his credential with the solicitude that the humble reserve for their identification papers.

The menacing lieutenant, his voice fortified more with brandy than military authority, shouted:

"We're looking for a blond blue-eyed man who may be a Jew swine. By order of the king!" He held up a knave from a deck of cards.

Colón's knees buckled. He became aware that, as his uncle Bavarello so elegantly put it, he had "made water." His codpiece filled with a warm, regrettable liquid.

The prostitute from Toledo, sitting before her inevitable dish of custard, looked at him with a sneer.

The lieutenant showed Colón the card.

"No, *mai visto*," said Cristóbal, mafiosally evasive. In his fright, he had reverted to his mother tongue.

The minions of the Brotherhood were Galicians and Andalusians. They had received their orders but did not know exactly what "blond" meant; neither were they sure

what color "blue" might correspond to. Furthermore, the
black knave in the deck of cards wore flat torero slippers, not
the spiral-toed yellow shoes of a dandy from Milano.

Cristóbal was sure it was a pogrom. He could not
imagine that anyone might need him, or that he might
benefit in any way. Genius is, by definition, skeptical.

The inspection party paused before the supine body of
Ulrich Nietz. They thought he was feigning. They prodded
him painfully with the staff of a halberd.

Nietz half-opened his yellow eyes, a Rousseau tiger
semiconcealed in a jungle clearing.

And then they beat him again when he tried to embrace
the lieutenant, calling him "Fernando, my king!" Hoarsely,
in his native language, believing he was close to death and
from generosity of spirit, he wanted to pass on the core of his
testament:

"*Gott ist tot! Gott ist tot!*"

He begged them to write down his words, then, clutching the leg of the puny Andalusian, he slipped back into the
bliss of his swoon.

The Andalusian, who had fought in Flanders, translated, with the typical Iberian ineptitude for languages:

"He says that 'someone taught God.' That's what he
said. That's a new one on me!"

•

Now it was the ninth day of the banquet for the Conde
de Cabra. Night was falling in the royal encampment and the
breeze was wafting tantalizing smoke from the braziers. They

were roasting calves' udders, stuffed kid, partridges, blood sausage, and large game birds—pheasants and turkeys—to shred and serve as tasty morsels on fried bread.

Corps of sommeliers were decanting Galician, Riojan, and French wines from double-spouted clay jugs into the crystal carafes on the royal table.

A merry orchestra was struggling to keep time to the cavorting of a troupe of Turkish trapeze artists: males with Nietzschean mustachios; females whose ample buttocks were resplendent in sequins and cheap but brightly colored stones.

Suddenly guards were running every which way, and crying the alarm:

"La Beltraneja! La Beltraneja! It's her! She's *here*!"

Captains stumbled through the dark to reach mounts grazing in the pasture.

The barking of the mastiffs and wolfhounds accompanying the Portuguese vanguard grew louder.

Doña Juana, La Beltraneja, riding bareback at the head of an entire troop, all bays, of unbelievable Teuton percherons.

They tore down the campaign tents, the open-air chapel, the royal latrines, the rows of braziers and tables; they even demolished the dance floor.

La Beltraneja, ironic, vengeful, implacable—but never happy, not even in her triumph and the humiliation of her enemy—rode one complete circle around the head tables.

She reared her percheron, groomed with braids even in the long hair of his fetlocks. She seemed ephemeral on that mammoth back, an anguished Muslim fakir abducted by a Velázquez charger.

"It's La Beltraneja. To horse! To horse! First Lancers cover the southern flank!"

Clash of swords. Whistling of arrows. One stray arrow from a crossbow crossed the royal field and with a melancholy *twanggg!* buried itself in the viola di gamba.

Captains spurred forward their horses, infantrymen began to close rank, but too late: the insult was complete.

Fernando had time only to remove his plumed hat and make a sweeping bow, as a vassal might greet his queen. La Beltraneja paled with rage as the huge, curvetting percheron's forefeet struck the ground.

The purpose of that strike by vanguard troops, whose Portuguese stench overpowered the mouth-watering smells from the braziers, was not armed triumph but defiance and humiliation; one last gallop through the camp, and they rode off into the shadows of the west. Their most experienced, and least cautious, mastiffs risked the glow of the embers to pilfer calves' udders and the last of the stuffed kid.

Isabel was beside herself. The Conde de Cabra watched, entranced, as she ripped her narrow green skirt from hem to groin, and with one leap mounted the nearest horse (unfortunately, as the red cockade betrayed, a circus horse; the Turkish trapeze artists counted on the steadiness of that reliable croup when they executed their double somersaults).

Isabel plunged into the darkness, orienting herself by instinctive female-female hatred. After a quarter of a league she saw the phosphorescent sweat of the troop of percherons now racing toward Extremadura.

She coaxed a supreme effort from a horse spoiled by commerce. She heard the hysterical laughter of La Beltraneja:

"I, the queen! I, the queen!"

Just when Isabel thought she had overtaken her, Juana, expert *rejoneadora* trained in the Portuguese school of bullfighting from horseback, checked her mount, elegantly swerved to one side, and spared his haunches the slash of Isabel's dagger. Insult added to injury. Isabel felt tears of humiliation. And as a last bitter pill, as she trotted back in defeat, she was hounded by stragglers from the Portuguese pack.

That incident signaled the end of a false *status quo*. Now the lines were clearly drawn; they were fighting a long civil war that would be the basis of the new order.

This was the gist of Isabel's harangue:

"You, Lord, Who knows the secret of our hearts, I beseech You to hear the sorrowful prayer of this Your servant. Show us the path of truth and legitimacy by which these kingdoms may be mine!"

Isabel knew she could not consolidate an empire, dominate the world, and contain the Turk's expansion toward the west without a bloody civil war. She knew that the fire that is lighted externally to subject other peoples and create an empire is but the flame of the fire within, the flame of civil war.

The final defeat of the Portuguese, following that outrageous incident, took place on the Duero, three leagues from Toro. Never had swords been animated by such fierce rage. Severed limbs, bloody wounds, riderless wild-eyed horses milling aimlessly about. As always, innocents were trapped in the cloaca of that old hatred.

King Alfonso had to flee to France. His virgin wife, La Beltraneja, retreated with her troop of percherons and exhausted dogs. She would lock herself forever in a convent, where to her last breath she signed "I, the queen" to requests for white garments and knitting wool.

•

Those were Spain's darkest years. The renewing fire of Fernando and Isabel was administered with the haphazardness of purest terrorism. Colón's goal was to pass unperceived during the four years of civil war that followed the unhappy interruption of the banquet in honor of the Conde de Cabra.

Cristóbal's brother Bartolomeo, also a part-time agent for Genoese multinationals, tried to sell Cristóbal's cosmology in the court of England. Abysmal failure.

Colón spent those years of terror in Córdoba, where he affected a nationalistic humanism. He became a regular in the Aranas' pharmacy on Calle San Bartolomé, where every afternoon a group of *conversos* met to praise anti-Semitism and criticize the negligence and bureaucratization of the inquisitors. From time to time they denounced some acquaintance, to ensure their own safety for a few more months.

As Torquemada and his wrathful Dominicans pressed on through city and countryside, a terrifying reality was coming to light: nothing was immune to the contamination! For an entire century, from the time the persecutions had become more severe, the poison of Jewish blood had been polluting the society.

Statistics on deportations and executions were frightening. In a single week in 1487, Torquemada examined 648 penises. He was tireless in his urological survey. "He stole hours from sleep," as one of the heroes of science was to say.

The adulteration had penetrated very deeply. Many Hebrews had taken refuge in the church; kosher meat made its way to more than one archiepiscopal table. Many new Christians gave themselves away with their fondness for cooking with sweet basil, frying with a frypan, or eating plain on Saturday.

Every public urinal had become a hub of informers.

In the court, in the judiciary, in the military hierarchy, one might see the hooked nose, the strangely shaped earlobes, or the cringing gaze that unerringly denounced the Hebrew.

Sordid commonplace terror was relieved by the wholesome violence of civil war.

In the Aranas' pharmacy, they could sense the circle closing. Beneath the intellectual nonsense, the laughter at the latest jokes, there was a perceptible undercurrent of anguish: fear at the sound of the boots of the Holy Brotherhood patrols, and of the Dominican torturers who were everywhere, begging and spying.

"No trials! The fire is the trial! If he burns, it is because he is a Jew! Blood Christians do not burn; they are the green wood of the Tree of Life!"

•

It was during those dark days that Colón began an important and strange relationship. It began with a shock.

In the twilight of the pharmacy (no one had yet come to light the lamps), he felt a seismic tremor: he saw Felipa Moñiz Perestrello. Pale and utterly beautiful. His heart pounded. He had to sit down on the cask of leeches. Ears buzzing, and feeling faint.

Then when he looked more closely, he realized it was not Felipa. It was Beatriz Enríquez Arana, a poor relation of the apothecaries, the daughter of modest growers of basil, garlic, and cinammon who had been executed by Torquemada—Beatriz's own uncle—who in them was destroying the proof of his own Jewishness.

Beatriz, who had hidden in the granary, was welcomed in the pharmacy like a person who, without having died, nevertheless possesses the serenity and detachment of a denizen of the other world. This is why no one bothered her with things to do or with signs of affection. Every ray of light— natural or artificial—that fell on her face seemed to glow like the flames of the stake.

She had a sweet, resigned expression, and from the day of her arrival, she helped in the most humble tasks. Out of delicacy, no one asked her to light the candles at dusk, or bring in an armload of wood for the oven. But she understood their concern, and with exemplary humility she would take the tinderbox and start the fire.

That was how Cristóbal verified that she was not his dead wife. He saw an enchanting profile, the body of an eighteen-year-old, and straight hair falling over her forehead as she knelt to blow on the coals to quicken the fire.

Three days later, as he observed her at the same task, Colón felt the stirring of a healthful animalism.

Considering his exaggerated—defensive—Catholicism, he may have wanted to demonstrate that because she was Jewish, and had survived, she was nothing but an object. He walked to where she was kneeling and confidently ran his hand beneath her dress. Everyone saw him. But no one could take his action as a sexual overture: she did not exist.

She looked at him in silence. Perhaps she understood. This would be a convenient relationship, above commentary. She was, after all, less than an object. She was vile; she could not even sell herself; she was lower than a Moorish prostitute.

She yielded to him docilely and sweetly, and never achieved orgasm (surely she felt she did not deserve it, or maybe, as Thomas Mann would say, "she feared becoming attached to life").

But even to Cristóbal, because of the metaphysical degradation, she did not seem real. "She seemed to be made of flesh, and yet . . ."

Without sorrow Beatriz watched the day that was ending, and without joy she greeted the day beginning. It was not Oriental wisdom. Simply put, she was tired of being afraid and of imagining her own violent death.

She was convinced that death was the best way out of what was worse: torment.

Her life was so desolate that no one expected her to complain if the soup was cold, or if she cut her finger while chopping the parsley.

And yet no woman would ever have the hold on Colón that she had. This nonrelationship, based in a Christian zealot's contempt for a condemned Jewess, would last twenty years (until death).

Each coitus held the secret enchantment of an orphic voyage, a descent into the realm of the departed. She dwelled in the land of death. She was a condemned Jew whom the executioners seemed to have forgotten after not finding her house at their first attempt.

They were together (although not together); she followed three steps behind, forever silent, slender, available.

When they entered the pharmacy, she took her place behind the counter, to serve the customers; he took the best chair in the corner reserved for conversation.

The fact that she had predeceased him created a certain distance between them. Once he had to travel to Murcia. When he returned to the pharmacy, he asked her:

"What, you still here?"

She nodded, lowering her eyes, as if she had survived by chance, or out of mischief.

In the pharmacy or at home, she invariably had within reach a modest valise containing the simple prison costume she thought she would be allowed in the dungeons of the Holy Office before she donned the cap and robe that was *de rigueur* for being burned at the stake.

When Colón expounded on the inarguable need to eliminate Jews, she seconded him with a gesture from behind her counter. He spoke of purity of blood, of responsibility to country, of focusing everything around One Kingdom, One People, One Faith.

After nine months, with less than astounding punctuality, Hernando Colón (the historian) was born. Cristóbal named him Hernando in homage to the king.

She held up the small bundle wrapped in linen swaddling clothes and, in the presence of midwife and neighbors, explicitly handed him to Cristóbal, as if saying, "Here. He's yours and yours alone. I did give birth to him, but I'm only a Jew."

But Cristóbal's uneasiness mounted. He felt spied upon, observed. In those days, as during any time of terror, one never knew whether one was being called to wear the hood of the executioner or the victim.

He did not suspect that his ambitions were melding with the ambitions of others.

The pogrom grew to undreamed-of dimensions. It would end in the expropriation of wealth and land. In the long-feared mass expulsion.

The diaspora was looking for somewhere to go.

For some time men like Santángel, Coloma, the Marqués de Moya, and other powerful *conversos* had known they must find an adventurer capable of leading Jewry into the New Israel.

Their plan had two goals: to obtain new lands and to obtain non-Jewish gold—gold not from their own pockets—to pay for Fernando and Isabel's ambitious plan: conquer the Moors, invade France, dominate the papacy through the Borgias, and, ultimately, possess the world.

There are no extant details regarding the meetings of the financiers (very few important facts were written down, hence the essential unreliability of historians).

What is fact is that mysterious emissaries began to hang around the Aranas' pharmacy.

And today we are clear as to the reason for the years of delay Colón suffered through before reaching the center of the dextrorotatory galaxy of power: he considered the ambitions of both the crown and the transnational agents to be frivolous, of minor importance, predictable human greed. Repetitions of the same old ideas.

On the other hand, he, the descendant of Isaiah, as it was known, sought only one, the essential, mutation: the return to Paradise, the land without death.

He knew that the enclosure Jehovah had erected around the inexperienced Adam could be breached. That the wall could be leaped. Yahweh had not spoken the last word, and, at the last instant, He would restrain the Exterminating Angel, fascinated by the daring and ingenuity of man.

In sum, he knew that Prometheus would rescue the bleeding and sorrowful Christ.

His conviction was charted on a parchment of unborn kid, with a clear representation of the spot in the wide Ocean Sea where reality opens toward transreality and allows the initiate to pass from the insignificance of human time into the open space of an eternity without death.

But of course he could not reveal such a secret to simply anyone. He would run a great risk. The greatest truth carries the greatest risk, thought Cristóbal.

•

The Spanish pope consolidated the cycle of regeneration of a Church debased by overly pious priests, a cult of death, and the long sleep of the convent.

Rodrigo de Borja, by now the Supreme Pontiff Alexander VI, made his entrance into the plaza of San Pedro preceded by his troupe of black contortionists and a solemn orchestra playing music more military than religious.

Alexander, attired in black velvet, was riding a white horse. His dagger and sword had gold grips. The agonizing Christ on the small crucifix on his chest was Chinese jade.

Beside Alexander rode his lover, the marvelous Giulia Farnese (whose marriage the pope had blessed as a means of keeping her by his side).

They arrived from the Castello Sant'Angelo, where they

had presided over a popular and charitable banquet (to which the prostitutes and beggars of Rome had been expressly invited). The odor of paprika, garlic, and saffron hovered over the length of the Lungotevere.

In large shallow pans brought from Valencia, the plebeians—who until then had known only pasta and roast *porchetta*—had been treated to supreme chicken, rabbit, and seafood paellas.

Cooks from Alicante had created a delicate "fruits of the sea" rice for the pontifical table.

Lucretia Borgia followed the pontiff and Giulia Farnese; she was dressed in strict Spanish mode (black dress, embroidered mantilla—although her ruffles and Gypsy shawl were slightly à la Lorca).

Also in the party were Cesare Borgia, the Holy Father's son; Cardinal Venier; the Prince and Cardinal Orsini; the Archbishops of Naples and Sicily; and assorted Venetian lords: Morosini, Grimaldi, Foscari, Marcello. The Princes Colonna and Patrizzi. The official executioner, Micheletto Coreggia, and the Borgias' poisoner, Sebastian Pinzón.

The plaza has been enclosed with large boards painted in the Vatican colors. A stage has been erected for the principal guests, and a box, with a canopy, for the Holy Father, his lover, and Lucretia. They have improvised a replica of a *plaza de toros*.[6] But a serious note, one that scandalized Mommsen, is that the only matador will be Cardinal Cesare Borgia himself.

---

[6]Author's note: For details on that memorable entertainment, the participants, and the bulls, see *The Civilization of the Renaissance in Italy*, by Jacob Burkhardt.

He fought the first, unusually gentle, bull on horse-back, and dispatched it with a single thrust of the lance. The second bull was energetic but disoriented; he gained confidence as the *corrida* progressed. That kill was achieved with a single two-handed blow that proved Cesare's fame as a beheader and his dexterity with the two-handed sword.

He knelt to receive the third bull as it emerged from the *toril*, with more spectacular effect than risk, but the uninitiated Italian platform party shouted until they were delirious.

He killed the fourth with a rapier, establishing a tradition of delicacy. He went in over the horns with courage and cunning, managing to avoid the last desperate toss of the bull's head.

The fifth rushed in prepared to gore the guts from the horses, provoking swoons among the marquesas of the papal party. Cesare calmed the shouting awakened by the fury of the bull by dedicating it to the public with a sweep of his cardinal's biretta. This was a paragon of bulls, jet black, sharp horns—one perhaps slightly lower than the other—with commendable spirit and breeding. Now Cesare attempted a maneuver no one had seen, one that drew admiring *olés* from the informed Spanish military: with a purple cardinal's cape, he challenged the bull and then stood his ground before its charge, capturing the bull in a swirl of his cape, which he then flourished above his head. For an instant, ephemeral but of magical intensity, he had achieved a fusion of man and beast, composing a figure of sublime beauty whose grace transcended their long and dark opposition.

Leonardo, the military engineer from Vinci, could not contain himself, and made hasty sketches in an effort to capture that barbaric and delicate rhythm. He filled six sheets of his notebook (which unfortunately was lost when the city hall of Forlì burned to the ground during the Second World War).

The last bull, a roan with tremendous horns, gave Cesare the opportunity to exhibit his courage in new ways: this one he fought on foot, with his cape curled around his arm. His father, the pope, exulted in his admiration for such Dantean *virtù*. He lost control. In the silence of the Vatican ring the pontifical Spanish voice boomed out:

"Get him away from the barrier—you're giving him his way. Keep his head down. Down! *Natural, natural*. That's it, with your left." Cesare chose a rapier for the kill, and effected it with two well-placed half-thrusts, then a final *coup de grace* that was unfortunately a little low.

There were thunderous cheers from the common people, but strong if subdued protests from Christians from other parts of Europe accustomed to exorcising cruelty in different tongues.

Clerics with onion-shaped bodies and crippling piety were indignant.

They did not, naturally, see in the bulls a renewed symbol of harmony in the struggle that opposes human to animal. They did not know that the ceremony has a different meaning for every situation and every spectator: the bulls are a tarot. The eternal figures arrange themselves in different combinations, and can be a warning, a prophecy, or a lesson.

Alexander VI left with Giulia Fornese; he had recognized the symbol of the beast of evil: the terrible unarmed prophet Girolamo Savonarola, with whom an epoch of hatred of the body, of envy of sex and grace, would be ended.

During the last passes before the killing of the fourth bull, he had, in his heart, made the decision to have Savonarola burned, to scatter his ashes on the air of Florence, as the obscene monk had burned Venetian engravings of beautiful nudes at the portico of his parish church. It would signal the end of an epoch in the Church.

The fiesta that night was spectacular. Never had such inventive lights and fireworks been seen. They had been constructed especially to lionize the aristocracy of Venice: great cardboard gondolas, skillfully illuminated, seeming to drift down an imaginary Canalazzo, carrying choirs of damsels and ambiguous youths singing a song that caused passing nuns to cross themselves:

> *Quanto e bella giovinezza*
> *Che chi fugge tuttavia!*
> *Chi vuol esser lieto, sia:*
> *Di doman non c'è certeza.*

•

The banquet for the Conde de Cabra was resumed after four terrible years. The spiral of power, decentralized during the civil struggle, was restituted in Córdoba.

Colón's eagerness to join a *picada* was diminishing.

Secretly, he put his trust in the Genoese merchants and in Biblical design. Those were years of reading and rereading. He read the Bible as if it were a family history.

"David is so amazing! That Isaiah, so profound!" he would exclaim, while at the window the ever-silent Beatriz spread her hair to dry after washing it in flower-scented water (to mask her aroma of death from Cristóbal).

In the afternoons, card games with the pharmacy philosophers. Sometimes he closeted himself for purposes of creativity: Cristóbal thought himself a poet, and he knew that in order to gain lasting value any great adventure—private or public—must end as a great book.

In the pharmacy there was talk of the floats paraded at the banquet.

They had heard that the Association of German Armorers, natural rivals of the Flemish and greedy for a market of great potential, had presented an enormous mechanical dragon which when wounded by a pasteboard Saint George released a white (flesh and feather) dove, cunningly and cruelly trained, that flew desperately but unerringly to take refuge in the bosom of Queen Isabel.

It was obvious that mastery of mechanics and horology was bringing the world to the brink of an unprecedented technical revolution.

The main dish at the banquet was unforgettable roast partridge in lemon sauce, of which the chronicler Fernando del Pulgar wrote:

"If once they flew free above the fields of Balza, so now they soar like swallows in the roofs of sovereign mouths, covered in a gossamer tulle of tart lemon, and gilded over the flames of the orange tree. Firm of meat, tender in death, they enjoy the happy destiny of having given pleasure to royalty."

But a climate of conjugal discord was preventing the pleasure of earlier days.

Aldonza Alamán continued to pilfer Fernando's affection; he no longer had any interest in Beatriz de Bobadilla, who had wearied him with her arrogance.

Fernando always invited la Alamán to accompany him at military ceremonies.

Isabel, for sympathy, and in accusation, often appeared as a penitent. She wore hairshirts. She ranted in Latin.

Her rage found a target in La Bobadilla: she succeeded in denouncing her and forcing her into marriage with the governor of the Canaries. It was an elegant way to remove her from the court; she expunged her by granting her favor.

Two weeks earlier, Isabel had given birth to Juana la Loca; she was not very old before she demonstrated her strange and tragic nature. The court priests, astrologers, and seers saw in her worrisome signs of the Trastamaras.

Isabel knew that she had given birth to weaklings, and that Spain would require a long reign beneath her iron hand.

The Infante Juan, although extremely intelligent, was so sensitive that on one occasion when his horse ran away with him, he refused to tug at the reins for fear the bit would injure the horse's mouth. (He was very nearly killed.)

The tension at home grew to the point that when Fernando received news of the offensive of the Great Turk, who had leveled Rhodes and was threatening to extend his iron scimitar curtain to Otranto in the south of Italy, he resolved to set out with forty thousand men to put an end to the Moorish problem in Spain.

That was how the last offensive against Granada was spawned.

The chronicle records the following particulars of the exploit. Defeat of the Conde de Cabra in Moclín. Later, Fernando's army is halted by a mountain between the strong-

holds of Cambiz and Alhabar. Isabel and the Bishop of Jaén
contract six thousand men with shovels, and they remove the
hill that is impeding the movement of artillery. In twelve
days the task is complete; Fernando triumphs.

Then Málaga. And the overthrow of the Turkish fleet at
Malta. The resistance of Almería. The Cross of Caravaca. The
siege of Baza and, finally, the fall of the merry kingdom of
Granada and the poet-king who wept like a woman over what
he could not defend like a man.

After 777 years of Moorish dominion, everything was
under the control of Imperial Catholicism.

•

Everyone knew that the cycle of the sea was about to
begin, although the fire of the inquisitors' stake was not
dimmed.

Once the holy war had ended, what necessarily had to
begin was international evangelism.

There was skeptical conjecture in the pharmacy.

One day about noon, finally, they heard the sound of
horses and rattling swords outside the door.

The errand boy peeked out: the street was filled with
the Holy Brotherhood; there was no escape. Men in black
with white crosses were converging upon them. Was it a
general pogrom, or selective?

Beatriz Arana knew. Silently, with her unfailing humility, she finished weighing the pound of leeches for the widow
of Torres, cleaned her hands carefully, with particular attention to the mud under her fingernails, smoothed her bun

before the cloudy mirror in the back room of the shop, and picked up the valise of one-about-to-die.

Serenely, she spoke to each person there:

"Goodbye, Bernabé. I'm leaving now, Señora Torres. Farewell, Uncle. Until we meet again, dearest Cristóbal. . . ."

She walked to the door with unaffected calm, but found it blocked by the leathery jowls of the Brotherhood.

"Step aside," they ordered. "We are looking for a Colombo Cristoforo, Christovao de Coulomb, or Colón the Mallorquín. Blond, with blue eyes. By order of the royal house. We have orders to bring him to court."

Beatriz, disappointed not to confront death once and for all, moved aside.

Colón, full of self-importance, left without a goodbye. He was foolishly confident they would not kill him. He felt his opportunity had come. He was a gambler, and was sure he held the winning card.

He climbed on the mule with assurance, and rode off with the silent guards, who had orders to leave him in a special place.

He was taken to the former Mosque of Córdoba. To the Patio of the Orange Trees. The men of the Brotherhood retired. He was alone, still straddling his mule. He heard the constant murmur of a fountain. A hint of coolness drifted through the heavy heat of the siesta. From time to time, the mule switched its tail to frighten away flies.

He took courage; he dismounted and walked to the discreet door of the seventh wonder.

He walked into an almost cold and definitely shadowy woodland. Antennas of slim columns. He moved forward timidly and uncertainly in that palace of a god unseated by politics.

From the darkness, clear as a bell, came a roar of laughter that broke into waves of echoes.

He inched forward like a cat in a new house. Not far away, among the forest of marble columns, someone ran a few steps and was again still.

He was struck by a terrifying intuition.

In the darkness he thought he saw a slim body pirouetting in dance. Heard naked feet on the cold marble.

A singsong voice murmured tauntingly:

"Co-lón. Co-lón. Co-lom-bo . . . *Bo!*"

It was a caricature of the other, the sacred, voice that once had called to him from the sea.

A burst of laughter. Immediately, a commanding voice, a man's voice, and again silence.

Then in an opening in the colonnade, he saw a moving silhouette, a cloud of tulle, or a Greek tunic. It was a woman, dancing.

A magnificent woman. Cristóbal felt fear, curiosity, and desire.

Her hair fell long and straight. The sound of her dancing feet, rising and striking the ground as she whirled, took his breath away. He thought he felt hers.

He had no doubt: it was She. He fell to his knees. He could not control his excitement. It was a kind of a sacred terror. The terror one feels at the sudden appearance of a deity.

The circle of the dance grew tighter. The swaying of her body and cadence of her feet were those of a Gypsy flamenco dancer. Her mute rhythm prefigured music. It seemed to him that a smile never left her lips.

Surrendering to fear, he lay prostate on the stones of the patio.

Twice the dancer circled around him, then stopped by his side. He felt the sole of a foot as cold as the mosaic resting on his burning, panting, plebeian chest.

In the darkness, Colón's face crumpled, but he could not achieve the release of tears. He felt something new: his sex was retracting like a snail at the scent of danger.

He risked a glance along the surface of an admirable calf, then the length of a strong thigh. Even higher: a bluish shadow in midnight darkness.

He was shaken by a savage desire not centered (curiously) in his genitals.

That presence, and the foot resting on his chest, was sweeping him toward an ineffable physical experience.

He could not know he was on the threshold of an erotic expression that culminates in what some scientists call extragenital ejaculation, or intraorgasm.

If the normal urethral avenue is blocked due to ecchymosis, the millions of spermatazoa anarchially reverse course, enter the bloodstream, and race through muscles and organs in a marathon cross-country (cross-*body*) trial. Because of the ancestral call of the species, they are programmed to seek an outlet and, specifically, "the other."

Colón felt as if his veins and arteries were brimming with the bubbling wine of Champagne (cider, perhaps, might be more appropriate in his case).

He felt the beginnings of relief, the lightening of anguished desire. His eyes glittered like gold in the darkness. He felt as if the tiny little genies of sexuality and fertilization were swarming, subcutaneously, from his big toe to the tip of his nose.

He felt millions of faint but perceptible tail lashings, the struggle of life to seek the light. As they filled his pores, Cristóbal was overcome by uncontrollable laughter and a generalized tingling sensation.

Then he entered the second sublime phase of panorgasm. He felt his skin rippling as if he were a rug being shaken out a window by a stout Portuguese serving girl.

He achieved celestial heights.

His ears closed like someone blasted into space. His eyes rolled back in his head, like an epileptic's.

It was only an instant, but a lasting delight. One instant, but more intense than the entire lifetime of an ascetic or a Latin professor.

He was damp from seminal dew, bathed in a milky whey, exuding a slight aroma of crushed tarragon; his arms were like lead, he was paralyzed with fatigue.

Today, in the light of psychoanalytical knowledge, it would not be difficult to explain the incident: the plebeian Colón suffered a genital block in the presence of royalty. His was an inhibition based in class inferiority.

Seeing the queen, in person, his flesh shrank, and he was incapable of rising to action. (That is why the great Alejo Carpentier errs when he describes a complete and uninhibited sexual union between the navigator and the sovereign. Carpentier is led to this forgivable error by an admirable proclivity for the democratic. But the scene he depicts is absolutely unrealistic. The plebe, physically, was totally intimidated. His metaphysical daring, in contrast, was absolute, hence his ability to achieve the liberation of panorgasm.)

Colón and Isabel were a sculptural composition, motionless amid the forest of motionless columns.

Colón had been anointed Admiral of the Ocean Sea (he would receive eight thousand marvedís, and would be permitted the perquisites of "don" and the golden spur).

Then Isabel resumed her dance, whirling in silence—as before, in carefully measured circles—following in reverse the spiral she had traced in approaching him.

For a second time, he heard the mocking laughter one might expect from a common peasant.

Then there was only silence, and he may have lost consciousness.

He awakened to the kicking and prodding of the Holy Brotherhood:

"Get going! Rowdy! Filthy Hebe!"

They laughed; they continued to pummel him. He tried to smile at them, to be one of the boys.

The light in the external courtyard was blinding. They threw him at the feet of his mule. They told him he would be paid beginning the 1st of March, and that on the 11th he should present himself in the newly conquered lands of Granada to join the royal retinue in their triumphal entrance.

Then they left, still spitting lupine seeds and laughing. Beasts. Clearly administrative types.

What has been narrated here, so important to the Destiny of the West (as they say), took place on April 9, 1486. Colón realized that the rite sealed a monumentous pact. The queen was to be his secret accomplice in the ultrasecret adventure of Paradise!

•

The eagle-men and leopard-chieftains regarded him with distrust. They were steadfast worshipers of Tazcatiploca, the warrior god, ancient enemy of the wise and astute Quetzalcoatl. But the Mexicatl Teohuatzin, the high priest, expected the warriors' reluctance to accept the true theology. It was known that "the warrior thinks with his feet, counts with his arms, and—it is inevitable—loses his head."

But they were young and handsome. Athletes of the will, unhappily captive to the Efficiency Principle.

They were in the Place of Initiation of the great temple of Tenochtitlán, occupying a long bench against a wall painted with the insignia of eagles and jaguars.

It was a splendid morning. Clear air. Purified air that had arrived with the breeze from Teotihuacán, the Place-Where-the-Air-Is-Clear.

The decadent sun—which already had lost its testicles to attacking black eagles, emissaries of ethereal night and primordial chaos—was shedding its pale warmth.

The blood of the thousands of warriors sacrificed at the inauguration of the temple of Huitzilipochtli had not fortified the anemic star.

The high priest gazed at them with serene authority, and said:

"No. No. Bearded will be the men who will come from the sea. Reddish will be the beard of one man. They are very near (we have been informed). No. They are not *tzitzimins*, the monsters of the dusk that wait behind the eastern sky to devour the last generation. No.

"Those who come now are the last of the minor gods. They come from the Great Sea. Quetzalcoatl sends them, he who foresaw their coming.

"Hear me: they are bearded and generous; perhaps all too human. . . ."

The eagle-warriors and leopard-warriors looked at him with the unemotional wonder of men educated in endeavors of body and weapons. They respected theocratic order. None dared air his doubts.

Continuing, the Mexicatl Teohuatzin recalled to them the sacred poet:

Every moon
Every year
Every day
Every breeze
Walks and passes.
Moreover, all blood
Reaches the place of its quietness.

He foretold the imminent future with the authority of a professional visionary:

"Oh, they are marvelous beings, those who come! The children of change. Generous! They are driven by infinite kindness; they will take the bread from their own mouths to satisfy our children's hunger. I know that their human god commands them to love as themselves those near to them. They are incapable of bringing death: they detest war. They will respect our women, because their god—infinitely kind—commands them to desire no woman who is not their own. (In this they are particularly rigorous.) They worship a book written by sages and poets. The god they adore is a small man who was beaten and tortured before he was put to death by soldiers. They identify with the weak. They love the weak!

"Hear me when I say that they despise war, violence, rape. What is their strength, you will ask. I say to you: kindness and love. In kindness and love is their strength.

"If they see an injured man, they kiss his wound and cure him. In their charity, they feed the hungry. They lead the blind. They despise wealth, because in wealth they see the trap of the *tzitzimin* devils.

"It is known that if any man strikes one of them, with humanity he will turn his face to be struck again. Yes, they go even that far!

"They do not, nevertheless, disdain the days of life: they know how to reproduce in great number their food and belongings and houses. They command the lightning of the sky and store it, but only for peaceful purposes, in tubes of metal as long as an arm. . . .

"And now I ask you, warriors! If they triumph, will not the victory, perhaps, be ours?

"This is why, in his wisdom, the lord of Texcoco, in the year 4-Calli, ordered the schools of war to be closed.

"A cycle of gentleness is upon us. Why shall we need arms? It will be the Sun of brotherhood and flowers. It is fitting that we recall the song of Huexotzingo:

> *It is thus I shall depart?*
> *Like flowers that wither and die?*
> *Nothing shall remain of my name?*
> *Nothing of my fame here on Earth?*
> *At least, let there be flowers!*
> *At least, let there be song!"*

III

---

water

CHRONOLOGY

1 4 9 2 – 1 5 0 2

A departure that will last ten years. The gibbet-cross (Spanish patent). Virgins at wholesale. Hammer and sickle. Uncommon presence of Jehovah. "One alone seeks Paradise; the others are fleeing the Spanish hell."

1 4 9 2

The reign of the Bloody Lady. Attempt of the admiral to flee through urinary channels. Circe: paroxysm and vulvar peril. High sea. The two directions of the Occidental dialectic.

1 4 9 2

September-October. Secret signs. Mare Tenebrarum. Confluence of nothingness and being: ambiguous apparition of the dead. Images of futurity. The Rex and the Queen Victory. Armor-plated. The menstral and its pernicious effect on discipline. The Mayflower. At sea: a rumba by Leucona.

1 4 9 8

August 4. The omphalos of the world. Delights. The Earthly Paradise! The naked admiral. Entrance into the Land of No Death.

I B E L I E V E they are simply fleeing that hell," he said to the distrustful Santángel, Jewish agent of the multinationals at the court of Spain, who himself was investing a million maravedís in an undertaking in which few had any faith (it was not much money; one could afford to gamble). Santángel asked him, with flat, expressionless eyes:

"And you? What do you believe in?"

And Colón replied with what little modesty he could muster:

"I believe that I am the only one seeking Paradise, along with lands for those who are unjustly persecuted. . . ."

Santángel believed the "unjustly" was redundant. But he knew that madmen are poetic by nature, when they are not in the grip of a mania for exactitude.

Fact: Cristóbal was now standing on the quarterdeck of the *Santa María*. August 2, 1492. A bright moonlit night. That departure was to last ten years (till May 9, 1502). The admiral saw the same activities—different setting—on the *María Galante* (Cádiz, 1493) and *La Gallega*. Provisions being loaded on: shovels, picks, pulleys, winches, Bibles, wheels. Nature there "is not dominated by man." They are convinced they will transform crocodiles into leather trunks, jaguars into ladies' coats, serpents into hoses for sprinkling. They are preparing a broad and powerful offensive against nature in the name of *doing* and against mere *being*. Decadent.

"Move along! Get those stores on board!"

The Pinzóns are everywhere, overseeing everything. They know who is idle and who is busy.

"Faster! Hurry it up, there!"

They secure the cargo with straps and ropes. They adjust, shift, and distribute the load. They appraise the balance they must strike among the bowels, the bow, and the sails of the ship.

The dock is crowded with soon-to-be widows, eventual orphans, and adventurers for sale.

Coils of rope. Tallow. Bags of salt. Sides of dried meat. Strings of strong garlic. Barrels of pigs' feet in pork fat. Stacks of tuna and dogfish so desiccated they are mere sketches of fish.

Sacks of flour are wrestled on board. Near them, high on the bulkheads beyond reach of the seas, large deerskin pouches filled with gunpowder.

The life-size cross is too large to be stowed below-deck. It is lashed down near the kedge anchor. The pale, pasty body gleams in the moonlight, splashed with blood of vermilion paint. An authentic crown of thorns, but not on its brow; the crown is tied with a cord to the spiked nail through one hand: like a puppet's hat tied to the back of a Gypsy cart—not to get lost in the shuffle.

Embraces. Laughter. Weeping on the dock. Gypsy children gnawing into the bales and bundles meant for the hold. Prostitutes shuttling between the dock and a grove of trees on the point. The guards of the Holy Brotherhood, chewing and—like automatons—spitting out pistachio shells. Grayish and colorless men, albino cockatoos.

The admiral is feeling queasy again. Persistent diarrhea. Eleven times they have emptied the bucket from his cabin. Even in the dark, he can see the malicious smiles and winks of the crew. Oblique allusions to "him from Genoa." Iberian resentment. They would like to confuse sensitivity with fear.

Out by the grove, denied access to the dock, beset on all sides by human vultures, stands a chorus of Jewish mothers. Loud voices, betraying neither resignation nor anger (all Jews must leave Spain by August 3). They are offering their sons for the fleet—to no avail.

They have reached the coast after surviving atrocious robberies and abuse. Some carry pieces of gold and valuable gemstones in their intestines, to buy the lives of their children.

Irrepressible, the mournful chorus chants the ancient poem of Immanuel ben Solomon:

Oh, God, though death come at Your hand
I shall place my hope in You.
In You shall I find my refuge.

They have no choice. They will have to negotiate with the Moorish pirates who announce their presence with great bonfires on the beach, on the Ayamonte side. They will endure punishing enemas of seawater and gunpowder. Impatient in their greed for pearls and gold, the pirates will slash open the elders like Swiss customs agents ripping open a suspicious suitcase. They will rape and sell the delicate young Hebrew girls schooled for the sabbatical Talmud and melodious flute. They will blind the young boys and chain them to water wheels in the Magreb.

Colón listens as the roll of the crew is called. Pinzón checks and strictly controls those embarking on the adventure:

"Juan de Medina, tailor! Why a tailor? To stitch the sails! Pass. Reynal, Juan. García Fernández. Fernando de Triana. Move along. Faster! Step forward, one by one! Tejero, on the word of Juan de Moguer. Pass. Abraes. Ruiz de la Peña. Are they all Basques? Pérez. Next."

Rodríguez de Escobedo, the secretary, demands special quarters and certain privileges. "A place where it's dry, so the official documents will be safe."

Luis de Torres comes on as a translator. He knows Arabic and Hebrew. He will be able to communicate with the peoples of the Indies and with the pioneers of the distant tribes of Judea.

Chachu, the bosun, oversees the cargo.

Cooks, caulkers, ropemakers, master sailmakers, painters. Even a goldsmith and jeweler, shrewdly sent aboard by the agent of previously mentioned sponsors, the house of Spinola.

The Italians gather at the rail to talk: Juan Vezano, Antón Calabrés, Michele da Cúneo, Jacomo Rico.

From his quarters, the admiral notes the arrival of a messenger on horseback. The horseman tells the guard he has come from Seville. In the moonlight, he is a dusty specter, an ashen ghost.

He boards, and reports that he is carrying a last message from Santángel.

He drapes his cape and hat across the railing, and transmits to the admiral the final message from the *conversos* of the court:

"The B'nai Israel send the following information on the yellow Jews you will find in Cathay and Cipango. We have unimpeachable confirmation of the kingdom of the Khazars. Their leader, remember his name, is the Shah-Kan Bulan, who died, but even as an angel continues to lead them. It was Hasday ben Saprut who went in search of the Khazars. There are people of the ten tribes beyond the River Sambation and the Euphrates. . . . Try to contact them, they will help our people in their persecution, we have no doubt of it. . . . You will have proof of their existence once you touch the island of Kish: they are guardians of the sacred mirror of the Temple of Solomon. But do not look into it: it will steal your image. It will suck you into the beyond. Take care not to be tempted. We are now in 1492; it is the year signaled by the Cabala, the year of redemption following persecution.

"You are the envoy! The Hebrews of Asia await you in order to resettle the promised land, for all of us. Discharge your task; reach the River Sambation, and ignore the mission of some of those we send with you. On the shores of the Sambation, with the help of Jehovah, we shall found Novaya Gorod. Hurry, leave before the deadline expires and they can kill Jews without fear of punishment! Remember that if you fail, the triumphant monarchs of the night will execute the final solution. Do not worry about expense. *Eretz Israel!*"

He handed the admiral the highly secret maps he had brought in a large leather cylinder.

He rushed down the ladder as if pursued.

Colón had no opportunity to disenchant him with his doubts.

As at other, similar, times, he felt far removed from the simple motivations—imperialistic, evangelistic, or mercantile— that caused others to push forward the adventure of the Indies, be they kings, entrepreneurs, or Jews threatened by the stake.

He was entirely alone. He could communicate to no one his ultrasecret—his ineffable—mission: to seek the ocean passage that would allow the initiate access to the formerly unreachable—and long-lost—dimension of the Earthly Paradise.

He knew that those lands sullied by the weakness of Adam and the perfidy of his female companion lay somewhere on the planet, and were known to some few initiates.

That place was still the Land of No Death. Surely there were marvelous gardens innocent of the Fall, without ensnaring apples, without talking serpents, without guilt. Inhabited by other Adams and women with long, beautiful hair, women as naked and slim as the dead proto-ancestor of Lady Godiva that had been washed up on the beach of Galway, in Ireland.

The admiral had noted in his Secret Diary: *"Virum et uxorem in duobus lignis arreptis ex mirabili formam."* Admirable bodies, long hair, golden skin. They were dead because they had fallen—surely through some amatory mischief—from the gentle climate of Paradise into the clinging mists of the pale, marauding Irish. The admiral had gone down to the beach, where he could wonder at those naked bodies surrounded by stray dogs and freckled priests sprinkling holy water. Suddenly, he understood: that man and woman were not angels. They were our primogenitors, unblemished by original sin.

To reach the sacred continuum without beginning or end; that was the only liberation, the only empire worth man's struggle. All other human efforts were meaningless reiteration.

As a descendant of Isaiah, the admiral knew that he was the bearer of an awesome responsibility: to return to the place where that trap of consciousness, that net woven with the two threads of Space and Time, no longer ruled.

It was not a question of repeating Adam's immature behavior. Not a question of repeating the momentous theft of the apple, but of maturity: give the apple back!

Sail always west, following the course set by initiates. Would the Lord God's angels with their flaming swords destroy them all? Would he be able to leap the wall of Paradise, as Enoch and Joshua ben Levi had done?

The admiral felt the enormous weight of his terrible responsibility. All the solitude of a mission that went far beyond the earthly ambitions of the most ambitious heroes. He was besieged by doubt, and no little fear. Again he felt the meteoric convulsions in his bowels.

He believed, without false modesty, that his challenge, his gamble, was of a level worthy of Abraham, or Moses, or David.

He was racked with ague—cold sweat and shivers. He was the Chosen One. It seemed as if he were carrying the whole universe on his shoulders.

There was still time to run away.

He imagined it: he gathers the essential papers (the charts of the route to Paradise, and his notes from the Bible and Cabala). He slips away into the darkness. "I'm going to stretch my legs on the dock," he tells the Pinzóns, who are guarding the gangway.

Leave everything behind! Flee with Beatriz and the boy, and in absolute anonymity begin the delights of a life without greatness. Open a pharmacy in Flanders, or a butcher shop in Porto. Flee from History!

He went to his stateroom. After he had used the bucket, he assembled his important papers, all the notes of a long lifetime of seeking the absolute.

What relief! To betray them, to abandon everything only a few hours before sailing.

He imagined it: "Where can the admiral be? Where is the admiral?" Shouts. Confusion. And he would already be on his mule, enjoying the cool night air on the road to Córdoba, anonymous, free, without a care. Blessed relief!

He would bring up Hernando in the peace of mediocrity, educate him in the retail business.

But as he left his cabin he felt a portentous wind on his face. The clouds were swirling strangely. He fell to his knees, stunned by a terrible intuition. Panic.

Fear and trembling. On high, in the deep folds of night, a Presence was growing. He lost a sense of his surroundings; the sounds on the dock faded; his ears were attuned to a stratospheric voice with a virile—though not baritone—timbre, saying to him:

"Oh, man of little faith. Rise up, for it is I. Have no fear. Be not afraid; trust in Me. Your tribulations are writ in marble, and not without reason. Would you deny the God of all mankind? The God who singled you out from birth, and caused your modest name to resound in the highest circles of Power? Listen, now, to what I tell you: I have given you the keys to the limits of the Ocean Sea. And you would disappoint Me? You would hasten toward a bullock's fate, when you could be an eagle? Do not forget that I made the shepherd David King of Judea. You, I made admiral and a lord with a golden spur. Onward! I await you!"[1]

---

[1] Author's note: Text recorded by the admiral in a letter, from Jamaica, to the king and queen.

Colón knew both fear and pride upon hearing the revelation of the *mysterium tremendum.*

He slumped against the gunwales like a beheaded swan. Lifeless, boneless, empty.

Then little by little he made an effort to compose himself; he was a scrubbed shirt trying to regain the shape of the hanger.

Meanwhile, the crew had laid out the main topsail on the dock, and were painting on it a large cross and the initials of Fernando and Isabel.

"One alone seeks Paradise; all the rest are fleeing that hell." He was numbed by his privilege.

A group of Central European Jewish women, who had fled czarist pogroms only to find themselves caught up in the Iberian persecution, formed a despairing chorus, yellow kerchiefs knotted beneath their chins:

Novaya Gorod
    Novaya Gorod!
Gute Winde
    Gute Winde!

•

Four young priests, coquettishly, are trying on cassocks embroidered by provincial aunts. Prettily, they spin on their heels, hands clasped upon their chest. *"Introibo ad altarem Dei,"* they say. Impishly, they applaud each other's style.

With pulleys and sweat, the stevedores load on the gibbet-cross. Built of heavy wood, designed for a dual purpose, it will be implanted on Hispaniola (this article, of Spanish design, has the necessary episcopal license filed in the Vatican). It will be the climax to the *via crucis* of Holy Week, and, frequently during the year, scene of lesser hangings of thieves, murderers, and subversives.

Padre Las Casas, serene in his march toward certain beatification, is bidding his sisters and female cousins farewell. They have brought him sweets for the voyage, and red knee breeches (actually, ordinary trousers puffed with elastic) clearly for episcopal consumption, which the young missionary accepts with due modesty. And an indulgent smile.

Fray Buil is in charge of the copies of the Inquisition's *Procedures* and accompanying matériel: pulleys, Neapolitan boots with compartment for boiling oil, two cheap sets of ritual cap and robe for victims of the stake, Solingen nail pullers, molar crackers, testicle roasters, several pairs of Chinese rats for breeding stock. Also pickaxes for the ecclesiastical patrols that will have to demolish *intihuatanas* and other heathen idols.

Agitated, perspiring, Padre Squarcialuppi and Padre Bonami hurry aboard fretting that they almost missed the ship:

"Credevi che no ce la facevamo!"

They have with them the portapyx and two demijohns of consecrated grape wine, to serve until grapes can be grown in the lands across the sea.

And Padre Valverde, fussing about with the shackles for the stocks:

"Has anyone seen the reliquiary containing Santa Lucía's knucklebone?"

Bibles, catechisms, five reams of blank papal benedictions initialed in the name of "Aloysius-Cardinalis-Katzoferratus."

Tinny violins, to pacify the peoples of the Indies in processions.

Tubes for an organ. Collapsible baroque altars, with fat-bottomed, mass-produced *putti*. Abundant Turkish, almost by now Bourbon, Catholica. The first great audiovisual production of the West; the first *son et lumière*.

In motionless double rows on the dock, a dozen and a half new virgins, their wax faces wearing an expression somewhere between not-too-bright and flirtatious: young Portuguese laundresses on communion day.

They will be enthroned in their sanctuaries: Canta, Guadalupe, Mutoto, Rosario. Some will have a career: they will grant miracles, or be Commander of the Armies (and be carried on the shoulders of a remorseful colonel—frowning, veins swelling on his forehead—escorted by the Italian cardinal and North American consul).

Gypsy urchins lift the tunics embroidered with false bottle-glass gemstones—*ad usum indianis*—and, although there are no undergarments, nothing, in fact, to see but hastily sanded wood, that primary nudity nevertheless incites them to masturbate like a chorus of monkeys imitating violinists in the allegro movement of the "Flight of the Bumble Bee."

"Never mind, they aren't consecrated," Padre Pane murmurs, in his impotence.

●

Ulrich Nietz and a group of mercenaries try to swarm over the handrail. Ulrich waves to the admiral on the quarterdeck, but Colón pretends not to see. He sees only what he wishes.

Dr. Chanca pushes his way through with the chests of medicines and the mini-ironmongery that compose his elementary surgery. He is carrying two boxes of mud-packed leeches and, as he passes, bumps into Landsknecht Swedenborg. He drops the boxes; the cupping glasses—so vital to arresting lockjaw and curing diseases of the night dew endemic in tropical waters—shatter on the dock.

Ximeno de Briviesca, the official supervisor, argues with the doctor, skeptically counting the grosses of Belgian condoms (trademarked *Paris*), for which demand has so suspiciously increased. He has the boxes opened, in spite of protests, and the dried-up, flattened little fetuses are revealed in their bed of rice powder. Pale little ghosts, like thin ladyfingers in a French bakery. They are still being made of sheep gut, with a tiny knot at the tip (soon American latex will be on the way). At first they were carried in accordance with Virgin Mary theology, to sidestep the prohibition against "carnal contact." The large numbers now being exported are due to the fiery diffusion of syphilis (which by a semantic triumph of Spanish diplomacy is being called "the French sickness," or the "malady from Naples").

A three-sheets-to-the-wind nobleman afforded one of the more amusing scenes of the last stages of departure: Giménez de la Calzada, who fell from the boom into the water and was saved by eight dressed-to-the-nines prostitutes chattering like parrots and wriggling their fingers in the air. They throw the noble the cord from a Franciscan's habit and prevent him from sinking to the bottom.

Who was who? There were Jews disguised as monks, their underdrawers stuffed with watches and silver spoons;

priests dressed as musketeers, traveling as agents of the Inquisition or Vatican; and a plethora of spies from the English court who had signed on as flamenco dancers.

The pimps, saddened by the parting, were singing ballads that evoked their dear mothers, or the virgin of Triana. La Diabla and the formidable Sword Swallower are trying on each other's chiffon scarves, provocatively plumed berets, and carnival masks.

"Who pinched my box of permanganate salts?" bellows La Italiana.

Each of them dreams of her own brothel, with an English bar and attached gaming room. Each hides her madam's cameo in her stained garter.

The admiral observes the harlot-racket, the general hubbub, with total indifference. He knows that authority is maintained with distance.

Behind him, in the cabin with the half-open door, is Beatriz de Arana, who has come to say goodbye.

They have passed a mute and intense afternoon of lovemaking, with little thought beyond that.

By now the dock is a bedlam. Pandemonium. Undesirables are beginning to filter through. If they are officially signing on whores and hired thugs, why not philosophers?

The admiral knows that *La Gorda* and *La Vaqueños* are trafficking in human beings. His informants have told him that the scum of the docks, who have almost nothing to lose, are stowing away, boarding in the dark on the far rail. Then these undesirables hide among the bales of cargo, in improvised pens.

That is where a one-armed former soldier, twice rejected in his attempt to be engaged as scribe, is hanging around, and a mad Frenchman who only yesterday was pontificating that intelligence is the most evenly distributed commodity in the world, but that what is lacking is *method*.

They will succeed in slipping down to the orlop deck.

But the most terrible and most closely watched by the Holy Brotherhood are the Tartars with the shining eyes.

It astounds the admiral that theology has so effectively, and so beneficially, stimulated the textile industry.

The naked American must bear his share of the blame.

Colón recalls a verse from Genesis that his father, Domenico, used to quote during their Sunday quarrels, trying to convince him not to choose such a perilous life: "Unto Adam also and to his wife did the Lord God make coats of skins, and clothed them." That was as he was about to throw them out of Paradise.

There was no room for doubt: the Lord was the first tailor. But Domenico erred in not seeing the dangers of tailoring without moderation, or life as a shop clerk. What destiny does not hold its dangers?

But it was too late to raise these questions: the passion for Paradise had obliterated any shred of prudence. The die was cast.

Beatriz had dressed. She appeared on the bridge wearing her usual gray gown and mantilla, and carrying her ubiquitous valise of one-who-is-about-to-die. She said to Colón, without embellishment:

"Perhaps we will see each other when you return. In a few months . . . or years. If I am here, you will find me at the pharmacy. As long as I am, Hernando will make progress in Latin, I promise. It always seems to me that you are the one setting off for the beyond. Strange, isn't it? And when you come home, it seems you are the one returning from death. . . ."

He watched her make her way across the dock, skirting crates and the insolent stares of the accountants and magistrates waiting to embark. Bogus gentlemen, paperpushers in tricorn and tailcoat, clutching their seals and goose quills in preparation for their court battles in the House of Contracts. Bourbons to the pore, even before Philip V. Nevertheless, and the admiral must recognize it, they are the bureaucrats the empire will need to recover from the mad delirium of the discoverers and conquistadors.

He observed that everyone stepped aside for, even fawned over, the surveyors and notaries. Ever since the status of "property and domain" had been exported, everyone was fighting for it.

No adventure of conquest was worth its oats if the thing was not duly measured, demarcated, assessed, and recorded.

On a corner of the dock, alone and friendless, like lepers, the butt of the obscenities of the whores (who never accepted them), were the two executioners, father and son, Old Hood and Young Hood, famous in Seville and indispensable to this venture.

They were jealously guarding their best steel and rope. Their wives, deeply moved, but dressed in black and wearing veils in order not to be recognized, refrain from kissing them.

•

As the dawn of August 3d, 1492, crept near, its rosy fingers unbuttoned the Jesuitical cassock of night. More than a day was dawning.

Sunrise was ushered in to the jubilation of hundreds of sparrows and August swallows nesting in the nearby trees.

With jollity masking panic, veteran sailors were singing:

Blessed be the dawn
And the Good Lord who lends it.
Blessed be the day
And the Good Lord who sends it.

The daylight emphasized the fragility of the three small ships: the *Santa María,* the *Niña,* and the *Pinta.*

Colón was as profoundly shaken by this departure as he had been at his first, the time he set sail for Chios (Domenico and Susana Fontanarossa, the lighthouse of Genoa, the scapular with the wafer of camphor).

Tows manned by the roustabouts took up the hawsers at the bow, and slowly the three vessels lined up toward the sea.

The all-ashore bell shattered the air.

Who had ordered them to cast off the mooring lines? The Pinzóns, the Niños, Juan de la Cosa. They were in league. The admiral was a foreigner. They suspected him of magic, pederasty, congress with the devils of the sea, misappropriation of public funds, even witchcraft.

He heard snickers when he appeared on the bridge in his large brown admiral's greatcoat, his Venetian hat and colored spectacles, and his yellow shoes. But the muttering and singing stilled as the men fell to their tasks.

"Hard to port! To port!"

"Hoist the foresail. Heave! Heave!"

"Sheet home the foresail. Taut!"

The crewmen labor in their bare feet. Breeches, and loose-fitted fishermen's blouses. And a wood-handled knife around the neck.

The first pounding of the bow against the sea. A straining beast contrasting with the lassitude of the river.

On the shore, a gentle landscape of beaches and groves. In the distance, he thought he saw a lonely, pensive boy standing in the cold morning air. But no, it was imagination.

Suddenly he fell into a harsh, early-morning depression. He went into his cabin and lay on his bed (a rabbit hutch, really). An unbearable sensation of vulnerability. A desire to vomit. He tried, but without result. His eyes filled with foolish tears.

The cradlelike movement of the ship had triggered his internal disorders. Shadows surged from his memory: a stormy night, a man digging a grave; an ax, and a pale corpse. It was like a black lightning flash. An orphic abyss opened by the pitching and rolling.

Again he was swamped by evasive dream-ghosts. He could not resist the pleasure of imagining himself a traitor and fugitive: he slips over the railing and swims for the coast. Shouts. "Admiral! Admiral!" They look for him in his cabin. They find the maps of Paradise, but mistake them, stupid clods they are, for charts of the harbor of Naples. Michele da Cúneo cups his hands to call out plaintively: "Cristoforo, *dove sei? Per carità!*"

Martin Alonso boastfully announces he is temporarily taking command. There's an opportunist for you. *Un grébano!*" protests Jacomo the Genoese.

It pleases Colón to picture them: feeling swindled, staring at each other in their incompetence, paralyzed without leadership. Cheated in their greed for real estate, for stolen pearls, for urinals cast in gold.

The creaking timbers and the strong and even rocking betray the fact that they have moved into open sea. Rhythmic shouting:

"Heave, heave, heave!"

"Haul up the mainsail!"

"Belay the backstays!"

"Haul. Heave. Haul!"

It was too late to desert. Escobar, the cook, is at the door to advise him that it is eleven o'clock (in his anguish, he must have fallen asleep). He hands Colón a cup of broth and offers the traditional salutation:

"May God grant us a good voyage. May the ship have a safe passage, Admiral!"

Colón stepped out onto the bridge, and breathed the pure salt air. The enormous, sedate mares of the wind inflate the sails, blowing from a favorable quarter.

Later at his desk, he began, in his easily recognized handwriting, the Secret Diary that his bastard son Hernando would burn beyond recognition, and from whose ashes Padre Las Casas would recover a few, only rational, passages.

SUNDAY, AUGUST 5. As far as the Canaries, nothing unusual. They call this sea the Gulf of Mares, because this is where horses leap overboard, maddened by the pitching and rolling of the ship. It is caused by the great waves of the Ocean Sea beating against the headland of Africa.

Frenzied, eyes rolling wildly, the mares, manes and

tails awash, swim for their lives, until they sink in the infinite sea.

Martín Alonso Pinzón, along with Quintero and Gómez Rascón, are conspiring. Surely it is they who sabotaged the rudder of the *Pinta*.

The admiral has spies, and knows that some want to turn back, because the route they will be following—from the Canaries westward along the line of the Torrid Zone—can only lead to warm shores.

They, ambitious husbandmen, are seeking green, showery lands like those of Burgundy, where lettuce and leeks will thrive. Most of all, they want lush pasture for their cattle.

They are motivated by petty ambitions. But they are as tenacious and terrible as ants (woe unto the gardener who underestimates them).

AUGUST 9. Heavy seas. Despite the opinion of the bosuns, the admiral refuses to strike the sails. He wants to test the ship before the Canary Islands, before they reach the terrible, the true, ocean. He wants to test the mettle of everything from joyful mainsail to the jib, from the helmsman to the cook.

The admiral asks for a washtub to be brought to his cabin.

The warm water does not splash over excessively, except now and then from an exceptional broadside.

The admiral verifies his ability to float. He knows, from multiple experiences, that he is inherently amphibian.

In the miniature sea of the tub, a microcosm of the Ocean Sea, he studies the laws of the waves. With eyes closed, he muses upon the secret bridges of unity only the wise know how to cross. Mysterious bonds between the macrocosmos and our minute planet.

In the tub, the waves of the sea are reproduced—tamed, diminished—with a sloshing that ridicules the orderly movement of a piece of bobbing sponge.

The admiral acquires precious knowledge about the habits of God.

SUNDAY, AUGUST 12. By night, in the distance, the fires of the volcano on Lanzarote. Towers of fire. The hand of Jehovah still at His work.

Land is sighted in six days. The pilots are astonished: that is half the usual time between the Canaries and the Continent. Only two split sails.

The *Pinta,* crippled by its broken rudder hinges, must enter the offshore currents with caution. They will have to rig less canvas, and reinforce the pintles on the tiller.

If the conspirators Quintero and Pinzón intend to insist on the route inspired by their agricultural ambitions, they will have to deal with the agents of the aforesaid Spinola, with Soberanis and Riverol. They may even have to change ship.

Husbandmen of the sea. They do not divine the interests moving behind the scene.

They believe, but they do not understand. And when they do understand something, they cease to believe.

•

The Domain of the Bloody Lady was the current name for those islands once called the Fortunate Isles.

It was a harsh coast; black porous rocks, mineral foam formed from congealed fires.

Something dampens the joy of a crew with land in sight.

A stilled life, almost surreptitious. The only exception, the bonfires of the guard posts.

About midnight, from atop the rocky promontory, a shattering, echoing scream, the howl of a Guanche chieftain quartered and hung from the tower wall of the tyrannical Bloody Lady.

A warning to the rebellious, to any championing independence. Repression of indigenous, nationalist forces was at its peak.

The Canary Islands are the pilot program of an expanding empire. There they are conducting experiments in large-scale, civilizing extermination. First Rejón, then Peraza and his murderous bishops. Now the widow (self-made?) Beatriz Peraza Bobadilla is in command.

She is no longer the scandalous adolescent known for her bronze thigh guards and intricately engraved purity enforcer. She is twenty-seven years old, and she is the Bloody Lady.

In a justifiable attack of jealousy, the queen had forced her to marry Hernán Peraza and, with him, to govern during the savage conquest of that oceanic base which—everyone knew—was still smoking because it was one of the last of God's works (according to Padre Marchena, completed on Friday as night was falling).

Living, breathing land. Fusing metals. Great oceanic monsters. Mineral vapors. A new and luxuriant vegetation that drinks from cool, ferrous humors. In six weeks, palm trees reach adolescence.

All the land is stolen from the natives, the Guanches, and sold in Seville at a good price. The Guanches themselves, tamed, are auctioned off as slaves. The Canaries are, in fact, the first of the twenty-some parcels into which America will be subdivided.

As described, Isabel had punished Beatriz with the favor of a governorship and marriage to the murderous Peraza. But her jealousy was belated. Fernando had already slaked one of his last sexual thirsts: he had possessed her while she was locked in her steel armor, availing himself of the red velvet crotch piece, and cynically dangling the key in front of the apertures of her visor. (This had taken place during the days of the banquet for the Conde de Cabra. It was the same night that she had eyed the aerialist Apollo shedding gilded cardboard with every orbit.)

Mutual fury exploded between Isabel and the irresponsible adolescent, Fernando's perverse "little swallow," the Huntress, who livened the gossip of the court habitués with her nightly escapades: running naked among the halberdiers and penitent friars, shouting for them to help her find the key for her miniscule chastity belt.

The two women's hatred united them in life until 1504, when in Medina del Campo one of the two would die, poisoned by the other.

Fernando did not excuse La Bobadilla from her obligatory privilege, and from that moment she cultivated a fierce hatred of men. Her husband, the cruel Peraza, was not spared that sentiment.

She lived alone in the tower, served by her maids and her fearsome Galician Guard. She raised wolves and mountain lions. She ate the meat of wild boars and deer from the high sierra.

Occasionally fishermen brought manta rays and shark fins to her rocky castle. Her cooks marinated them in bitter lemon, in the Japanese fashion, and prepared thick soups that intensified her lust.

Her sexual demonism was legend. Fishermen sailing near Gomera at night, perhaps following a school of dogfish, told tales of the horrible cries of her lovers, victims of her merciless eroticism. Pulleys, whips, stocks, quantities of studded leather, cypress switches soaked in vinegar and brine. Hooded accolytes.

Love tends to be red or yellow; in her case it was hard and black as jet.

At the end of the night, most of her lovers—fishermen, strayed sailors, captive Guanche chieftains, altar boys with precocious pastoral passion—were thrown into the sea from the north window of the tower (as the Comtesse de Nesles would do from her bedchamber above the Seine).

It was a true challenge for lovers. In spite of her reputation, it was not easy to reject the invitation of that beauty. In those times of sexual repression, who would deny himself the chance to be tortured by a naked woman? Perhaps they believed she would fall in love with them, or that they could domesticate her with tenderness.

Those who did survive her love were under orders to keep their silence or to suffer mutilation of all organs of communication.

Núñez de Castañeda, who boastfully commented on her personal habits, was invited a second time to the palace, and hanged. An ass appeared in the town plaza carrying a corpse with its tongue tied like a belt.

•

The sailors were green with fear. No one wanted to leave ship. The men of the *Pinta* went into port, but only because they had to.

They felt they were being watched, although they saw no one. The terror was so palpable in those islands that even the scum in the holds were afraid of being arrested. The guards, in their off hours, hid from other guards making their rounds. *Quid custodet custodes?*

Peralonso Niño asked them:

"Do you smell it? Don't you smell the odor of sulfur rising from the bowels of the earth? There are caves in those mountains to the south: they are the gates of Hell. . . ."

He had been there three years before on a Venetian carrack engaged in the Guanche slave traffic.

Colón decided to go ashore, to reassure them. He wanted to take on fresh meat and water.

At dawn, he ordered his yawl and disembarked with all the Genoese. Without much skill—animals were not as yet so wary of the human presence—they brought down a stag with enormous antlers and, with no little struggle, by binding the four feet, managed to carry it back down to the beach.

That decided the men. Throughout the day, until the sun had set in the west, they feasted on abundant meat and island wine.

Even so, they thought the gesture by their Italian captain pretentious and demagogic.

Tongues kept wagging among the crew. What was this business of changing the sails on the *Pinta?* They would be more than a month in that dangerous port. In that place that reeked of sulfur, where the ocean foam seemed more like boiling earth, and where apples tasted like iron.

Why had the admiral, always so distant, wanted to show himself off as a hunter? Whom did he want to impress?

Why had he stood for hours outside his cabin on the poop deck, with the sun beating down on his plumed hat? No one had any doubt: the filthy Jew was waiting for his chance to sell them all, bound hand and foot, to the Bloody Lady. He would then turn the ships to deep-sea fishing and trafficking in Guanches. He would ingratiate himself into the role of Supreme Pimp for La Bobadilla. Could anyone believe that a swine like that would turn his back on opportunity?

Two days later they saw a deaf-mute signaling from land. He brought a message: "Admiral. Dinner at nine. Her excellency the governor."

He spent an hour getting ready. The men realized that their admiral's naiveté exceeded the permissible.

At seven, he appeared on the bridge; more than attired, he was decked out: golden admiral's cape, ornithological hat, ornamental shoes with the gold spurs indicating his high rank.

No one thought he would ever again be seen on the *Santa María.*

"She will kill you, Admiral. She will poison you. Be careful, she's a witch," Excobar warned him, but the admiral was deaf to his comments.

He hesitated for a moment, but decided to leave the map of Paradise in the false bottom of his trunk. As he stepped into the yawl, he told his men:

"Get on with the preparations as I ordered. Be sure the water is good," and, looking at the Italians, *"Mi raccomando!"*

He heard the muttered insults of the crew:

"Clown! Asshole! She'll fry your balls—if you have any!"

They thought he did not understand their Spanish.

He marched along behind the deaf-mute. It was a difficult climb to the tower. He clung to the heather for security. Twice he lost his footing and dangled from roots. Frivolous lizards and solemn iguanas observed them from the Tertiary Age.

He remembered, uneasily, a passage from Saint Paul's Secret Apocalypse: "And I set out with the angel and he brought me toward the setting of the sun . . . and there was no light in that place, but darkness and sorrow and distress."

When they reached the summit, they had to pass through the territory of a lioness who surely had had her fill of human flesh. She yawned indifferently, as if she were still in her native Sahara and any presence was therefore strangely baroque.

He reached the iron door to the tower. From the merlons hung the hides of executed victims. It was obvious that La Bobadilla administered the law with exemplary and energetic didacticism.

He realized that the mute had disappeared.

He had the urge to sing, or whistle loudly as if walking through a cemetery on a dark night.

Even though the sun was shining brightly.

The Galician Guard, or the GG, as the terrorized islanders called them, were not impressed by his rank. They led him to an interior patio covered over with an arched stone ceiling. Not satisfied with removing his clothing, they were gross enough to slit open the seams. What were they looking for? They performed their task silently, industriously, like customs agents acting on a reliable tip.

"Are you looking for poisons? Stilettos? What do you want?"

They did not reply. Sterile, expressionless faces. Boring. A mile of pampa stretching between their ears. Slits of eyes. They seemed to be eternally peering between the slats of a Venetian blind. Half-hidden steel-gray eyes, grimly Celtic.

Once he was naked, they scrubbed him down. Seawater, with lye and disinfectant.

He tried to protest, but realized that this was merely an impersonal, routine annoyance. They acted with an efficiency and silence that bespoke experience and good teamwork. Stocky but agile, they scrubbed him as if he were a cart that had just dumped the manure for the garden and now was to be decorated for a pilgrimage to the shrine of the Virgin del Castro.

Curiously, Colón did not feel offended. It was like the strict ritual for being admitted to jail, or a Jewish cemetery.

They dried him with a piece of sailcloth, and lent him a comb made from a cuttlefish bone. They provided him with sandals and a hooded robe of fine linen. Administrators, they made sure all belongings were inventoried and—eventually—returned to his heirs.

The GG placed him in a chair at the end of an almost monastic table. Then they took up positions in the corridors, and only intermittently did he see a pumpkin-shaped head, a blank face, peering into the hall.

Four beautiful young girls attended him. One of them handed him a silver goblet in which the harsh wine of the islands seemed to burst into pleasant coolness.

Then he saw her. She was preceded by two officials, who immediately disappeared. She descended the staircase with true majesty. She surpassed her fame: there was an aura about her, a kind of anguished hush. His appetite, the taste of the wine, even the sound of the flute on the lips of the adolescent Greek girl playing on a raised dais: all faded.

Tremendous hips. Tiny waist. Planetary, Picassoesque thighs, but fine ankles as delicate as the wrists of a Viennese organist.

Robed/disrobed, veiled/unveiled, in a kind of gauzy Hellenic tunic. Sandals of gilded leather. Thick black hair loose on her shoulders. Large green eyes, closer to the stalking panther than the fleeing gazelle.

"Hips like a Lacedaemonian," Colón thought to himself, practicing compliments he could tell her in bed.

A gold band held her hair back from her face. It matched the sandals. No jewels. Nothing but a necklace of something like small ivory shells, like a string of tiny dried figs (Colón later learned that they were the clitorises of village and town girls who had the misfortune to have relations with her lovers—whether before, during, or after her time).

Without ceremony, she took her place at the opposite side of the table. She acted as if she had been receiving him every day of her life. A true sophisticate.

Except for the armor of the departed Hernán Peraza, which looked, hanging on the wall, like one of the tin puppets in fashion in Sicily, nothing in the hall suggested repressive medieval constraints. Amphoras with fawns, tri-clinia, bronze handbasins, a bust of Socrates or Caesar (it is never clear which). Mosaics, a marble table, gold and silver cups. Everything rather Roman, or Greek. A proliferation of rare birds in controlled freedom: pheasants, a Nile ibis, Malayan cockatoos, a gold-throated eagle.

Appetizers, mainly seafood. Pepper goat cheese. Grape leaves with curds. Dry, cool wine.

As she ate, she seemed indifferent to the long silence. Colón, in contrast, began to feel uncomfortable, and decided to offer an observation:

"Isabel, our queen, is much thinner. . . ."

The sentence hung in the air, naked, unfinished. His attempt to present himself as a regular at court, even a confidant, was patent. He regretted having said it, but could not take it back. She merely raised an eyebrow and breathed a single word.

Colón perceived that he had chosen the worst possible subject: naming Isabel was like speaking of rope in a hanged man's house.

A new attempt:

"Mmmm . . . many problems? Umm, political, I mean. I saw the hides outside the door. . . ."

She listened tranquilly, with a receptive but ironic smile. Then for the first time he heard her voice:

"It is not easy, Admiral, to make Christians of them."

Her reply was gentle, but she was unapproachably remote.

"Is this where she hanged Núñez de Castañeda?" Cristóbal wondered. "Would it have been before or after dessert?" He contemplated the high beams, but saw no marks of violence.

The girls acting as wine stewards filled their goblets.
Two girls brought in a stuffed kid. Salads, puréed kidney
beans, roasted peppers.

She was watching, imperturbable, as he chose the leg of
the kid and greedily sank his teeth into it. After three
mouthfuls, he wiped his hands carefully on his napkin, and
took a sip of wine. Vulgarian that he was, he crooked his
little finger with affectation.

She never lost her terrible aplomb. She even watched
dispassionately the gaffes of the uncomfortable plebeian who
was hovering in the territory of vulgarity and bad taste.

"Yours is a great undertaking, Admiral," she said
condescendingly.

"Indies. Spices. Cipango. The Great Khan," he listed.

"It is farther than you believe. Everyone who lives
around these islands knows about the warm lands you are
seeking. Many have been there, carried by the sea. . . . But
none, on his return, has known how to explain things as he
should. Your accomplishment will not be originality, but
publicity. More than that . . . *they* have sailed near here
several times in their strange boats. They are timid and
delicate, I warn you. They are doomed to lose the world
because of that delicacy. One of them, whom the Guanches
killed because they thought he was a god, told that they had
discovered Europe in 1392. They landed in three different
locations. . . . It seems . . .

"Well. I'm not sure. I do know they reached Porto, the
Azores, and the Canaries. They were not interested in continuing any farther. They do not sail with the wind, they master
the sea. They believe there are rivers in the sea, and that
sailors must learn to follow them. They may be right. We do

not interest them, that much is clear. Who *would* be interested in a world increasingly more perverted by democracy and public education?"

A fresh fruit course was served. Betraying a sweet tooth, La Bobadilla served herself two dishes of custard with the nonchalance—beyond elegance or pure animalism—of a wild beast going down to drink from a spring.

As they were ascending the stone stairway toward the "observatory," as she called it, she said to him with irony, one hand tracing the sign of an orbit:

"Would you like to see my shell collection, Apollo?" Colón was disturbed that she had recognized him, remembered him in a moment from less happy times.

They were never out of the sight of the stocky, pumpkin-headed Galicians, who regularly peered between the draperies, then withdrew.

From the landing on the stairway, she tossed a handful of pistachio nuts to the pheasants strolling through the dining hall. She set free a white mouse as dessert for the royal eagle, which swooped from its perch with elegant and discreet cruelty.

Shortly before dying (Valladolid, 1506), Colón made a statement to Padre Gorricio: what was the event he referred to as "the most intense experience in my life"?

May we take as truth the notes of the ship's boy Morrison who, fifty years after the fact, took down the account of one of the Galician Guard?

Michele da Cúneo reports that Colón returned from the castle "stained with love" (*tincto d'amore*), transformed.

One of the serving girls was willing to offer a comment, once she learned of the tragic death of Beatriz Bobadilla in

Medina del Campo. She said that as La Bobadilla watched Colón bite into the leg of the roast kid, "she knew she was in the presence of a real man, a different kind of man."

La Bobadilla climbed the stairway before him. Intimate glow of oil lamps and candlesticks on the tables. Comforting, stimulating wine. The passion of garlic and seafood from deep, salty waters. Trembling veils, stirred by her footsteps and the breeze from the sea. Tender memory of the torso of a pathetic Apollo whirling erratically above the banquet, scattering bits of gilded pasteboard and leaves from his laurel wreath. Tenderness? Or thwarted desire that had been lying dormant, awaiting its moment of fulfillment? (We must remember that she had watched him through the visor of her helmet, and that she was locked, completely naked, inside her steel armor; Fernando had whispered in passing—such an objectionable sense of humor—that he had thrown the key into the lake. All these details, which escape the superficiality of all the chronicles, have a direct bearing on that strong and indescribable chemistry from which desire and hatred are born.)

They entered a cool, dark room. Colón felt engulfed by her, as if by shadow, as if by dream. La BobaTyrant employed with true mastery the science of approach and withdrawal that fuels ardor.

It is rumored that she was expert in the use of drugs, and other forbidden arts. Prudently, before climbing the hill to the tower, Colón had asked Escobar to prepare him an infusion of *moly*.

She held up the shells against the moonlight: tiny Gaudí cathedrals. Perfect, each different. She made him hold one to his ear, to hear the merry and distant cries of the

Nereids in the depths of the ocean: the sounds of a girls'
school, in the memory of an incurable romantic.

She took his hand and guided his finger through the
spiraled concavity of a *Nautilus silurensis,* to let him "feel the
ivory softness of God's bizarre creation." Colón felt sweat
beginning to trickle down his neck. An uncomfortable defect
of hypersensitivity.

He sensed her radiations. Although she did not move,
and was some distance away, her body advanced toward him,
obliterated and commanded him.

Glimmer of the moon upon the sea. Shimmer of antique
silver. Moonshimmer on silverglimmer.

He could scarcely breathe, he felt that she had invaded
him, that it was an offense to nature that their bodies were
vertical.

As he turned, he saw that they were in a bedchamber:
there was a huge bed, large enough for three couples. It was
covered with snowwhite lambskin, contrasting starkly with
the deep black of the silk sheets and many pillows.

They were enveloped by that blackness: a moonless, uncompromising night. An ardent night that would
last three days and nights. We know, through friends
of Colón, that there were no prolegomena. The Genoese
had sufficient experience of the ports of his world to
know that courtliness is not the quickest way out of your
breeches.

We can imagine that overexcitement threatened the
lovers' pleasure during the first hours of their encounter.
(A young, frightened bull charging through bedchamber
and hall, until finally it falls, gasping, depleted, perhaps
destroyed.)

This was serious lovemaking. They were as somber as two notaries preparing the most important document of their lives. (One laugh, during that ritual, and everything would have collapsed like a castle of playing cards. Nothing more nihilistic than an inopportune laugh.)

The story the guard told Morrison, in addition to having surfaced fifty years after the events took place, suffered from the young Galician's incurably unhealthy two-dimensional view of sexuality. Two-dimensionalism: a substantial lack of projection, of body consciousness, a product of the strict virginology of the era. Furthermore, even had he seen them, there would have been no adequate words to describe and interpret the strange figures Cristóbal and Beatriz produced in the darkness. For the young Galician, those were shadowy Chinese ideograms projected by a Gypsy illusionist. Fire-breathing dragons. Centaurs. The ox with two heads.

The fact is that Colón took risks. Defied the reputation of the BobAutocrat. It was said that, being vulvadentate (molars and two powerful incisors guarding the gates to her intimacy), she was in the habit of leisurely devouring the sex of those lovers who ventured to enjoy her delights. It was also told as fact that when in rut she had congress with the (regional) leader of the wolf pack. The hours went by but the GG were not summoned with their detestable paraphernalia.

More and more sure of himself, Colón expanded his territory and gained ground in that delicious bed. The rich panoply of Onan began to yield its most precious fruit. (From so much imagining the wildest extremes of carnal love, one ends by actually experiencing it.)

Beatriz de Bobadilla felt inclined to abandon her bloody sadism and yield instead to the joys of submission.[2]

For once, La Bobadilla did not have to call on the apparatus of erotic torture to assuage her "penis envy." In the loveshrine, without discussion, the admiral's phallitosis-free *lingam* was accepted as the epicenter, the omphalos, of the city of concupiscence they had entered.

Monumental, abused, nostalgic, and solitary, that penis rose up in the darkness with the self-assured pride and excessive satisfaction of genius long denied but at last recognized.

Actually, it was Colón who took the sadistic initiatives. He tied, for example, two "mortifiers" (a knotted seaman's cord popular in the brothels of the Mediterranean) onto the shaft of his sex.

Toward dawn, the *lingam* became entirely a coparticipatory bridge. That phenomenon had been produced that German sexologists would call *Verfremdung,* the distancing or objectivization of the sex, a depersonalization that transforms it into a pure copulative instrument that is introduced into *both* bodies and about which there is no sense of ownership or domination. A fleshy and physical bridge that unites the "I" and the "you." A no-man's-land. A dual-purpose entity. Nonappropriable. The penis ceases to be the incubus *par excellence.* As symbolically it detaches itself from the male body, it becomes a valuable instrument for the female, who

---

[2]Author's note: The events of that long amatory journey refute the daring theses of Jean-Louis Cesbron in his much discussed study *Colomb, Amait-il la Discipline?* (Paris, 1966).

can manipulate it at will—like a demiurge that demands no ritual adoration, no loyalty. A demiurge already stripped of illusion.

The novelty of domination was so great that at one point during the night La BobaTyrant cried out, in what was already a Caribbean accent:

"Good pussy, mon! This is helluva good time!"

He knew intuitively that she longed for death (erotic and figurative, that is) at his hands. He stepped up his phallic aggression to its highest power. (That was most probably the moment they reached level 8 of lechery on the Hite scale.)

Like every Duse, she demanded of her d'Annunzio that they approach the realms that border on death. Reach the pinnacle of pleasure on the very threshold of physical break-down (like those impassioned and elegant tubercular nineteenth-century courtesans).

It was lust, pure sensuality unsullied by any stain of love. Two bodies inventing their own law of violence-tenderness without the unwelcome intrusion of metaphysics (that aged Western nun expounding, logorrheically, on the color of birds!).

She considered it a strange if tolerable eccentricity that the admiral did not remove his hose.

Their deep sexual harmony was the basis of the unexpected clemency of Beatriz de Bobadilla, who refrained—throughout that amorous interlude—from calling her dreaded GG (who had fallen asleep near dawn, heads together like hastily harvested watermelons, and were snoring in the corridor).

At some moment before dawn, when Colón went to the window to breathe deeply and to look for lubricants and something cool to drink, he saw in the distance the stern (rape oil) lantern of the *Santa María* anchored in the cove, and heard the voice of the watch announcing the turning of the hourglass:

> . . . *o'clock, Good Pilot and Captain,*
> *Good was the hour that's gone,*
> *And better the one that's to come!*

All that seemed very far away. A monastic world with all its concomitant rites, struggles, and illusions. A puerile world.

It was on his return to the bed that they attempted the ultimate.

They had been forming a succession of intricately intertwined figures. We know that she thought she would go mad as he, sex gourmand, a starving hound, sucked and nibbled her tempting popliteal hollows.

Between sheets that blacked out any gleam of light, Cristóbal nonetheless saw the glow of La Bobadilla's phosphorescent humors. They were like a line of lights which seen from the sea announce the remote shore where an unknown but certain happiness reigns.

In her pleasure, she secreted a mercurial moistness that as it evaporated left the pleasing combined aroma of musk and of a warehouse whose principal commerce is sea salt, jute, and blond tobacco leaves.

In that sort of Arabian tent in which they were enclosed as if in one of El Bosco's oranges, the admiral observed a fine white mist issuing from his lance when he emerged from his immersions; this mist rapidly evaporated, leaving on his glans penis, in fact, along the entire trajectory (veiling the tattoos Colón had submitted to in the ports of Thule and Chios, more out of imitation than any other reason), a fascinating deposit of crystallized salts. Tiny gems that glittered—ephemeral and beautiful as fireflies—in the darkness of the loveshrine.

(Neither of the two ever knew that those gems are the only known proof to this day of what we loosely call love.)

Their bodies, silent and sure as two trapeze artists who have worked together for many years, had kindled like two dry logs placed on a fire. By dawn, they had achieved the ultimate configuration, one at which the poet Ovid had failed, and the same that would frustrate Casanova: the unsupported double *trimesí*—also commonly called the "distaff pharaoh,"[3]

Michele da Cúneo would note down the admiral's words: "In the depths of my being, I felt a pleasurable invasion of hundreds of ants (the small red ones that cause prickling but do not bite). Something unique."

Cries. Deep moans. Perhaps a blood-curdling howl, like a wolf that stumbles and plunges into the abyss.

---

[3]Author's note: The *trimesí* would be considered in the famous *Kamasutra* as the ultimate possibility of amatory complexity (without the aid of accolytes); the greatest sensitivization, even exasperation, of the serpent Kundalini that snakes up and down the vertebral column and is the generating center of desire and erotic pleasure. Very probably it corresponds to the "Indrani position," or "apical union," that is accompanied on the part of the female by the sound *"jinn."* But we have no description of this figure. The *Kamasutra* says: "The lovers continue with frenzy, without concern for excess. Passion blinds them. A moment comes in which the union merges into something unreal, as if in a dream."

The truth is that when the guards rushed toward the room they found nothing but two unconscious, exhausted bodies; on their faces was the beautific expression that comes only after an attack of epilepsy.

Came the morning of the third day. A really glorious day. He slept until eleven, when the sun struck him full in the eyes.

The four maidservants filled the bedchamber with laughter and the sound of their sparrowlike voices. They had brought fruit and clear mountain water in a sweating silver jug. A large glass of jenny's milk icy with snow.

A "porcelain" blue sky; below them, an incredible azure sea. (The caravels, three catafalques adrift.)

The four girls, who saw to all personal needs in the palace, warmed a bronze tripod of water for the bath.

Bemused, he felt as if time had stalled in a gerundial "now." The usually ephemeral dot of the present had expanded into a still, cool lake. He took a bite of honey-sweet melon, and held cool milk against his palate.

He liked being *cafishio,* irresponsible, cool, free of rank or title.

The maids submersed him in the tub, laughing at his nakedness and stupefaction. Skillfully, they bathed his sex in cold, light oil and wrapped it in a small towel of Irish linen. Four pairs of youthful hands mischievously fondled him beneath the water.

At moments, he drowsed with delight, and a thread of saliva, a sign of Buddhistic harmony, joined his mouth with the surface of the tub water.

He was immensely happy. Not only had she not killed him, she seemed transformed in a dress with *broderie* ruffles, her hair combed into two schoolgirl braids tied with blue rosettes. She was wearing a straw bonnet with flowered ribbons. Nothing more feminine. Almost girlish.

She was pale. To her the moment was a bead in the necklace of the long night of love. She smiled. She took a silver goblet and delicately crouched over it. He heard the calm whisper of her urine (urine, yes, but enamored urine!).

With magical normalcy, she handed him the goblet and he drank. They gazed at each other. More accurately, each fell into the abyss of the other's gaze.

The laws of amorous delight alter the senses. They had shared a profound communion. That liquid had been consecrated as it passed through the *via triumphalis* of the sexual love uniting them.

Both felt the pleasureful prickling of desire. But she, wise and very female, picked up a wicker basket, and said:

"I'm going down to the market. Which would you rather have, spider crabs or broiled lobster?"

Colón swelled with pride. That act of "going to the market"—modest, domestic—filled him with triumph; he was a lion that had just appropriated new territory, along with its attendant lionesses. He lay there with half-closed eyes. Conqueror. Master. Randy as a billygoat. He mused upon happy and immoral possibilities: dressing in flowered shirts and high heels and managing a busy brothel in Tenerife. Noon on a terrace filled with jasmine and geraniums. Sea breezes. Turkish silks. A profitable slave traffic to the Continent. High finance: opening a branch of Centurione and forcing out the Soberanis and Riverols.

"Prometeo é morto," he cried, as if awakening (in Italian,

which was the language of his subconscious, of his financial dealings, of his occasional sincerity).

The Galician girls laughed, and continued to lather him. What could they know of his depths?

•

Colón's decision not to stay in Gomera and marry the tyrannical widow is, in historical terms, inexplicable. We have no documentation. Failures and fears are not confined to posterity.

Strange that a rather vulgar and pragmatic hedonist, a social climber (who regularly repeated the words of Cicero: "I do not understand the man who, having everything, wants more"), had so quickly abandoned that power base.

It is told that one of the servant girls whispered to him: "There is nothing as treacherous or dangerous as a woman who schemes behind your back. . . ."

It seems it was not the first time that Beatriz de Bobadilla had used submissive sweetness to lure her lovers into a feeling of security. She pretended to be all sweetness and light, but once the careless fellow gained confidence and became too demanding, too domineering, too macho, all her terrible punitive power would erupt: the pigtails and rosettes would be replaced by martial metal, braided leather, and studded scourges. This, in a certain way, had been the sad case with Núñez de Castañeda: overly confident in his ephemeral phallocracy, he was crushed by the deadly repression, the instinctive vengeance, of the spider who devours her mate.

Michele da Cúneo believed that the Genoese had inter-
cepted some wink, some secretive dialogue, between Beatriz
and the chief of her guard. It is also likely that curiosity had
led the admiral to discover the palace torture rooms. That is
the more likely probability.

Did they fear—Colón as well as Beatriz—Isabel's revenge?

Did the basically shrewd Colón sense that power in
those Fortunate Isles was far from being consolidated, and
that the guerrillas were more active than anyone supposed?

Might not the fact that they had achieved *trimesí* by the
end of the first twenty-four hours have left them a little
empty? What is the length of a love, of a relationship, of a
marriage? When does what always dies between a couple in
love die? Probably the time of love is achronic, like time in
dreams, and those days were thirty years; we can imagine
that in the last ten, Colón and La Bobadilla fell into a
boredom of cooking pots, yawns, household bills, and indifferent lovemaking, like the majority of couples in whom the
milk of love loses its savor and becomes tasteless and watery.

Whatever the reason, on the 6th of September Colón
left behind him forever the lovenest in Gomera. His men,
who had decided to continue the voyage without the leader—
the foreigner—designated by the crown, watched him labori-
ously descend the rocky cliff, aided by the same cretin who
days before had led him up.

He waited while they dispatched a yawl for him (there
was some hesitation, but the men from the company nipped
that in the bud), and when he climbed aboard, with the
spirals of his picturesque shoes as limp as two yellow snakes
he had crushed on the path, he said only: "All men to their
posts! We sail today!" And to Juan de la Cosa: "We follow

the agreed course: due west. Did you find the proper hinges for the *Pinta's* tiller? I assume everything is in order. The water here is excellent. . . ."

His equanimity caused great indignation. As he climbed the ladder to his cabin, he heard an unidentified voice:

"Genoese pig!"

And he, almost indifferently, with the serene aloofness of the leader who uses the occasion of gross behavior to instill a lesson:

"Without me, without my cunning, you would have been worse off than pigs. The BobaTyrant would have made you her slaves! Keep that in mind; now shut your mouths and look to the sails!"

•

Horrifying griffins. The Giant Octopus. The Killer Whale. Now, now it must be confronted. The abysses of the unknown Sea. The fury of the wind; the realm of demons.

It seemed to a distraught Colón that God had unleashed His wildest fantasy. Divine perversity, that punishes as it bestows. Let pain be your triumph. Curiosity your damnation.

Espinoso brought him a bowl of beans with sausage and dried beef. A glass of harsh wine, the kind that has no effect. As a sweet, a handful of almonds and raisins.

"You will be hard pressed, Admiral, to maintain this course."

"Did I ask your opinion?"

"No, but the men say that this route can only lead to warm lands, whether those of the Great Khan or someone else. They say it's madness, that it's as if you were going out of your way to find dry, barren lands like those we left behind in Trujillo and Badajoz and Extremadura. Pure madness! Such land will only yield olives and garlic. And with prices already so low! If your excellency does not correct the course there's going to be hell to pay. Admiral: get it in your head: in warm lands, in the tropics, all you'll find is people too poor to cover their nakedness. Where it's hot, it's *poor*."

It was easy to see he was a messenger. That he was speaking the opinion of Pinzón and his men. Ants! Dwarfs! What could they know of the Voice? Of the secret mission of the descendant of Isaiah?

SUNDAY, SEPTEMBER 9. The crewmen have not steered a steady course, but veered a quarter northwest. Sometimes as much as ninety degrees.

They seek a northerly course toward temperate and fertile lands.

They believe either that the admiral will not notice, or that he is too weak to discipline them. They are mistaken. This is the one point he cannot concede. He signals the ships to approach, and summons their captains and pilots. For a real tongue-lashing.

Rodríguez de Escobedo, the secretary, is called to the bridge. He checks his appearance in the mirror tacked to the mainmast. Combs his beard. Solemn, always with his Homer in his pocket.

The Pinzóns arrived, Niño, de la Cosa, Quintero. All the Genoese and the royal paymaster, Sánchez de Segovia. Colón wants his wishes to be clear, stated in black and white in the presence of the Scribe of the Realm. No ruses from now on. There will be no change in the course herewith solemnly noted and in accord with the mandate of their royal highnesses; *due west.* Due west along the line of the Tropics.

Discontented faces. But now deception and unauthorized variations in course will be difficult.

The official document is signed. The meeting is called to an end.

The admiral returns to his roundhouse. He climbs into his tub. He meditates on the forces of the sea.

ELEMENTARY AMPHIBIOLOGY, SEPTEMBER 10. Word of the admiral to his officers: nothing worse than to forget. Yet men, even sailors, forget their amphibian origins. Have they never studied their feet, the palmiped hands that have lost their membranes? Their buttocks, stubs of vanished dorsal fins. Are they blind to the evidence?

They will never learn to navigate if they do not return to their essence.

Men must forget what they praise as the mark of a good sailor.

The admiral orders the main course to be rigged so the ship rides low in the water. He wants the ships to blend into the substance of the sea. For them not to be dry, mere visitors on the ocean.

He orders that several leaking seams not be caulked. He wants water in the bilge, wants the men to hear it sloshing with the roll of the ship, the way he listens to it splash over the edge of the tub and run along the cabin deck.

Navigate like gulls. Like sailors from the Bay of Biscayne. Never far from the mass of the sea. Never in opposition to it. Never dry. He recommends that the men not try to keep dry, to stay wet, if possible. They will avoid colds, although they do not believe him.

The gull—the admiral preaches—does not look to the winds to change. It *is*, whatever the wind. He has similar praise for the nautical adaptability of Galician fishermen.

"Any other way of thinking," he proclaims sententiously, "is for the French."

Juan de la Cosa starts to reply, but refrains.

Colón submerges his head in the tub and floats face downward, like a dead man. All that is visible is an arse as soft and white as the buttocks of a Belgian nun raped by soldiers and drowned in a Flemish canal.

He floats a long time; he amazes them.

Then he states that in the bosom of the water he communicates with the Ocean Sea, and that only challenge can conquer fear.

Sing in cemeteries, he recommends. Whistle in the moonless forest.

The wind is howling and the ship is breasting heavy seas. The bow shattering teeth of foam. Fringe is flying, lace, the slobber of a madly galloping colt.

When the admiral steps out of his cabin, the insolent wind whips his hair mercilessly.

Drenching drops of salt. Strings of melted silver.

Shrouds and halyards are humming. The billowing spritsail, the "nose bag," tugs valiantly at the bowsprit. It is a stubborn mule straining in harness, its ears laid back by the rain and wind.

As soaking halyards are whipped by the sail, they are

wrung out and dried. They smoke from friction with bitts and belaying pins.

The reins of a runaway horse.

Deep sobs were wrung from the mast holes of the foresail, mainsail, and mizzen—strained to capacity. The masts are again slender tree trunks standing amid the fierce thrill of the storm.

Thudding hoofbeats as the hull pounds the seas.

"Look lively! Man the sails!" shouts the admiral. He runs down the ladder from the quarterdeck to the main deck. He shouts orders to the uninspired men, who act as if they do not hear him. They loaf about as if waiting their watch. Staying out of the spray. Somber, bored, playing cards. "Get up! At once! All of you! Sheet the sail! Tighter! Heave away!" he cries. He himself takes the forestay.

The ship shudders. A filly in season. A stringed instrument in a passionate *allegro.*

Now the wind is singing hoarsely through hatches and lockers. The stays and shrouds are chords of an enraptured harp.

The wind moans and sobs.

The admiral shouts, exhorts. He longs for a whip, anything to shake up the loafers. Wretches!

He climbs to the forecastle and receives a benediction: foaming waves, cool on his face and chest. He stretches his arms before him, face streaming water. He feels he *is* the ship.

"Yahweh! Yahweh! Yahweh! Hallelujah!" he shouts. "Sheet the sail! Tighter! Look to the mainsail! Haul the main topsail higher, that's it!"

Tumultuous gallop across the fields of the sea. Abandon. Celebration. Ecstasy. Capitulation to space.

As he returns, soaking, to his cabin, he sees them exchanging grins and winks. They think he is mad. Most of them are lolling against stores on the poop deck, picking their teeth, dreaming of an orchard of their own, or of stealing pearls from the idol in the Imperial Palace.

Blessed common sense.

SPACE AND TIME, SEPTEMBER 13. The return to Heaven from Earth must be affected along the same path Adam followed in his ignominious and deserved expulsion.

The world in which we think we live is writing that must be read in reverse, before a mirror.

Space and Time are the names of the exterminating angels that expelled us from Eden. They must be watched with great cunning. Only they can indicate to us the return path to the desired Gates.

(Is that what you want, Adam? To measure? Count? Till you can't count on anything? To study the science of Good and Evil? Stubborn geodesist! *This* is Space, and Time is *here.* Get it straight, stupid! Take care, or they will crush you. They will roll you flat, squeeze you dry, like the dear departed—God rest her soul—Felipa Moñiz Perestrello. She ended up a portrait her ungodly husband hung above the carving board in the dining hall. Adam: entangle yourself for all time, if you wish, in the net! Or exclude yourself, if you want. Measure carefully!")

But there will be one, one of the line of Isaiah, who will lead them all. Never will so many have owed so much to one man. The Hero.

He will liberate them from their unique suffering.

Christ was a minor demiurge. He could have done much more. Save bodies, for example. Save here on Earth. Here in the pain on Earth. All he did was show the path by which souls might return.

But this is understandable, given his celestial nature: his body was pro forma, a virgin born of a Virgin. His flesh insipid. Christ did not sweat. (The admiral notes this with the greatest respect. He recognizes that Christ was the God of the Jews' best possibility to make himself known throughout the world.)

The sea is still strong. The wind, safe. Time, variable. Occasional clouds and drizzle. The men lick their hands and the wet brass. Some hold out the blade of their knives to receive the angel of the rain.

Mess is announced. General jubilation concentrated about the firebox. Stewards are filling the wine jugs.

Officers—the secretary and the paymaster—sit at their table near the helm; the seamen lounge against the coamings of the hatchways or coils of rope. They all have a favorite place, their territory. Like cats.

A ship's boy runs up and down the decks with a little bell (as if everyone were not already waiting!).

"To table! To table! Sir Captain and Master and good company. Table is set. Food is ready. Long live the King and Queen of Castile, on land and on sea!"

Merriment. Laughter. The usual disorder around the firebox and cooking pots. Jokes.

A good day: mutton stew with lentils. Soup of rice and dried fish. Roast peppers. Large pieces of biscuit.

Harsh wine, not yet turned bitter.

They gnaw the bones happily. Use their bread to wipe the last grease from the plate.

Dried figs.

Cards, a siesta, or watch duty.

SEPTEMBER *14. THE BRANCH OF FIRE ON THE SEA.* Toward dusk the skies cleared. That night they saw stars they had not seen for several days.

A moonless night. The awesome movement of the stars. (The men whisper that many constellations seem to be falling below the horizon. The pilots try to clarify matters. Calm the men.)

Incredible splendor. An abyss that humans can see from the spine of their dark planet.

In the west, they watched a marvelous branch of fire fall from the sky into the sea.

The men point to it with fear. They believe it is an exploding star.

Several arms of fire around the center. It is the unmistakable sweep of the flaming sword. The swastika of fire.

The admiral falls to his knees in the dark solitude of the bridge, in response to that clear and direct manifestation from the Divinity.

"Oh, God. You Who cast us out from Your house now are indicating the way home. All praise be to Your name."

Devoutly, he closes his eyes and sees in the night of astral space the unequivocal movement of the sword, just before the bow, almost a projection of the center line of the ship.

Arise, shine; for thy light is come,
is risen upon thee . . .
but the Lord shall arise upon thee,
and his glory shall be seen upon thee.
(Isaiah 60: 1, 2)

The sea is ever deeper and more foreboding. Its calm does not soothe anyone's terror.

The Admiral, conscious that they are disheartened and alarmed, enters false information. Each morning, for the day's run, he reckons fewer leagues than they have made. You have to put blinders on a horse when you expect to confront fire, or a savage bull.

This is not the sea they have known, the Mare Nostrum that man plies with relative confidence. This is the Mare Tenebrarum in all its grandeur.

It is a living animal that only human ingenuity can domesticate. It needs no special malevolence to destroy men: its mere being—a mammoth, savage deity—is sufficient.

At dawn, off the bow, they sight two or three whales followed by a clientele of sharks.

Their presence is menacing. The sailors stand in small groups, whispering terrible tales, superstitions heard in the ports. (Are the monsters in the sea or in their souls?)

The realm of demons is best left undisturbed. The admiral recommends discreet silence. Leave off the boasting and foolishness of days on land: the laughter, the quarreling. He has little success. They do not understand.

The spider, the scorpion, the serpent, are aware of their evil. The creatures of the sea, who conserve the dimensions of a different era on earth, work their evil automatically, like mindless children; in short, like Dutchmen.

Griffins, which fly from undiscovered islands to devour sailors' flesh, are a hybrid of eagle and lion. The Giant Octopus, which so often has dragged ships down into its abyss, is a squid with eight tentacles. It is known that it prefers the light of the full moon, but if it devours men it is from extreme hunger, for lack of anything better.

They enter a spatiotemporal region never seen by human—except accidentally or in the unconscious. The admiral understands that it is natural that in this intermediate zone between nothing and being, between the known and mystery, the dead—at times with true insolence—make their appearance.

The admiral has experience, and knows what to look for. They walk constantly among the living, but it is at dusk when their milky color is most defined.

He knows the dead must be denied, and that if allowed they will claim all the space and time of the living, driving them mad. Treat them like dogs: ignore their threats; never show fear.

They are clinging, opaline presences. Astral protoplasm with an unholy nostalgia for life on earth. Nothing more.

At close quarters, the dead have the stale smell of cloistered nuns, like slightly damp snails.

The admiral refuses to acknowledge the dead, to know them any better. Even though he knows they are there. He senses them from his cabin: perched in the rigging, legs swinging; sardonic, demanding, calculating. Unable, basically, to tell what they have seen, if, in fact, they have seen anything. Indecent exploiters of the somber reputation of death. Always with an insistent desire to scatter signs and portents.

But the admiral will not look at them. His fear is stronger than his curiosity. He knows that the dead abduct, but never liberate. That they spread fear and disdain for life, when actually they are devoured by a rabid envy of healthy bodies and senses.

The admiral stares at the deck. If it is night he squeezes his eyelids tight. He tries to sleep, thinking of bright scenes filled with people.

When he feels he is about to lose the battle, that they are about to emerge in all their milky splendor, he rushes from his cabin, hurries down the ladder, and begins talking with the helmsmen on duty.

These are the only times when he expresses himself freely, speaks of pleasant, even entertaining and sincere, subjects.

Because of his fear of the dead.

To the degree they are increasingly insecure, the men find propitious signs tailored to their desires.

They bring the admiral seagrasses borne on the currents, and show him a live crab nesting in them. They place it on the planking of the deck and nudge it to make it move. They feed it crumbs. They splash it with seawater. They adopt it. It becomes a talisman to ward off their fear.

They estimate that the coast—the fertile lands they seek—is very close. They believe they see flocks of migratory birds (on that auspicious September 18). With exuberant cries they welcome the sighting of an aged pelican, surely lost or abandoned by the flock.

On the 20th there came to the ship, about dawn, two or three land birds, singing, but before sunrise, they disappeared.

Their eagerness is so great that the eyes of many shine as if bewitched.

The compass declines northwest: unmistakable proof that they are approaching a region of the world where the usual spatiotemporal schemes are disrupted. The needle always seeks the true, therefore they are uneasy.

The sea rises very high. A dark sea, heavy as mercury. Strong seas, but in the absence of wind; this disturbs the pilots, who communicate by shouting from the crow's nests of the three ships.

They do not understand. They have never seen such a phenomenon. But the admiral welcomes it as another unspoken but unequivocal sign from God. As in the times when Moses led the Jews out of Egypt, the sea is parting, rising into walls of water, even though there is not a breath of air.

The admiral gives thanks, eyes half closed. The Dialogue continues; that is the important thing.

SEPTEMBER 25. *THE FALSE ISLANDS.* The wish is so strong that it becomes illusion: finally someone shouted from the *Pinta,* commanded by Martín Alonso Pinzón, that land has been sighted.

Visions of their fear. The admiral capitalized on the opportunity. He accepted the mirage, and joined in the exultation. He dropped to his knees on the bridge, in a pathetic pose, and led the chorus singing *Gloria in Excelsis Deo.*

Men swarm up the rigging. Wave their hats. They all see the islands of golden sand. "Just like Guinea." They see palm trees. They name several species of phantom trees.

Taking advantage of the sudden calm, some dive from the rigging. The Mare Tenebrarum is behind them!

They mistreat the sea as if it were a sleeping lion, kicking and splashing. They are convinced the worst is over.

Their thoughts turn to self-interests and dreams of what they will find ashore.

Even the most excited sleep with calm. They are no longer thinking of mutiny, but of plantations (at sea, they want to be ordinary husbandmen; in the fields and tailor shops, they dream of the sea).

But the dawn reveals no coastline. They sail on.

They are not greatly disappointed; they conjecture that soon they will sight another archipelago.

In the regions into which they have ventured, the wind responds to different laws.

Saint Paul was right when he said that the Prince of Darkness powers the air.

Nothing is more terrifying. The storm precedes the probable breaking up and fall of the skies.

Thunder. Lightning. God is more refulgent in his fury than in his calm.

The admiral, thinking of God—God the Father—as the storm begins, recalls the fury of his grandfather in the village of Quinto; when he lost at *chinchón* he threw bottles and chairs through the door in a drunken rage. Roared and slobbered. And had to be thrown in a ditch of cold water to be calmed down.

The winds alter the seas: wild waves and water spouts.

The tiny ships career along terrible racing mountains. With their white sails, they look like little scraps of paper.

"The thunder is rolling its boulders."

Run with the storm. Run. Gallop with the waves! Don't be afraid! Don't fight it, it would be futile.

But they do not understand. They want to furl the sails. Cast oil on the waters. Lower floating anchors. In short: transform the ephemeral space of their three vessels into three solid, safe islands. Impossible! One cuff from the sea and they would be lost.

The admiral makes himself heard, urges them to give themselves with joy to their gallop over the ocean. To transmute rape into an act of triumphant love.

To ward off the fury of the wind, the sailors tie knots in anything they can put their hands on, even the tails of the rats.

Hypnotized, they recite the prayer *Ad Repellendas Tempestatis.*

They send a delegation to the admiral. They even dare climb his ladder without permission. They know he has a bag of knots sold him by a seer in Scotland. They want him to use them now, tossing handfuls to the four cardinal points.

They tell him: "The foremast and mainmast are bent like reeds."

The admiral retorts: "Innocents! When a person thinks he's in bad trouble, you can be sure he knows only the half of it."

They implore him to put on his Franciscan habit, and to ask for the aid of Tata Pancho. Traditions of the sea.

The pilots do not want to steer toward the center of the storm, that forge of thunder and lightning blazing on the horizon. That smithy of celestial fire. That volcano pointed toward the earth.

Instead, they throw their weight against tillers to steer away, driven by pure animal fear.

The admiral shouts to the man at the helm:

"That is the only way we *can* go. To where the demons sleep! To their cave! Only there can we be saved! In the heart of Evil! At the center from which devils come!"

At the eye of the cyclone, when they reach it, there is calm, a gentle silence. All about them they see swirling black clouds laden with fire and ice, pursuing each other like the Erinyes.

With great difficulty, the admiral climbs to the crow's nest, defying the storm winds, and releases handfuls of torn paper to study their spiral course. He shouts what he has learned to Juan de la Cosa, who is standing at the foot of the mainmast, but the storm blurs and sweeps away his words.

The admiral knows that the wind is moving in a spiral, like the stars of infinite space, and like seas when drawn down to the terrible abyss of the Maelstrom.

The stature of the admiral increases during these terrible tests, in these new dimensions where they are all so vulnerable.

He has one great advantage over the ordinary man: he believes more in man's original peril than in a protector. He does not ask the storm to abate, nor the sea to become a meandering meadow stream.

He believes that there is no end to difficulty, or that if one difficulty ends, a greater trial will follow; that is why he is strong when others weaken or complain.

Beside him, his men—who scorn him—are dwarfed; they assume the color and size of their fears.

The admiral is splendid in his solitude. Now—close to what only he can sense—he spends many hours on the bridge.

When the rains stop and there is only a rain of lightning, he appears on the poop deck, in expectation of the Saint Elmo's fire.

Like many geniuses, and in no small part due to the encrustation of salt and plankton on his skin, he is from time to time bioluminescent.

As the enzymes on his brow and face are oxygenized, visible sparks can be seen in the dark night (like those of a blinking lighthouse, the kind the English place at the mouth of their ports to guide the return of the heavily laden ships of plunderers and pirates).

His detractors and enemies say that he is illuminated by the luciferine his body produces.

The men of the crew do not love him, but they respect him. Awed, they spy on him from behind bulkheads and masts.

At times he looks to them like a gigantic firefly.

SEPTEMBER 27. STRANGE THINGS HAPPENING. Pérez the cobbler and the royal paymaster Sánchez de Segovia request a conference with the admiral.

Pérez says that while relieving his bowels over the gunwales of the port "garden" he has seen a group of lights. Several overlapping strings of lights moving along the horizon. He says it was an enormous ship of terrifying size, as tall as the Cathedral of Seville. The illuminated mast reminded him, he says, of the Giralda during the week of the festival of the Virgin of the Seas.

He knows how to read (he is a visionary and mystic like almost all cobblers). He swears he read the words "Queen Victory" on the stern of the monster that passed spewing showers of phosphorescent foam.

Sánchez de Segovia believes him, and that is why he has brought him to the commander. He says that he himself has noticed that strange things are happening. He believes that they are not alone, and even dares suggest it would be better to return to Spain.

The admiral does not reply to such insolence.

The paymaster advised the admiral that a climate of slander and suspicion reigns on his ships.

"This is a bottomless barrel, a keg of serpents." Many, it seems, are beginning to see the dead appearing in the rigging. Some do not want to go to the gunwales to tend to their needs, because mocking demons are lurking there. (He recounts two anecdotes of questionable taste.)

The most alert have observed that the days are not lasting twenty-four hours, but thirty-two, even thirty-three, and that in this region of fear each league seems like four miles.

They sharpen their knives. Meet secretly. The paymaster says the men believe that the admiral has powers of the devil. That the boldest even speak of tarring him and burning him at the mainmast.

There is truth in what he says. The men, in the face of such mutations, take refuge in the idea of returning, by violence, if necessary.

The admiral requests the paymaster to carry out a full and thorough investigation and to present it in writing. He rewards Pérez de Cádiz, mystic and cobbler, with a sugar lump, as he would a noble steed. He himself holds it to the man's lips.

•

That voyage, once begun, will exist in a ten-year continuum.

The admiral soon understood that his goals demanded a flagrant rupture with the established spatiotemporal order. That the appearance of the world would be affected in major ways.

It was a new set of events, and new circumstances would emerge from them.

The spatiohistorical horizon was shattered once and for all by the bow of the *Santa María*. It was like ripping open one of those grab bags sold at the Ferragosto fairs. The Pandora's Box of reality.

People, ships, began to slip through the rent in the spatiotemporal veil, human scenes that the admiral—as a visionary—had to accept without trying to seek explanations that would exceed the modest possibilities of the age.

He was at once on the bridge of the *Santa María* and that of the *María Galante* (which would set sail in 1493 at the head of a flotilla of fifteen large and several smaller vessels), and of *La Vaqueños* and *La Vizcaína* (1502).

His task became enormously complicated. His skepticism and patience in the face of the mysterious and the unexpected rescued him from the perilous fatigue of astonishment and subsequent search for explanations.

On Saturday, October 6, from the bridge of the *María Galante,* he gazed into the past and watched the departure of the three caravels (sailing toward the famous October 12, 1492); he was aided by a lens-fitted tube given him in Barcelona, on the occasion of his triumphal return, by a Flemish optician, Monsieur Zeiss, who was offering them to the court in return for an exclusive patent.

He saw himself on the quarterdeck of the *Santa María,* peering into the mists of the future to identify the outlines of the *María Galante!*

The men of the crew crowded against the gunwales, hung from the shrouds. Trying to peer through the layers of fog.

They say they have heard neighing from the sea, and the unmistakable bellow of a bull. At dawn, the crowing of a rooster.

On board the three tiny ships there are only men, and furtive rats.

They mutter about demons, about the mythic sea horse.

In fact it was the bull tended by Joan Velmont aboard *La Colina,* destined for the celebration of October 12. The animal had burst out of its improvised pen and was spreading terror and festival excitement (Spanish style) as it charged back and forth along the deck. It was like San Fermín day in Pamplona. Cries of *olé* accompanied each fruitless effort by Joan Velmont to get the beast back to the orlop deck. The neighing is from the horses, whose terror of the sea is added to the fear awakened by the brute.

In the rigging, the uproar produces a fluttering of doves, sparrows, and breeding partridges.

A valiant ship's boy is trampled, hemmed in against the bulkhead at the bow.

The bull bellows, excited by the scent of the milch cows aboard *La Gallega.* Angry protests from the husbandmen; the bull's horns have ripped apart the seedbeds of edible plants that transform the gunwales into floating gardens.

Finally, the torero, feet firmly planted beside the hatch to the hold, challenges the bull. When the beast charges, he

performs an elegant pass, swirling his cape triumphantly as
the animal tumbles into the darkness of the bilge. General
applause. Accolades. The torero is lifted to their shoulders.

Velmont is invited to eat at the table of the pilots and
officers.

Now there are several who, like Pérez de Cádiz, says
they have seen strange ships with lights ablaze.

The admiral himself has observed them. They are large
sailless ships transporting quantities of passengers and goods.
Some have enormous metal chimneys, and leave a trail of
curious smoke that seems too uniform to come from a fire.

One of the ships, the *Rex,* left a mantle of lively music
as it passed. It was dusk, and the admiral could see clearly,
sitting beside a kind of large pool surrounded with brightly
colored parasols, a group of young men in straw hats, white linen
jackets, and long straight-legged trousers. The women's straw
hats had bands of flowers around the crown. Several are
holding drinks with straws in them, and lemon slices. Synco-
pated music (the admiral has no way of knowing it is the
rumba "Peanut Vendor," played by Leucuona). He watches
with fascination, like a peasant on the fringes of a fiesta,
feeling a hint of envy for the frivolous and easygoing life
of the happy bourgeoisie of the first decades of a future
century.

Intuitively, the admiral avoids examining these phenomena in too great detail. He reacts against falling into the
abyss of these dangerous future events with the same healthy
instinct mules display on a mountain trail.

He knows that he could lose his reason forever. And he
is a prudent man.

But the frequency with which these ships fallen from future time appear is truly disquieting. They cut insolently across the stern and bow of the *Santa María,* without due respect.

He has observed that he never sees them directly ahead of the *Santa María's* bowsprit. It is as if they depended upon her battered wooden prow to cut the veil of time. At moments when the *Santa María* is becalmed, or on a long tack—whenever the normal course is interrupted or delayed—the ships from the future circle aimlessly.

This was the case with the good ship *Mayflower,* laden with terrible Puritans on their way to Vinland, that circled the *Santa María* as if she had a damaged rudder, or a one-eyed, distracted pilot steering obsessively to port, like a donkey turning a water wheel.

Similar phenomena occurred with the ships of the English pirates Sir Walter Raleigh and John Hawkins, lovers of the Virgin Queen.

North, toward Novaya Gorod, as well as south toward the River Plate, steam somber ships loaded with immigrants from Sicily, Italy, Extremadura, and Ireland.

Grist for the labor mills, for interbreeding and bastardy, moved by dreams of a modest existence.

At night he hears the singing of Ashkenazi Jews. The *canzonetta* of the Neapolitan who will seduce the daughter of a Hungarian rabbi and engender a managerial class for New York. The Turkish woman from Ankara who will have a child by the solemn man from Extremadura, who dreams of a son who will be a notary, or owner of a large estate or coffee plantation.

The breeze carries words the admiral cannot understand: fox-trot, Andes, Immigrant Hotel, Río de la Plata, *milonga,* "There's gold in them thar hills, Jim!"

One night a great sailing ship hove into view: Christian Dutch trading in Negro slaves to be auctioned—with written guarantee and to the highest bidder—in Hispaniola and Portobelo.

The stench, the *catinga,* was so great that whales abandoned the region between the line of the Tropics and thirty-five degrees north latitude.

But in spite of everything, from that tragic ship came a melody, a deep, rhythmic chanting, that would not be subdued.

That fate would be the result of a humanitarian recommendation from Padre Las Casas: "If the Negroes have always been slaves, and have so little soul, why not import them from Africa and save the Indians from such a wretched destiny?"

OCTOBER 9 AND 10. "All night they heard birds passing." Inky blackness. The wingbeats of what must surely be migrating birds.

They are following the same route as the birds, and that is good. Toward dusk, a rook, a mallard, and a pelican land on the ship.

They probably saved the admiral from the desperation of men haunted by visions and presences. The conspirators were divided: many believed that land was near, and it was worth waiting a few days more before mutinying.

The royal paymaster has presented his report, duly sealed by the secretary. Of the strange things happening on board, half are due to conspiracy, the other half a mystery.

The officer, who values order above all, is dismayed. It is as if he had proved that the world moves beneath our feet.

That all connection with the order of the mother country had been left behind.

But in any case, for the moment the threat of insurrection is averted. Pinzón himself brings the *Pinta* alongside, almost close enough to board, and shouts to the admiral:

"Your excellency, toss us half a dozen of those trouble-makers. And if your excellency lacks the stomach for it, my brothers and I will dispatch them for you!"

Iberian simplicity. The admiral, always ambiguous, replies:

"Keep calm, Martín Alonso. We are proceeding well with these gentlemen. In a few more days, if land is not sighted, we shall reconsider the course. . . ."

But there are other conspiracies to concern him. The paymaster has lists of names, veins of subversion spreading in all directions. He counsels:

"Don't trust them, your excellency. They have friends at court. They did not enlist to follow the command of God, or the king and queen, but to betray the System." Does the admiral believe they come in the name of Spain? He is mistaken! In truth, they are trying to escape civilization and Christianity. Fleeing from Spain and Europe. They are saboteurs of the System.

He unrolls and reads his list of names:

"Comendador Bobadilla, Margarit, Fray Buil. Guevara and Riquelme. Ojeda, who is even preparing his own flotilla, and, as the crowning blow, has signed on one of the Berardi managers named Amerigo Vespuccio, a relative of La Bella Simonetta. Plus the Porras brothers, Francisco Roldán, the pharmacist Bernal, Fonseca . . ."

These men on the one side. Although they may seem innocent, they carry subversion in their bone marrow. On the other, many strange types, like the mercenaries, whose language no one understands and whose intentions, therefore, are difficult to analyze.

One of them is greatly to be feared, one Mordecai, who hides in the bilge of *La Vaqueños* and the *Correo.* He lives in darkness, among the rats' nests. He tells the men they are equal, that they should unite, that private property is a kind of thievery! It is obvious he has misread Saint Thomas, and that humble man from Assisi. He even says religion is the opium of the people. Does the admiral realize that?

"Mordecai?"

The inspector continues:

"It spreads like an infection. Some of his men tried to saw through the rudder post of *La Vaqueños.* We are sure of it: we found the sawdust. Fortunately, my agents arrived in time. A vessel with a sawed-off rudder breaks up like a flower in the wind."

There is also a family of Flemish Gypsies, children of Hegel, hiding in the belly of the ship. They come out only to speak with the dregs among the crew: the resentful, the ill. They promise them Paradise.

"Paradise," the admiral asks in alarm. And Sánchez de Segovia replies:

"Well, in the figurative sense. They say that man must have his Paradise on earth, and that they will lead him toward it."

The admiral is beside himself:

"Bring this Mordecai to me, and the others! Search for them in the holds! Double the guard! Torture them! Throw them overboard!"

•

The night of tropical calm follows a day of infernal heat. Sun beating down: limp sails drooping like melted candle wax.

Heat so intense that dry leather grows supple, even spongy. In the holds, only the Galician peasants have not shed their clothing. Men and animals desperately struggle up to the deck, only to encounter scorching sun and boiling air. Befuddled hens take a few steps on the deck and fall feet up, eyes staring.

As the plants in the seedbeds wilt in the heat, despairing gardeners—witlessly—moisten the thirsty leaves with seawater. It is like putting salt on the lips of a feverish man. The tender leaves shrivel, crusted with salt.

The hammered iron of the vessel's nails, mortise plates, and hawse holes expands and becomes malleable. Bombards burn as hot as if recently fired against invisible enemies.

On July 13, the admiral wrote in his diary that he feared "lest the ships should burst into flame; water casks and wine barrels swelled, wheat burned like fire, bacon and salt meat roasted to no man's benefit."

A colt went beserk and had to be thrown overboard. In its frenzy—contrary to instinct—it started swimming south toward the line of the equator, proof that its delirium was total, since by instinct animals swim in advance of, or back toward, the course of the ship. (Or could it possibly have scented land to the south?)

Its bay mane was visible in the motionless sea, and then, nothing.

The admiral knows that at the point they have reached in the cosmic aperture, the horrendous heat is a positive sign. It comes from the fire of the flaming swords guarding the Gates.

After midnight, the heat moderates. The air cools to the temperature of the sea and begins to run as smoothly as a deer.

But it is not to be a placid wind. It will bring devastation.

"Menstral blowing this way!" shouts a lookout from the crow's nest. It advances toward them, as dense, humid, and sensual as the sirocco that might have enveloped a night of young love in Venice.

It is a wind that frees buried restlessness. "The smell of woman on the wind," as they say in Naples.

The admiral knows that its effect will be disastrous to the ravenous sexual hunger of his Iberian crew. There is a full moon, and he recalls an old proverb of Catalan sailors:

Menstral, and a full moon,
You'll pay for your sins all too soon.

The air is at once sweet and saline. A wind like sweat. It bathes faces in a milky dew. The admiral goes below decks, where the crew is lolling about like demented, flimsily clad novices.

The Iberian crew are as hot as caged dogs in heat. Their

sexuality erupts unexpectedly, generally in illicit manifesta-
tions: rape, masturbation, sodomy, in sum—it is painful to
say—in Catholic sexuality.

The admiral is well aware that the crew is risking the
Atlantic adventure to obtain women—to "unleash the hound"
(or "sharpen the saber" or "to look God in the face"), as they
say in the lingo of the bilge.

A calm night. Only enough wind in the sails to propel
the vessels forward at a swimmer's pace. Some men, in fact,
strip (an infrequent occurrence, as they seldom remove their
sweat-stained underdrawers or undershirts knit of Catalan
wool) and jump into the water. They paddle and splash, and
the boldest dive beneath the keel. They climb back aboard by
shinnying up the thick cable they had dropped over the
stern, like blacks in Guinea climbing a swaying palm tree.

Billowing sails in a moonlit night. Great pale breasts.
Now the ships are three Portuguese wet nurses on their way
to market.

As they have before, rarely, some climb the rigging to
the crow's nest and from there leap toward the canvas breast
of the sail and slide, as if tobogganing, down to the foot,
where they fall laughing onto the deck. Again they climb the
Jacob's ladder to the masts and, guffawing, repeat the game.

Enormous udders holding the wind. Taoist triumph of
the inaction that selects and directs impelling force. The sails
concentrate the female power of the ships. Great maternal,
remote females. Serene, majestic godmothers.

As if by chance, many older sailors begin to hang
around the port and starboard gunwales (what they call the
"gardens") to watch the young deckhands urinate. It becomes
a place to congregate, to talk.

The admiral realizes that they are under the spell of Aphrodite, the inescapable goddess of love born of the depths of the sea. If you listened closely, you could hear the rhythmic song of the sirens. Three of them, laughing and frolicking like dolphins, swim by the bow, their alabaster breasts gleaming in the light of the moon. To escape them, the admiral gives the order to tack. La Bobadilla had warned him that they must flee the voices of the divine sirens and avoid the realms in which they so sweetly sing. He knows that Aphrodite is watching them, filling their hearts with sweet reveries.

The moralistic paymaster demands they curb the crews' excesses; aboard the *Correo* they are coupling with cows, which moo disgruntledly.

The thirty prostitutes who had agreed to come aboard in Seville are offering their services—against strict orders to the contrary—in full view at the base of the masts.

Many undesirables and stowaways creep from the holds in various, often indecent, disguises. Amazingly, women's wigs materialize, embroidered underdrawers, even the dress of a Gypsy dancer.

The philosopher Jean-Loup Vasselin, author of the *Traité de la Modération*, joins those loitering about the ship's primitive pissoir.

As the night progresses, sexual bargaining heats up, with its eternal principal of give and take.

Inexhaustible, the number of the hypnotized sliding down the bosom of the sail increases.

The admiral does not yield to the repressive suggestions of Sánchez de Segovia or the secretary. Nor does he listen to the arrogant protests of Fray Buil. (Squarcialuppi and other

fainthearted and fluttery novices have escaped both his watch-
ful eye and the convent cells improvised belowdecks at the
bow of *La Colina* and mixed with the crew. He says it is easy
to recognize them: naked, a virtual striptease, beneath as
yet—fortunately—unconsecrated cassocks.)

Whispers and panting in the dark, heavy night.

One of the unsavory participants in the great westward
adventure is strolling along the deck, too warmly dressed in a
greatcoat and smelling of medications; he is speaking with
the deckhand Pérez, a toothless Aragonese in a tattered
undershirt, knife hanging from a cord around his neck, who
understands not one word from that refined Frenchman referring to his "Tante Léonie" and the bell tower of the small
church of Saint-Marcel-des-deux-Braguettes.

Persecuted and execrated love must resort to eccentric
postures and places. Some prove themselves to be true anal
acrobats.

Who, then, was the maddened Madrilenian dancing the
heel-tapping rhythm on the forecastle of the *Santa María*? Is
it possible it was Rodríguez de Escobedo, the secretary?

The menstral wind is the bearer of everything female.
The men exude woman from every pore: sister, nurse, prostitute, nubile nun, loving and hardworking aunt.

From the bridge the admiral can see the Quakers and
Puritans of the *Mayflower*, laboring, their faces shining in the
night. Obstinate, striving to ignore the affront of indomitable erections. Lutheran pastors' penises roar ominously from
the depths of their many-buttoned trousers.

Nor was Padre Las Casas spared the trying *rigor vitae*: he
knelt sobbing before the boom of the *María Galante*, assailed
by humiliating snickers from the hands on duty.

The paymaster and his four faithful halberdiers seize the opportunity of the menstral to track and attempt to apprehend Mordecai and his followers.

Proof of the revolutionary zeal and self-denial of those subversives was the fact that they refused to join in the erotic festival.

Just before dawn, on the topmast of *La Colina* was seen the messianic, Levitical figure of the bearded Mordecai in his soup-stained overcoat, sending luminous signals, surely in secret code, to conspirators aboard two English sailing ships headed for the southern hemisphere (they were the *George Canning* and the *Avon*—the latter bearing the profile of Simón Bolívar).

Too late! Mordecai, who has his accomplices among the crew, the troops, the undesirables, and the whores, scrambled down and disappeared toward the bilge. It would not be surprising if from there he slipped to *La Gorda*, the center for copyists of the subversive lampoons that were causing so much harm.

•

The admiral knew that the passage to the invisible is visible.

In his quarters, he consulted the secret map, product of untold years of searching, violation of correspondence, and intuition. (Everyone could read the same things in the sacred and profane texts, but only the Chosen One—he of the line of Isaiah—could formulate the final synthesis.)

He would have to steer a steady WSW to hold to the

line between the tropics and the equator. The ship—he was sure of it—was now sailing in the zone where in the year 565 Abbé Brendan had succeeded in *transcending.*

The admiral has no doubt that in spite of deviations and dead calms they are in the zone of the Aperture.

Would he be abandoned now, he who had, deservedly, received so many unmistakable signs? The strange fruits, the songbirds, the extraordinary heat, and, above all, the ineffable aroma on the night air: hidden jasmine, fleeting orange blossoms. Signs that rewarded his boldness in having deserted—from pure fear of the Devil—the enchanting perdition of La Bobadilla and dominion over her sulfurous lands. (It is known that the Mouth of Hell is adjacent to the Gate of Salvation. Dante knew it but erred seriously when he stated that the Fortunate Isles, the Canaries, were the Earthly Paradise. Poetic irresponsibility.)

The admiral spends long, obsessive hours on the bridge, remaining there even after nightfall. He orders the sharpest-eyed ship's boys to the crow's nests. (Although only he, he is aware, will be granted the privilege of the full vision.)

By the flickering candlelight, he reads his notations:

> *"Beyond the Ocean that surrounds the four sides of the interior Continent representing the area of the Tabernacle of Moses, there is another land; that is the location of the Paradise man inhabited before the Flood."* (*Cosmas,* Indicopleustes, *in his* Topographia christiana)
>
> *Coincidentally: "On the other Pole . . . four stars that had/Never been seen except by the first people."* (Dante, *Divine Comedy,* "Purgatory," Canto I)

*Why did Isaac and Jacob not speak and describe
their visits to Paradise? What was the secret that compelled them to silence?*

*"When he expelled Adam, God allowed him to
take with him saffron, nard, palms, cinammon, and the
seeds of many fruit trees."*

*"In Paradise, there are seven golden gates and sev-
enty thrones of gold and diamonds for the chosen of God.
The Third House of Paradise is wholly of gold and silver."
(Joshua ben Levi, who succeeded in entering Paradise by
means of a well-known and infamous stratagem. His
testimony, certified by the rabbis of Genoa, was decisive
in obtaining the guarantees extended by the Banca San
Giorgio, and the loan from the financier Santángel.)*

*"Beyond the tropic of Capricorn there is a habitable
land that is the highest and noblest place in the world; it
is the Earthly Paradise." (Pierre d'Ailly,* Imago Mundi)

But it is not gold or diamonds or pearls the admiral is
seeking. (It is not his goal to steal the golden gates of
Paradise, as if Paradise were some abandoned *casolare* on the
outskirts of Genoa.)

His proposal is lofty, grand, truly beyond expression.
He will return having conquered death! He will cast eternity
before Queen Isabel's feet. He will discharge upon those
golden shores all that is moribund in a gasping Occident,
like tons of filthy coal to be shoveled by the brazen whores,
murderers, and avaricious peasants on his ships.

(How shall he write it to the managers of the Banca San
Giorgio? "No man since the time of King David shall have
received grace that equals mine.")

He felt that the proximity of his objective allowed him to share the Secret with a select few. He summoned the ship's rabbi, Luis de Torres (until that moment enlisted as a translator); the cobbler given to visions, Alonso Pérez de Cádiz; and the royal paymaster. The admiral told them:

"Gentlemen, although you are of different state, I call you here as equals, in view of the most unusual nature of what I have to tell you. We shall soon reach land. What land? Naturally, somewhere in the Indies or the Orient—probably Cipango or Ophir. But—and this is what is important—we shall likely discover something much greater. Something truly portentous. Do not be surprised to learn that we have found the regions visited by Abbé Brendan, and thought to be inaccessible.

"These are lands that will be valued far beyond their mere geographic importance, their wealth and products. I trust in you and in your loyalty, and I am warning you to be prepared: it is not often that man is asked to bear the vision of Greatness."

The disguised rabbi, who was the only one of the three who seemed to have understood, fell to his knees, and murmured devoutly:

"*Eretz Israel*! The word of Jacob is confirmed: this world is the antechamber to the world to come. We must prepare ourselves in the antechamber, that we may be received in the great hall!" (The Talmud) And he blubbered and loudly blew his nose.

OCTOBER 12, 1492. GUANAHANI. The admiral spent the night in his captain's quarters. Finally, before midnight, he saw the sign of the flaming sword (although it was barely perceptible,

very distant, surely made by an indifferent angel after millen-
nia of routine guard duty). "It was like a small candle
someone was raising and lowering," he wrote in his diary.

A gentle wind, astern. He indicates the point on the
horizon to the men at the helm, but they say they see
nothing. The royal steward, Gutiérrez, however, confirms it;
he, too, thinks he sees something.

The admiral, before the imminent, closes himself in his
cabin and meditates.

He is afraid. Afraid of disillusion. Afraid of reality.
Reality, once again? And what if it really was only Cipango
or Cathay or Ophir with all their gold?

But now Rodrigo de Triana is shouting from the crow's
nest of the *Pinta*. It is two in the morning. Dawn in the
tropics; that rosy-fingered dawn painting the sky in halluci-
natory tones.

"Land ahead! Forward of the bow, admiral!" He waves
his shirt. His Andalusian voice rolls across the calm sea and
bursts against the gunwales of the *Santa María*.

Men swarm up the rigging. Pour from the holds. Shout,
laugh, pray. Sing the *Salve Regina*. Shave, as if grooming
themselves for a Sunday bullfight.

The admiral shuns the gross celebration. He closets
himself in his cabin. He has seen that nowhere on this coast,
which is now clearly visible, is there a prominent mountain.
Nor the violent sea surge that will suck the vessels into the
center of Paradise.

The coast they have sighted must be only the luminous
outer regions. The lands known to Abbé Brendan.

He sensed there were still long trials to bear at sea and
at court. That still it had not been given him to pass from

the periphery to the omphalos of Eden. That still he would see men chained to the same life, repetitiveness, the eternal misery, the crushed dreams, boredom, death.

He knew that he must continue to follow the paths of the sea, trusting in finding the right course, awaiting the true Aperture.

But he can say none of this; he must remain silent. He writes this famous passage in his diary (as transcribed by Padre Las Casas):

> *They shortened all sail but the mainsail, which is the large sail without bonnets, and lay to. It was a small island in the Lucayos which is called Guanahani. Immediately they saw naked people, and the admiral went ashore in an armed boat with Martín Alonso Pinzón, Vicente Yáñez Pinzón, Rodrigo Sánchez de Segovia, and the secretary Rodríguez de Escobedo, to give witness and testimony that he was taking possession of the island in the name of his king and queen, his sovereigns. "And in order they might feel great amity toward us, I gave to some among them red bonnets and glass beads which they put about their necks, and other things of little value that gave them much pleasure."*

AUGUST 4, 1498. THE OMPHALOS. In the real life of the admiral, the day that follows October 12, 1492, is—curiously—August 4, 1498.

There were days and days of burning heat. The deserts of the sea. Blazing waters. Nights of heavy dew.

The panting of tropical lands. America's air, the breath of a feverish dog.

The coast of the Paria peninsula in the distance. Monotonous golden band. Foaming ribbon of the joyful sea.

The admiral's head glows in the night; encrustations of salt and marine corpuscles that phosphoresce as they decay. His is a great head, like the rock crystal skulls buried with the chieftains of the exotic lands they are sailing past.

The morning sun blinds him. His eyesight is already perilously weakened, exhausted by his tenacious quest for signs of the Aperture, the epiphany. His half-closed eyelids are like tanned leather, protecting him from the glare.

There is little wind those days. The prow of the *Capitana* breasts clear, calm seas. In the distance, the white thread of the beaches. Green palm trees. Foam.

The admiral has not slept for thirty-three days. He scarcely eats. During the day he wanders about the ship, muttering, erased in the crushing, blinding light. From time to time he raves or yells deliriously. He confuses real people with imaginary beings.

His men, through these long years, have lost respect for him. They mock him. They make vulgar noises behind his back. They desire his death, but fear he will die (as is often the case with autocrats). The prostitutes taunt him from the deck of *La Vaqueños*.

He is not even well attended. He lives like a prisoner on the quarterdeck and the forecastle. During the long hours of infernal heat, only Landsknecht Ulrich Nietz remembers him, climbs the ladder to bring him a jug of fresh water. The Landsknecht is moved by the admiral's greatness to compose a brief poem:

Vast is the sea. My Genoese prow
sinks into its dense azure.
Nothing but your enormous eyes—
infinitude—watching over me.

Finally, the long-awaited day. The day toward which all his sacrifices had led: August 4, 1498.

The admiral writes in his letter to Queen Isabel:

No one may reach the Earthly Paradise, except by divine will.

Alonso Pérez sighted mountains, the peaks of three mountains; thus I christened the place Trinidad.

We are no longer sailing on a merely horizontal plane, as the pilots and crew may believe. We are ascending the path of the sea. At dusk the North Star is at five degrees. We are in the zone of grace. The climate is mild and gentle, and the trees are so green they surpass the orchards of Valencia in May. The people here are of good stature and whiter than those we have seen before. Their hair is long and straight.

We are ascending because the earth is not round. We are at the edge of the world, below the equinoctial line and at the point of the planet nearest Heaven. . . .

For three days they lay almost motionless, waiting. The admiral drowsed at the base of the foremast.

In a scratchy voice he told Luis de Torres: "Space will open to us. The ships will be impelled by a violent current of water, or wind, or both. It is the Aperture! Union. The place of transcendence!"

And it was so. At dusk on the 4th, they saw moving

toward them a great current of water like an opposing flood. Like the continuation of a great river.

The admiral wrote in his relation: "We were caught up in a great surge. A gigantic wave approached from the south with a frightening roar and threw the ship into the trough of the sea, causing a terrible outcry of fear and several wounded among the skeptics."[4]

The admiral would add, once back in Seville: "Even today as I write this, I feel the same sensation of terror. A crest of water rose up high as a mountain."

He kneels in his cabin. Gratitude of the Chosen One of God. He weeps copiously, and the large, sweet tears trace furrows in the saline mask of his face. Washed eyes wounded by light and sleeplessness.

He must slow his racing pulse as he writes the queen: "The Lord God made the Earthly Paradise, and in it He placed the Tree of Life. Thence is born a fountain from which issue the four principal rivers of Paradise. At this very moment we are being borne on the waters of the original fountain!"

---

[4]Author's note: The admiral's relation coincides remarkably with that of a different seeker, the protagonist of another memorable, although metaphysical, navigation, René Daumal. He writes in *Le Mont Analogue* (Chapter IV, "Entering the Dimension of Mount Analogue"): "We were thrown into the bow of the ship. There rose up a sudden wind, or, more specifically, a powerful inhalation that suddenly pulled us forward. Space sank before us into a bottomless crater, into a horizontal abyss of air and water twisted together in great circles. The ship's timbers creaked and groaned as it was hurled toward the center of the abyss."

He makes a rapid sketch in the margin of his famous letter, and adds: "As I have stated before, the world is not round but pear-shaped; it would be round except for the nipple at the top. Or it is as if someone had a very round ball, and upon it placed a woman's breast, and the nipple of the breast were topmost, nearest to Heaven, and below it were the equinoctial line. All this I describe is at the Orient edge. I call 'Orient edge' the place were all the land and islands of the world end. . . ."

He hears the seas growing calmer. They are entering!

Now the deckhands are less frightened, the prostitutes, the priests, the murderers set free in Cádiz and sent to civilize America, the philosopher undesirables, the hopeful husbandmen, now all are brave enough to walk to the gunwales and breathe in the sweetness of the air.

They are at the omphalos.

The admiral, imposing and entirely serene, stands on the quarterdeck and, with great majesty, as if performing a ritual that all will understand, removes all his clothing until he is entirely naked.

And this time he removes even his hose!

IV

e a r t h

CHRONOLOGY

1 4 9 8

Soft, gentle air. Beautiful, simple peoples. Landsknecht Swedenborg and the language of angels. Nudity in Paradise. Anacaona, Siboney, Bimbú. "They have come, the bearded gods from across the seas."

1 4 9 9

Ordinances of Nudity and Being. End of Guilt. The last mass. Ulrich Nietz and the birth of superhumanity. Colón reunited. Padre Las Casas and the evidence of the Absent God.

1 4 9 9

Roldán: the first revolution in America. La Diabla's brothel. Fever for doing. Angels in chains. End of a tragic theological error. Sacking of Paradise.

1   1   *Ahau*

Message to Tenochtitlán: "The great stone-pilers have arrived." Their savage mastiffs. End of a solar cycle.

1   5   0   0

Death returns to Castile. End of the Sect. Fernando signs the order to arrest the admiral. Rebellion of the dogs. Colón in irons. The Gates of the East dismantled and shipped to the Catholic University of Brussels.

———————————————————————

MAGNIFICENT April morning. For more than a week the court has been encamped on a picturesque plain not far from Almagro, on their semifestive, semi-administrative journey to Barcelona.

At dawn, horses, peasants, and dogs, captained by Fernando, had set forth on the hunt. They slew Manchegan wild boars in the swamps near Alarcón. Downed partridge and wild turkeys with their crossbows. For Isabel and her ladies it was a culinary fiesta: beef stewed with prunes, partridge in cider, bread pudding, eggs *à la flamande*, custards, suckling pig. For a few days they were liberated from the overbearing refinements of dictatorial French and Piedmontese chefs. Sometimes they themselves prepared food under the tutelage of the old women of the place. Laughter rippled across the freshwater plain to the tables where stern-faced officials were embroiled in affairs of state.

Now that state was an empire. No longer an agrarian-colonial kingdom. There was a Department of Cartography, and complaining German and Portuguese craftsmen were laboring in the open air, cursing the breeze that scattered their parchments and the frequent bird droppings that smeared the ink of their depiction of the New Lands.

Almost without realizing it, those men seated around King Fernando at brocade-covered tables were directing the course of the first world power. Resolving global questions as they recounted hunting anecdotes and read reports from their ambassadors.

Isabel, followed by the Marquesa de Moya, had just run from her tent to recapture her bitch Diana, who could not resist the attraction of Fernando's hunting dogs, penned and howling in sexual frustration.

Messengers had arrived at dawn with news of major importance. It had altered Fernando's good humor, so enraging him that not even Cardinal Cisneros or Andrés de Cabrera, the most faithful of his SS, could distract him.

He was exasperated by the possibility hinted at in a highly charged letter from the admiral: that an empire such as the one he ruled could see its best lands, along with their potential wealth, turned into holy and intangible possessions, as church enclaves and consecrated cemeteries already were. He railed:

"That damned Genoese! You send him in search of gold and new lands and he comes to us with a box full of angels' feathers tied up in a pretty bow!

"Is it possible he *has* found the Earthly Paradise? How could he have happened upon that precise spot? Nincompoop! A half-assed mystic and celestial demogogue!"

He asked that certain passages of the letters be read again.

"That about the woman's breast . . ."

Isabel overheard him. She was struggling with a recalcitrant Diana, tugging on her neck chain:

"Majesty, the truth is that our admiral *never* believed the earth was round. We were both present in Santa Fe when he told us his newest geographical secrets: that in the human realm the earth is flat, although it is spherical, if not perfectly round, in the cosmic order—like most planets. So he is not contradicting himself now when he tells us that the earth is pear-shaped, or like a ball with a superimposed woman's nipple—your excellencies will forgive the expression. But if what he tells us is true, it will change the order of the entire world. Rome would no longer be the seat of the Vatican, and only the mystical would have meaning. And no one would have the right to favor the banal things of this earth." She lowered her eyes submissively.

Fernando, growing more and more impatient, surreptitiously gave the affectionate Diana a hard kick in the ribs as she ambled over to sniff his crotch.

At his side, Aldonza Alamán, dressed in a *condottiere*'s bright uniform and wearing a black mask that revealed sparkling, mischievous eyes, was enjoying the underlying tension in the discussion between the royal pair.

"Is it possible, I say, that he really has found the Earthly Paradise? Padre Talavera, please!"

Padre Talavera stepped forward; until that moment he had remained in the background, leaning against a poplar tree and mingling with the less important courtiers (that was his clever way of being always on the front line in matters of state).

Fernando continued:

"That would mean that from 1492 until today, for six years and in spite of the hundreds of persons who have voyaged to America, the admiral's only goal has been to discover the Tree of Life! His only interest has been what lies within Paradise, not its external forms. That would explain why he deserted the islands, abandoned Hispaniola, leaving

them in the unfortunate state they are today. To continue
searching! He has burdened us with incredible expenditures.
If things are as he says, we should send the bill to the
Vatican! Padre Talavera! Has he really found the Earthly
Paradise? Is it possible?"

Padre Talavera hesitates. He does not know how to
answer. It is as if he had been told by an aged nun that the
Virgin Mary had handed her a message. Nothing more both-
ersome for priestly routine than evidence of the divine. (All
religions and creeds are born of the disbelief and nostalgia
that seek answers by challenging established literary canons.)

Father Marchena, standing beside him, spoke up:

"It is true that there are things that suggest Paradise
. . . several details coincide with the word of the Church
Fathers. The exotic fruits and flowers . . . the gentle breezes,
great rivers, naked white mortals!"

And Talavera:

"Yes, Father . . . that is true. But what theological
interpretation would be acceptable to the Church? What is
the status *today* of a place that was once the site of the Earthly
Paradise? Could mere man enter there, use that land and
exploit its riches? Is it consecrated land, God's land? I would
like an answer to the reasonable concerns I have heard from
his majesty the king. Whether these are viable lands or lands
exempt from human use. Is this place *res derelictae*? Or is it
still, even though intermittently, the domicile of God?"

This series of questions aggravates Fernando's impatience:

"In fact, the Vatican has no reason to review the matter.
Pope Alexander was clear enough in Tordesillas: everything
beyond a line three hundred and fifty leagues west of Cape
Verde belongs to Spain."

(Fernando was referring to the highly secret accord of Loches [Torrejón], which the pontiff had honored unconditionally upon accepting the cathedra of Saint Peter.) He glanced at the papal ambassador, who was prudently reserved in his assent. A sign that Fernando's argument was overly secular and graceless, and would neither convince anyone nor resolve the questions posed by the admiral's letter.

And to make matters worse, Isabel picked up the missives and began to read aloud:

". . . The trees grow in the most marvelous groves, the island is very green, the plants grow as lush as in Andalusia in April. The singing of the birds is so sweet that no man would ever choose to leave. Parrots flock so thickly they obscure the sun, and there are large and small birds so different from our own that one marvels. . . . As for the people, they are meek and fearful; they go about naked, as I have recounted, without weapons or laws. Their speech is the most beautiful in the world; they always smile as they speak. They love their fellow man as they love themselves. . . ."

Fernando could see that the queen was moved. It was obvious that she was slipping into one of her dangerous phases. The court was listening to her, enthralled. He had to interrupt:

"But before that, he speaks of gold. There is scarcely a page where he does not speak of gold! Now he knows that there is almost no gold in the islands, so he has abandoned Our projects and continued his search without proper authorization."

Padre Marchena ventured a thought:

"Is it not acceptable that someone sent for tiger skins should send back angels' feathers? It may indicate his honesty. Not wishing to contradict your majesty, we must not forget that gold, as so many Church Fathers bear witness, is a sign of the Earthly Paradise. We need look no farther than the Gates, which are wrought of gold—so the Bible tells us."

Many sincere Catholics among the courtiers feared that the Genoese admiral would leave not so much as the hinges. And no loyalty to the king could justify the sacking of Paradise.

"Gold and pearls and precious stones may be evidence of the realm of Paradise. Like a profusion of sulfur and serpents. No serious theologian would refute that . . ."

Fernando, irate, withered Padre Marchena with a glance. But Isabel nodded in agreement. She was clearly won over to the cause of Paradise.

Privately, Fernando lamented not having instructed Aguado to stop the Genoese and his relatives before they ever set sail from Hispaniola. That had been an error. With the keen political instinct Machiavelli would later praise, he knew intuitively that an enterprise had been set in motion that could have dangerous consequences: an empire based half on power and half on celestial air!

Furthermore, as the admiral's letters continued to arrive, the priests were gaining power. They might intrude in his affairs. Claim that decisions in America should be based on theology.

Isabel then asked:

"But is it not true that all our lives we have sought liberation from our earthly chains? Is it not possible that the good God is offering us the supreme privilege of a return to Paradise?"

Echoes of the admiral's secret ramblings were all too evident in her words.

"But once we are given proof, we grow fearful. We search on in the crass everyday world. We must not deny God's presence! Or His majesty! More lands, fewer lands, what matter! Empires fall and are forgotten. Courage! That I ask of you! Courage to rise to the height of the epiphany. Amen!"

She closed her eyes and in the stricken silence that followed her sermonizing recovered Diana, who was creating a disturbance beneath the table, and then retired with the Marquesa de Moya and her ladies. It was time to make caramel custards.

A grave crisis of state could be in the offing. Fernando summoned Santángel. This time the Genoese had struck a severe blow: he had disoriented the Jews who sought new lands to end the diaspora; he had betrayed the interests of his financiers; and he had shattered the unity (earthly, at least) of the empire.

Santángel listened to the king's concerns. They were justified. Fernando inquired:

"What do they say at the Banca San Giorgio? Don't they see the danger? Do they like being swindled?"

And Santángel, humble, convinced of the gravity of the problem:

"I shall write them this very day. I shall advise them today."

•

Soft air, bright sun, cool salty sea. Gentle waves wash ashore and hiss into foam upon a beach of golden-white sand. A coconut falls from a palm tree, breaks open, inviting, its delicious milk—a known fact—always as cool as the dew. High in the branches a playful monkey turns two pirouettes, waves, and disappears into the treetops.

The imposing figure of the admiral appears upon the scene. He is completely naked, his hair as shaggy as the mane of a decrepit circus lion. His pasty white belly droops slackly in three successive folds above white pubic hair (a sign of maturity, of years not lived in vain). Long thin legs support a massive torso: one thinks of a mosquito that has swallowed a chickpea.

"This is God's land," he states devoutly.

He is surrounded by officialdom and clergy in ceremonial garb. Banners of Castile. Trumpets and tambors. A seven-cannon salute booms out as the secretary reads the standard Proclamation of Possession. (The secretary disapproves. For the signing in 1492, the admiral had dressed in a cape of gold, plumed hat, and golden spurs.)

Flocks of parrots. Blue, yellow, and red parakeets. Some chatter in chorus, others protest in an indecipherable but sweet tongue.

Never-before-seen birds-of-paradise. How to describe them? To compare them to birds in Spain would be to reduce them to the sepia of scientific tomes.

The crew surface-dives in the shallow sea to observe fish with tails that fan open like Thai screens. Submarine birds. Clearly, colors in these lands do not discolor or fade as they do in cold seas. These are visibly friendly fish; they swim near enough to kiss the ankles of the ecstatic swimmers, who chuckle at the tickling sensation.

The breeze blowing off the sea creates an eternal harvest time; here a ripe papaya falls, there a pineapple, a mango, an avocado.

As Landsknecht Swedenborg confirms to the admiral, the only place one finds naked angels is in the deepest heart of the heavens.

And the ones they saw walking toward them beneath the midday sun, through the blinding glare glancing off golden sands, were completely naked, except for a few of the women in brief and far from opaque skirts.

The admiral was jubilant. Their nakedness was irrefutable proof. He rejoiced in his assurance, now beyond any turning back. He felt something akin to the poetic drunkenness of Dionysius.

Swedenborg tells him:

"Those who dwell in the farthest reaches of heaven are naked because they have always lived in innocence, and nakedness corresponds to that state. We also know that the language of angels is a melodious and gentle uninterrupted flow of words in which the vowels *u* and *o* predominate. You hear, your excellency? The number of vowels that accumulates in the phonemes depends upon the affective mood . . ."[1]

But the admiral pays little attention. He is dictating a passage in his diary to the secretary:

[1]Author's note: These and other references from Swedenborg can be found in his famous *Heaven and Its Wonders, and Hell.*

"As soon as day broke many men and women came to the beach, all of good stature, a very beautiful people; their hair is not kinky, but coarse and flowing like a horse's tail, and all have large heads and broad brows, and very beautiful eyes that are not at all small. None is dark-skinned; they are nearer to the color of the people of the Canaries. They brought balls of spun cotton, and parrots, and javelins, and gave it all for the least trinket. And I made every effort to learn if there was gold. Some of the elders came forward and gave great cries to summon the men and women who were timid, saying, 'Come see the men who have come from the heavens! Bring them food and drink!' "[2]

The admiral had no doubts: these were the lands that Father Frisson had spoken of on a long-ago rainy afternoon in Genoa. He said to the secretary:

"It is remarkable, but fear is unknown here. Not even in birds; look, they light on people's shoulders. Look there in the sea; you can catch a fish with your bare hands!" And he dictated: "There were dogs that never barked (strange mute dogs unable to believe that anything might be stolen). There were marvelously fashioned nets and hooks and instruments of fishing. Trees and fruit of unparalleled savor. Large birds and small birds, and the singing of crickets throughout the night, which gave pleasure to all. Neither

---

[2]This theological misunderstanding will have tragic consequences. In 1492 there were some 250,000 Indians in Hispaniola. In 1538 only 500 remained. The native population of America declined from 100 percent in 1492 to 5.9 percent in 1942. See Angel Rosenblat, *La población indígena y el mestizaje en América* (Buenos Aires: Editorial Nova, 1954).

cold nor heat; sweet, gentle breezes. Great forests, which were very cool."

The admiral notices that his men, increasingly remote from the sordid disputes of the workaday world, are beginning to smile. Murderers and robbers with terrible scars and evil, twisted faces, badly treated prostitutes, traffickers and priests, all smiling like bewitched children. In that atmosphere of calm and relaxation, many were converting to nudity, wearing only their underbreeches as they bathed in the sea.

Landsknecht Swedenborg points out to him that the air of Paradise is making saints of even the vilest among them.

"Little by little, all greed, ambition, and lust will depart from them."

•

The *tecuhtli* of Tlatelolco was standing some distance away in a palm grove; he, the *cacique* Guaironex, and other Taino chieftains were observing the gods from the sea. After a while, he decided to go nearer, blending quietly into a group of Indians with trained parrots. There he studied the newcomers at close range. They bore all the signs of the prophecies; Quetzalcoatl had predicted their coming. The *tecuhtli* prepared a message to be sent immediately to Tenochtitlán:

"The ones we have long awaited have reached the islands of the Tainos. With infinite kindness they have made gifts of brightly colored bonnets, tiny bells of ineffable musicality, and small brilliant stones mined from what is surely a highly prized mineral in their world. They are bearded, of an incomparable whiteness; they have a strong odor, and they know the use of fire and the wheel.

"They have the appearance of humans, but they are more than human. (They resemble only slightly the pale humans who inhabit the dismal, fog-shrouded lands far to the east.)

"So great is their goodness that they seem almost simple; they stand staring at the colors of the most ordinary birds, and they dive until they are breathless, only to observe the fish. They are amazed and dumbfounded by everything they see. And their greatest ecstasy and sweet surrender is reserved for the women; they crowd around Princess Anacaona, and one of them pinched—with no ill intent—the *cacica* Siboney.

"Certain of them are gods of high rank; others are lesser, roguish gods who must render them obedience and service.

"They are not—you may be assured of it—the *tzitzimin* demons that dwell in the shadows of the eastern sky."

Once the message was dispatched, the *tecuhtli* returned to the palm grove where Guaironex was marshaling the virgins for the dance of welcome.

The Iberians were splashing around in the irresistibly pure, cool water. Some were drying off in the shade of palms murmuring in the gentle breezes.

The noonday light was truly blinding. The admiral was squinting like a nearsighted man looking for a coin on a dark night.

Vapors rose from sand and sea. The slender trunks of the palm trees seemed to dance and sway. Then on the undulat-

ing air came the sound of drums and conch shells communicating the sensual, heavy rhythm of the *malleón*.

Through a blazing veil of air in which the human form
seemed to dissolve into pure brilliance, they saw moving
toward them a line of virgins preceded by princesses. Caonabo,
Siboney, Anaó, the ravishing Bimbú, gracefully dancing to
the rhythm of the drums.

A congealed silence fell over the men, not unlike the
stillness that paralyzes courtiers upon the entrance of the
pope. All conversation ceased abruptly. They were enthralled,
mute, mesmerized by the spectacle.

They prodded the blind Osberg de Ocampo unmercifully
for talking after the others had fallen into voluptuous silence.

"Shut up, for Christ's sake. Bunghole!"

"*Caram . . . ba!*" muttered the mercenary, as usual detached from the others' reality.

Anacaona was stunning. Skin the color of cinnamon and
copper. Legs parted, she circled to the steps of the *areito*. The
beat accelerated, and her hips gyrated with a rapidity that
stole nothing from her grace. A true pyrotechnical proto*mulata*.

She unfastened the strings of her *tanga* and stood completely naked. Ritually naked: a subtle symbol that she was
once again a virgin in the presence of the new gods and in a
new theogenetic cycle.

The admiral, immune to banal sensuality and with the
pontifical majesty of a true descendant of Isaiah, strode to a
nearby dune. There he knelt.

"Hallelujah! Hallelujah!" He gave thanks, with a warm
thought for Isabel, his partner in the adventure of Paradise.

In his heart, he felt he had reached the end of all
tribulation. On his knees, he felt the protective warmth of

the sands of the Paradise of Abraham, Isaac, Jacob, and—false modesty aside—Colón.

The vessels rode at anchor in the natural port.

An intense ferrying operation was underway. The Spanish were unloading the instruments necessary for transferring and reconstructing one world in another.

With great difficulty, they lowered the great cross that had been lashed down at the bow; the weight nearly swamped the small boat carrying it.

They planted it high on a dune—imagining a charming mount of Calvary—amid thickets of thin-trunked palm trees. It was the cross-gibbet.

The admiral, at some distance from the activity, thought it time to summon Fray Buil and Padre Las Casas. He watched them cross the golden sands. In their coal-black cassocks they looked like disoriented bats humbled by light.

"There will be no more death," he pronounced. "We are in the land of eternity. This is the House, that is, the Garden, from which Adam was expelled because of his error, and woman's innate evil. As it was prophesied, only by following a descendant of Isaiah may we return. We have transcended. This event will change our lives and the course of world history. You must be calm, and try to comprehend. Be prudent, like the ministers of God you are. Men of our ilk are little prepared. But gradually their murky souls will open to receive the light. There are already signs. It is important that you teach the men to use good judgment with the angels. Not to confuse their gentleness with stupidity. It has been said: angels can be terrible."

Landsknecht Swedenborg, one of the undesirables whom

both the priests and the royal paymaster held in scorn, began nodding excitedly. He was sprawled on the sand a few steps from the admiral, his heavy iron Scandinavian helmet pulled down to his eyebrows.

Buil glared at him, inquisitorially tempted. The admiral continued:

"The Apostle said: 'By one man sin entered into the world, and death by sin; and so death passed upon all men.' He spoke a great truth. But now we have the opportunity to make the return journey, from mortality to the blessing of a world without death. God loves symmetry: one man, Adam, was the cause of our downfall; now one among us will lead us back to the Garden of Eternity. I believe I am that one.

"Let us not forget the word of God: 'To him who overcometh will I give to eat of the tree of life, which is in the midst of the paradise of God.' And we have overcome the dark seas and now are enjoying the rewards.

"But do not mistake where we are: this is not the place of righteous souls, of the dead who have been redeemed. No. This is the house where man dwelt before his fall and condemnation to death. This is the Garden of Delights. Recall the poets. . . . I speak not of an eternal soul but of the wondrous eternity of the body. Guilt does not exist! Sin does not exist! Have you seen the men of the crew? Even the most despicable among them smile and dreamily close their eyes in rapture before the naked angels, the singing of the birds, the colorful cockatoos, and the playful monkeys that tease us with bananas but throw us peanuts. Praise be! Praise be to God!"

With the impudence of the just, the admiral knelt, exhibiting the notarial pallor of his backside to the priests,

who were already disconcerted by the untoward intrusion of
the divine into the routine of this vale of tears. The admiral,
as he revealed to them the reality of the Earthly Paradise, had
disoriented the specialists in delirium, who were like sparrows lost in a fog now that theology was invading the real
world. They felt a shiver of terror at the thought that
Jehovah might be nearby.

Noble, young, and sincere, Las Casas knelt behind Colón
and devoutly began to pray.

It was then that he observed the secret until that moment known only to Susana Fontanarossa, a secret Colón had
guarded beneath heavy woolen hose; between the second and
third toes on each foot was a thin connective membrane like
that of ducks and other aquatic-terrestrial creatures. The admiral was palmate, and—who could doubt it now—definitely
amphibian by nature.

•

In the eyes of Fray Buil, Landsknecht Swedenborg was a
heinous heretic, one of those independent and irresponsible
theologians who march alone toward the stake—even provide
their own tinder.

While the spiritual Las Casas was inclined to accept the
admiral's revelation, Fray Buil—a fixture in the Church,
whose only religious goal was to be a bishop—had strong
doubts. He was reluctant to accept any unwritten evidence of
the Mystery.

He felt an ecclesiastical repulsion toward nudity, even
that of a mystic. Now he could appreciate the derogatory

comments he had heard about Colón in Seville. And he understood the danger inherent in his relationship with the queen. Theirs was a convergence of Illuminati, of initiates in the sect of Paradise.

Nothing worse for the stability of the Church than those "enlightened" heretics, more papist than the pope. In relation to God, both Isabel and Colón placed themselves closer than recognized and ordained clergy. Buil was fuming with indignation.

And if that were not bad enough, that upstart Swedenborg, completely forgetting his place, was lecturing him. Where was the man's respect for class and orthodoxy?

"Yes, they are angels. And angels talk and go about naked only in the very heart of Paradise." (On the outer edges, they wear dazzling raiment.) "No, Padre, we cannot understand either their codices or their language. But if they want us to understand, they will make it possible."

"*You* may believe they are angels. But I do not believe that angels urinate without the least attempt at modesty, or that female angels reveal the slit of Beelzebub the way these women do when they squat," Fray Buil was sputtering. Swedenborg replied:

"Oh, but angels do fornicate and eat. Make no mistake, Padre, that is absolutely normal. Saint Augustine himself says so, and surely you take his writings as Church dogma: 'There in the Earthly Paradise, man shall seminate and woman shall receive semen when and however often necessary, as the organs of reproduction are regulated by will, and not excited by libido.' And recall, Padre, this comment by that same Bishop of Hippo: 'God spare us the suspicion that there is any taint of carnal appetite in the engendering of their children!' "

Swedenborg's insolence was insufferable. In Spain, the priest had seen people burned for much less. He interrupted:

"But are you entirely ignorant of what is going on here? We have found sodomites coupling shamelessly among the palm trees, forming the abominable brute with four legs and two heads. My informants have seen it. More than once. Two of them had the gall to perform their rectal acrobatics before *me*, a man of the Church! And what of those bloodthirsty animals the Caribs, who slip ashore at night to abduct and then eat the Tainos! What angels do you have in mind?"

Swedenborg, always serene, replied from the eminence of his liberated theology:

"I am surprised that a prelate as well versed as yourself should be unaware of the particulars of the teaching of Enoch, son of Cain, who was the first man permitted to return—temporarily but *in corporis*—to the Eden from which his grandfather had been expelled. (I expect God gave him that license in order to retrieve some important family memento.) Well, then. Enoch states that when the angels of Paradise came into contact with Adam's perverse daughters— always the woman!—they fell into an orgy of lust. And as is often the case with pimps, from overexposure to feminine flesh they moved on to homosexuality and bestialism. It seems incredible that this could have happened only a few steps from the Tree of Life! But Enoch's words are in the Bible. . . .

"I remind you of this, Padre, so that you will not be too hasty in your judgments. The sodomites your informants surprised are simply descendants of that very special order of fallen angels who, from having so badly abused women and having searched for them so long, find them finally beneath the skin of their brother. You surely remember, Padre, the acts we witnessed during the voyage, when we were in the spell of the menstral.

"As for the cannibals who castrate, fatten, and feast upon the Tainos, who are their ideal of beauty, they aspire to be reincarnated in those perfect and envied bodies. They prefer the testicles, it is true; they roast and eat them as a special dish, because they sense in them the origin of the seed of perfection. Why does the Catholic partake of Christ in the host? Is it not to hold Him next to his heart, deep in his being? We have seen many Catholics who are revoltingly greedy for God! Is that not true?

"And you must not forget the serpents the men hunt with such fascination. They, too, are creatures from God's garden, the same as the cannibals and sodomites."

They were prevented from continuing their dialogue, which, in any case, was growing dangerously heated. The admiral had clambered to his feet and was staring toward the shore. He issued the following edict to Fray Buil (who was resentful, but did not dare reveal his annoyance before the legal representative of imperial power):

"Padre, let the men increase and multiply. But let them do so without shameful pleasure and without fancy capers. Here there is no urgency. Lust is an offshoot of frustration. Yes, let them increase and multiply. And it would be appropriate, Padre, for you to remind them that God recommended that they eat fruit. Fruit that purifies the blood, instead of the meat dishes that fuel the appetites. Recall to them the word of God: Genesis 2:16. . . ."

Then, as sublime as, say, an ancient eremite (one who

has already achieved union), he walked in the direction of the grove, toward a cluster of thatched-roofed huts visible in the distance.

Las Casas and Buil stared at one another, priest to priest. They knew a gap was widening between them, but may not have sensed that their dissension would be so fundamental in the history of the Catholic Church. (Buil could not tolerate the fact that Colón claimed for himself the role of God's vicar, assuming functions traditionally carried out by the Church.)

Between the two priests nothing passed but that one pointed exchange of glances, interrupted when the admiral ordered everyone in his presence:

"Remove your clothing! We must all go naked! We must not stain the Garden of Jehovah with garments that recall the misery of the fall and the punishment of shame. Naked, I say! And pass down the order to the lowliest deckhand and wretches from the hold. We have seen an end to sin. Now let us see an end to clothing."

Las Casas, humbly obedient but clearly mortified, removed his cassock and emerged in all his hideous ecclesiastical pallor, clad only in billowing red muslin knickers, the gift of the provincial aunts who were unshakably convinced of his episcopal, even cardinalate, destiny.

Buil was outraged. How obscene to be asked to exhibit himself in God's purview (if, in fact, what the Genoese maintained was confirmed). And if it was not, it was unpardonable to request a man of the Church to humiliate himself to this extent.

He was wearing a fashionable cassock tailored in Seville, at Triana, by the same modistes who made the tricornered

hats of the most famous toreros. Down the front, from his
Adam's apple to the tip of his toes, ran a line of tiny covered
buttons. For the sake of diplomacy, or obedience to earthly
power, he reluctantly unbuttoned the first dozen buttons.
Curious, the admiral inquired:

"How many buttons are there?"

"One hundred fifty-five," the priest replied sullenly.
Colón, always drawn to Cabala and the magic of numbers,
murmured:

"One hundred fifty-five. Precisely the number of years
remaining to the end of the world—which will be by fire. . . ."

As he continued his way toward the trees, he met a
young Indian, or angel, who had been observing him closely;
the admiral asked in his Italianate Spanish:

"Tell me, *che*, big tree, *multo* big, *spectaculo*." And he
traced luxuriant leafage in the air.

Without hesitation, the boy turned and pointed in the
direction of a tropical jungle where a family of toucans
clattered a greeting with their yellow beaks.

"*Agrak . . . agrak*," the boy replied.

"Thank you, good friend," said the admiral and, with
absolute conviction, cried:

"Straight ahead! Do you see, Las Casas? They speak
Hebrew! I did well to bring Rabbi Torres."

The Indian boy, the athletic angel who had heard from
the lips of the *cacique* Becchio the good news about the
divinity of the newcomers, fell facedown on the sand in a
gesture of adoration.

Few people followed the admiral in his rash foray toward
the unknown: his faithful, Quintero, Escobar, a few bored
sailors, the priests Las Casas and Buil, and, led by La Italiana,

several prostitutes who had had visions of finding pearls the size of partridge eggs.

A few of the undesirables also tagged along because they preferred proximity to the admiral over the perils of unsupervised sailors: Jean-Loup Vasselin, the one-armed man the secretary had not wanted as amanuensis, Ulrich Nietz, and a group of the landsmen who had heard that deep in Paradise saffron was for the asking, the very best that fetched ten thousand maravedís the half-pound in the Antwerp exchange.

The admiral led the way, eyes cast modestly to the ground, not wanting to risk the temptation of looking ahead and seeing God. He kept repeating the words of Exodus: "Thou canst not see my face: for man shall not see me and live."

They walked deeper into the lush jungle. Orchids as beautiful as the birds and fishes, in vivid hues like a mafioso's cravat, or with muted Greek patterns. Huge butterflies that seemed to have been born of the delirium of Tintoretto's palette lurched drunkenly among lianas and tree trunks or fluttered exhaustedly, crushed by their own colors. Unintimidated or frankly hostile macaques masturbated like little Gypsies, or unleashed a barrage of green nuts. Velvety spiders so silky they could have been born in María Felix's hair. Whistling cockatoos. Flocks of pale lemon-yellow parrots. Warbling of thousands of birds. Flashes of elegant jaguars, which the admiral knew they must not challenge, but neither need fear, since they would eat man only if they could not find hyena.

"But there went up a mist from the earth, and watered the whole face of the ground." Much like the breath of a feverish dog.

And among so many species, and beyond the mire splashed with brilliant amethyst, aquamarine, and lapis lazuli, a horizon of tiny hairless, voiceless dogs which according to the lore of the natives absorbed dead souls having difficulty in passing to the great Unbounded. They were the only living creatures with whom God had been reserved or miserly when granting color. A striking anomaly in that part of a creation in which the Author, faced with romantic and baroque temptation, had lost control.

The admiral knew, and so informed Las Casas (although not in the vulgarly conmmercial sense certain authors have interpreted), that they would find nuggets of fine gold—an indisputable sign of Paradise—as well as onyx and fragrant resins.

"*Genesis* 2:12. Most important!"

He was looking for confirmation, signs, not vulgar gain.

Toward nightfall they noticed that the trees were taller and of exotic woods.

They saw a wondrous black-and-yellow anaconda; they knew by its size and splendor that it was indisputably the one that had spoken to Eve. Fortunately, it slithered off into the jungle.

Finally, on the slope of a gentle hill, they came to a clearing dominated by a jujube tree and a gigantic, stately ceiba. In the dusk light the ceiba projected a serene and terrible presence. It was the Tree.

The admiral walked around its trunk and then gave the order to make camp. He had his hammock strung in its lower branches. He counseled his followers to build lean-tos to protect themselves from the frequent tropical showers.

"Here the original waters are blended in a single continuum. We are at the brink of the Beginning," he explained.

He climbed into his hammock, sheltered in the bosom of the Tree of Life. In the reed net, the pale white Discoverer resembled an albino monkey in a trap, or a monstrous ceiba fruit in the clutches of an insolent medlar tree.

The admiral rested, not from the travails of the day but from the fatigue of centuries of death and dying. He slept soundly. He had returned. Far beyond the bosom of Susana Fontanarossa. Paradise was the end of entropy, of degradation, of a time of humiliating being-toward-death.

Two gentile angels, two natives eager to please the god from the sea, fanned away mosquitoes with palm leaves.

•

The Ordinance of Nudity, dictated by the admiral beneath the Tree of Life, arrived at the shore.

Work was already begun on the construction of the customs house (also warehouse), the church, the barracks, and the prison when the crier read the document based on abridged evidence of the return to the land of the Beginning, which was innocent of evil and, consequently, free of shame and prudishness.

What followed was a witches' sabbath among the ex-felons and prostitutes. A merry dance. The hellhounds of repressed desire swept along the coast.

Interpreting the new decree as license for vulgarity, the amazing Sword Swallower organized the other whores into a strolling sideshow. They did not take "naked' to mean totally nude, which could be pure, but cathouse tease: see-through pantaloons, garter belts, and corsets like the ones favored by cardinals in Rome.

Extremadurans and Andalusians threw themselves on the women like soldiers set loose in a nunnery. Clothes were strewn the length of the beach, scattered like trampled skunks.

Many could not bring themselves to obey the law: without clothing they felt they were no better than peeled bananas.

"The more freedom, the less pleasure," Squarcialuppi muttered enviously after vigilant observation of the vicissitudes of sin. "Look who has the last laugh!"

Sensible, conservative citizens were horrified. The royal paymaster was in a dither. Rodríquez de Escobedo, the secretary, discussing things with the few noble lords among them, like Núñez de Mendoza, said that not only had he not divested himself of his clothing but he intended to endure the tropical heat without unbolting a single plate of Toledo steel armor.

"We are not fucking savages!"

All this frenzy amazed the natives. They could not understand the sudden eccentricities of the gods. They yielded courteously to their needs. They were puzzled by the bearded ones' curiosity about ordinary parts of the body. And their panting effusiveness as they undertook the most natural relations.

They found it comic that in the enthusiasm of their pairings the gods imitated the exotic animals they had brought with them: they grunted like the hogs, they brayed pathetically at the moment of climax, and they trembled like jennies with the ague.

The Ordinance had an unavoidable corollary: the celebration of the last mass, with a *Te Deum* of thanksgiving as
they abandoned their human condition—that is, mortality.
The sacrifice of the mass, however, was lacking the essential
justification (masses are not celebrated in Paradise).

Ill-humoredly, and as if it were in fact Sunday, Fray
Buil prepared to say the final mass, over the protests of the
young priests and novices:

"Saved, these sinners? The Genoese is beyond pardon. A
heretic! Everyone's going around fornicating like rabbits!"

The mass was celebrated at eleven. There was a joyful
atmosphere of happy farewell to Guilt.

The *Salve Regina* and the *Te Deum* had a vaguely rumbalike
rhythm. The choir of seminary students had been listening to
the bone percussions and the *areitos* of the angels. A real
Sonora sound. The *Te Deum* ended with the entrance of
delectable princesses and virgins dancing in a hip-swaying
line behind the spectacular Anacaona, whose costume con-
sisted of a brief *tanga* of tiny quetzal breast feathers (a *luxe*
that among the Tainos was equal to European sable).

At the sight of a dozen marvelous angel asses swinging
in rhythm, the lecherous young monks and seminarians lost
the thread of their chant.

The non-Spanish theology students, Tisserand, Danielou,
and Caggian, wept disconsolately inside the large black stall
they had improvised as a confessional.

"Finis Ecclesiae," murmured Caggian.

But in spite of their protests, the Ordinance did not
create a forum for theological discussion: the sermon ended
with a decisive affirmation: "We are reunited into one."

Also suspended, for the same theological reasons, was

the afternoon bullfight. What were bulls but a spectacular consequence of the fall, of original sin?

The bull remained beneath its shelter of leaves and branches, and all Joan Velmont's protests to the inspector were in vain. He was to breed it, or slaughter it.

•

The Ordinance of Being arrived a week later. It created a furor because it profoundly altered the plan of the Iberians. It, too, was issued from beneath the Tree of Life, brought by an emissary, and announced by a crier.

It was more difficult to comprehend than the first.

The admiral proclaimed that they were now in the Open, where all human *doing* was irrelevant. The paroxysms of activity the Caucasoid Europeans had set as a standard of conduct was, according to the Ordinance, a mark of damnation, of life after Paradise. (Adam had done nothing before being expelled for—provoked—erotomania.)

Labor, therefore, was declared pointless; it had evidenced itself among the whites only as an attempt at divine emulation and an objectionable demonstration of skills, Babelian pride, and diabolical rebellion.

Pure and simple, the admiral was condemning work.

The decree forced the paymaster to burn wheels, hammers, sickles, shovels, rope, pulleys, lathes, knives, weights and official measures, scales, administrative records, weapons, musical and inquisitorial instruments, and all similar articles.

Resistance to this Ordinance was strong, the protests nearly subversive. This was worse than nakedness; this was living naked hours, face to face with the reality of existence but without the refuge of habitual distractions.

Only the naive, and confessed ne'er-do-wells, willingly handed over their tools. The husbandmen, inveterate kulaks, buried their sickles and whetstones like dogs burying a disputed bone.

What few tools remained were collected by speculators, who soon would resell them as "imports" at American market prices.

It became clear that the admiral wanted them to devote themselves to harmony. To calm, leisure, conversation. Meditation, the arts that elevate and delight (no Pascalities, no Kafkaizing). And love, but love devoid of cupidity. The de-dramatization of life. Relaxation.

He was asking them to accept the gifts of Paradise as natural. Why hoard pineapples and mangos, as those wishing to be greengrocers had done? Why make them into preserves? Why more than one woman? Why a half-dozen langoustes, if two and a good lime were enough?

Simply *be*! Be serene, and appreciate the easy fruits of Eden. Be and let be. The admiral's hammock would become the symbol of this stage of joyful return to the maternal bosom. Admire the sweet song of the birds, identify the thousand nuances of those feathered artists. Appreciate the profusion of delicate orchids. Why frighten away the panther with glowing coals when he comes only to kill his daily deer?

He recommended tobacco to them, an innovative vice. Consumption of coconut milk and a preferably but not stringently vegetarian diet. Although he did warn: "Avoid red meat, for it nurtures evil."

*   *   *

After two weeks everyone began to feel that without evil nothing had meaning. The world seemed faded, the hours empty. In fact, this highly touted Paradise turned out to be an insipid antiworld, too bare and too diurnal—because now night was not night. Living naked and free of Evil was like arriving in black tie and tails to find that the party was already over.

They had been born and raised to strive for good. To fall, and rise again.

The state of salvation decreed by the admiral upset them both physically and metaphysically.

"*Being* is boredom, an opiate!"

Bad-humored priests wandered up and down the beach, sleeves rolled up and cassocks unbuttoned, picking up exquisite seashells. Utterly bored without confession. Although they were followed by naked peasants clamoring for mass and catechism. Some prostitute or other, availing herself of their demotion, would brazenly ask if they wanted to "take a little walk."

Neither nudity nor *being* rid the seamen of the restiveness they brought with them from reality, from the world of the fall. From ten in the morning on, they prowled around camp. They formed parties to go from the coconut grove to the reef and back. Without enjoying it. In their nakedness, they looked as if they were waiting for a group medical checkup.

They yawned. They asked a hundred times, "When do we eat?" And without their *salsa*, or garlic, or wine and red meat, deprived of their bean and bacon soup and their stews, everything they ate tasted like hospital pap.

The song of the "thousands of birds" the admiral had

praised said nothing to them. Not even the antics of the monkeys seemed amusing anymore.

Loafing, yawning, they dreamed up the idea of making rubbers from the latex of the rubber tree, and they began to slaughter hundreds of goldfinches, redbreasts, gulls and cuckoos. Just for target practice.

But the disease of *doing,* so essential a component in the misery and pleasure of Occidental peoples, continued to infect them surreptitiously and by night. During the day, the agrarian workers slept like lumps in their hammocks, but by night they went to their plots to clear brush and hoe until daybreak. Once the land was tilled, they summoned the surveyor and the secretary and asked them to draw up and record the proper deeds of ownership, for which they paid double the official fee.

Overtly subversive priests—Buil, Valverde, Colángelo, and Pane—candidly and enthusiastically made consecrated wafers (necessarily of maize).

All the Colóns (brothers, children, nephews, and cousins) were in open rebellion, cursing the evidence of Paradise. They had come all the way from Genoa, attracted by the fever for fame and riches the admiral had described in a famous missive to the king and queen: "Now all, down to the very tailors, seek permission to make discoveries."

Jacome Rico and other Genoese representatives of the multinational agencies could see the days passing by without appreciable profit. Paradise was toppling every reasonable criterion of marketing. Those objective experts proved that an undesirable and alarming "zero growth rate" had been reached. For the moment, they decided to delay communicating that information to the central office.

A broad sector of dissident entrepreneurs, from the cheese-maker Bavarello to the gold prospectors, began to fawn over the mercenaries, captains, and sergeants. Plots were hatched. Even the executioner, Old Hood, was enlisted for being a hex.

Francisco Roldán, one of Bartolomé Colón's guard, a swarthy mustachioed type with lank hair, began to figure prominently in local affairs.

Boldly, he assigned himself the title of "colonel" (an Italian denomination seldom used in the Spain of that day). Defiantly, he began wearing a frogged jacket and a spiked Prussian helmet.

He was in league with La Diabla, and conspired with cronies in the brothel-cabaña the latter had talked the angels into building on a rock beach called Cabo de Piedra.

Roldán received visitors in his hammock, smoking large rolled cigars and drinking a mango liquor, suffering the sweltering heat in order to show off enormous epaulettes fashioned from gold fringe taken from the portable high altar, now in storage.

It was there that Roldán began to speak of "nation" and "dignity."

In a brief time he had become the strongman. His ascent to power seemed inexorable.

•

In spite of protestations, the Ordinances were being observed. No one, as yet, dared dispute legal authority.

The celestial nudity dictated by the admiral was opening a breach in the bastion of ancestral modesty. The Spanish were slowly approaching a collective unbuttoning. They looked like infants born of their armor and doublets. More than naked, they seemed incomplete, like plucked chickens. Their bodies radiated the offensive pallor of years of light deprivation. Some were reminiscent of catacombs penetrated by sunbeams.

After two weeks they stopped blushing when they looked at each other. As is wont to happen, an immoral and obscene vanguard sprang up, paralleled by a conservative rearguard openly hostile to the Ordinances. Among the latter were Buil and Núñez de Mendoza and the other nobles. Colonel Francisco Roldán was now appearing at gatherings—they had to stomach it—on the arm of La Diabla, who wore black from head to toe and displayed her madam's cameo on a black silk ribbon around her neck. (She was not practicing any longer; she now spoke in terms of "the couple," and had instructed the nieces of the *cacique* Becchio in arts of broad application: the "puppy dog" technique, and the "Duc d'Aumal.")

But the truth was that the selfless and moderate love preached by the admiral and explicated by Landsknecht Swedenborg had deteriorated into an obscene bacchanal. There was a mania for how often and how many. No one rose to the level expected in Paradise. Men of good will, like Las Casas, were hoping the orgy would abate. It was as if a flood of dogs of desire had been loosed in a single place and at a single moment. (People had not removed their clothes or indulged in free love since the conversion of Constantine!)

In a few days' time the men were exhausted, drained. Nevertheless, they would stagger to their feet and again chase after angels and tumble them among the dunes.

They came to know the rage and misery of physical limitation. Some, exasperated and reckless, goaded their senses to the edge of the abyss, experimenting with every exotic possibility. But they, too, ended in enervation, in *nada*. They resorted to the brews and pomades of the native shamans, but alleviation was ephemeral. They suffered the punishment of satiety, one of the Creator's most subtle and terrible weapons, or, in the terms of the scandalized Padre Buil, "the antidote of sinful pleasure."

This state of affairs affected even the Church. Padre Squarcialuppi, previously so loyal to the hierarchy, basing his justification in the texts of Saint Augustine and Saint Thomas, hung his cassock on the branch of a willow tree. Followed by four seminarians, he joined in the bacchanal. At first there was a flurry of interest occasioned by the perverse imagination the priests had brought with them from the seminary; then those ideas, too, were diluted by repetition.

Squarcialuppi's desertion, for which Las Casas, always faithful to the admiral, was to a degree tolerant, was cause for heated exchange among the churchmen. Caggian and Pane argued that the seminarians should be excommunicated, that a minister of God must not go naked even in Paradise. In his own defense, Squarcialuppi made a distinction between the Heavenly Paradise of the blessed who are reborn in body but not cursed with shameful appetites, whether carnal or gluttonous (see Saint Thomas), and the Earthly Paradise to which they had been led by the admiral, and which was accurately described by Saint Augustine in his *City of God*. Here, Jehovah's "increase and multiply," *Genesis* 1:28, was entirely applicable. This was the verse from which Squarcialuppi had drawn inspiration for his erotic adventure. It corresponded with Swedenborg's ideas.

The hierarchy heard that argument with hostility, and accused its adherents of being judaizers and loathsome millenarians. Judgment was left *in suspectis*, and torture and inquisitorial fire held in abeyance in the expectation that the Ordinances of the Genoese would be declared null and void.

Roldán had to be restrained by Padre Buil: he wanted to proceed without further ado.

The Iberians were faced with a number of specific problems. How to derive maximum pleasure from those marvelous naked women who smiled as they offered themselves to them? How to transform into delicious violation their completely natural and placid submission?

After a few days, nostalgia for sin and evil made everything seem boring. The act became mechanical and intranscendent. Not even worth talking about. There was no place for traditional sadomasochistic play.

Caravans of adolescent girls kept arriving from the interior, eager to yield docilely to the gods from the sea.

Then, strange events began to take place, the first erotic brutality that was to proliferate to the state described by Las Casas in his own hand: "The men could not control their abuse; they ravished the island women in plain view of their fathers, brothers, and husbands, abandoning themselves to defilement and assault."

These men from beyond the sea began to dress the angels in "European petticoats and gowns," even though they themselves might be nude in accordance with the Ordinance.

La Diabla, who had a sharp nose for business, dressed two of her pupils in the robes of the Little Sisters of God's Charity and other, totally uncomprehending, native girls as European ladies or merry Basque milkmaids. In two days her earnings had soared. Appointments were required three days in advance. Although outside the cabañas of the brothel there were dozens of naked native girls, the demand for her girls was so great that she had to hang a sign above the bar: *Notice to our distinguished clientele. Two turns are strictly forbidden without additional payment. The Management.*

In addition to the clothing, a second form of violation began to occur: physical cruelty. In the women's screams, the men again found the machismo they had lost through the absence of objects to be dominated. Sighs, lashings, moans. All too soon, that path led to death: one early morning, the first cloudy day in those ever-blue tropics, they found the delightful princess Bimbú disfigured by torture and hanging from the left arm of the cross-gibbet.

•

Cradled beneath the branches of the Tree of Life, the admiral rested from the age-old fatigue of the Occident.

He drowsed, taking pleasure from the harmonies of the songbirds, learning the forgotten dialogue of the plants. He was oblivious to the mischievous tricks of the monkeys and the curiosity of the pilgrimages of angels coming to see for themselves the gods from the sea. The visitors left him cassava bread as an offering, and brought him freshly opened coconuts.

Landsknecht Swedenborg, meanwhile, interrogated them in Hebrew, and wandered about in a happy daze at being able to substantiate his theories on the origins of angel parlance.

Las Casas, deeply distressed, tried to reconcile the earthly theology he had learned in the seminary with the realities of a celestial Eden on earth.

But the one who was profiting most from the great adventure was Ulrich Nietz, who for two decades, ever since his long-ago arrival at the Vico de l'Olivella, had followed close in the footsteps of the admiral. It had not been in vain. He had in fact reached the only land where he could put to a definitive test the philosophical intuitions he had maintained at the risk of his life, arousing the fury of "reasonable people" and the angry fire of inquisitorial orthodoxy.

He knew that his ideological subversion was the most daring since the time of Christ's earthly adventure. He had proclaimed that God was dead.

That Sublime Ancient, irresponsible, playful, autocratic, cruel in His indifference, enchanting when painting butterflies or sketching a leopard, had died.

God was dead. But men lived on, diminished, like worms upon a mountainous cadaver.

In those naked Indians who stared with healthy amazement at his mustaches and chestnut, yellow-streaked eyes, in their simple relation to nature, Nietz saw Man, at last free of the deviations and humiliation imposed by the defunct Tyrant. Ulrich knew that Jehovah, the God who occupied every inch of the Judeo-Christian Occident, had in fact been a triumphant demon, an annihilating demiurge.

But the time had come for the definitive proof. Rejoicing, the Landsknecht made his preparations. At dawn he gave thanks in his guttural German, and bathed in the sacred cistern of the Tainos. He made an impressive figure as he emerged, gaze uplifted, wringing water from his dripping mustaches.

Without entering into a polemic with his admired admiral—who was still prostrate in his hammock, confident of God's imminent return, even if briefly, to His abandoned garden—Ulrich Nietz prepared an expedition of decisive importance. In a manner of speaking, a gnostiological excursion.

With the help of the *cacique* Guaironex, who provided guides, and with the collaboration of Rabbi Torres, who spoke fluent English and Hebrew, he plunged into the jungle in search of traces of Yahweh.

His party marched through swamps that metamorphosed into tall exotic trees draped in mantles of orchids. They had to negotiate with irate families of macaques. They accepted conditions of passage set by a pride of jaguars. Finally, they came upon the Sacred Hill, a large stone outcropping, an unexpected dome in the middle of ferocious jungle growth.

On one side they found a portico of white stone devoured by lianas. The Landsknecht had no doubt: this was the famous East Gate through which Adam and his companion had left in disgrace to look for work.

Torres had to give the German credit (they communicated, haltingly, in university Greek). Here was proof of the secular abandonment of a garden whose proprietor was deceased. The Indian women of the vicinity had the bearing, the typical indolence, of children that have been raised without benefit of a paternal hand. There was not the slightest trace of a strong and authoritarian presence.

Nevertheless, with the perseverence of entomologists, they spent two nights watching for signs of Supreme Dominion, of its power or survival. Without result.

They decided to provoke Jehovah through the avenue of his well-known wrath: Torres, the Jew, defecated upon a cross, and the German Nietz urinated on the Star of David. But there was no gathering of the conventional storm clouds, the skies did not grow black and rain down terrifying lightning bolts. A stupendous day dawned, greeted by hundreds of larks and cuckoos.

Nietz howled with pagan joy. This was the birth of man, finally liberated from the Tyrant's oppression. Of superman.

"Greece! Long live Greece!" he shouted.

He turned toward Rabbi Torres, who suddenly—Sephardic beard and timid prescribed nakedness—seemed insignificant and mean. He could not control the impulse to punch him in the jaw. Immediately remorseful, he helped him up and begged his pardon, as Torres searched in the mud for his eyeglasses.

Ulrich Nietz had known forever that man is a thing to be surmounted. Now it was time to return to the customs of his ancestors: to be slothful and brutal, to live with danger, to recover the space stolen by worshipers of death!

•

The *coup* was in the air. The first military takeover. The Ordinances had prepared fertile ground. Erotic satiety and high prices in La Diabla's brothel "created the historic conditions" (as Mordecai, the undesirable, would say when commenting on events).

The paralysis of *being* was replaced by conspiratorial fervor. Combined economic and erotic interests were at the root of the *doing*.

At eight o'clock on a Monday morning Colonel Roldán stepped out in his gold braid and the boots polished by La Diabla's pupils. He marched from Cabo de Piedra to the protocathedral. He was followed by Adrián Muxica (future feared minister of the interior), Diego de Escobar, Pedro Valdivieso, and the apothecary Bernal, who now stoutly defended the free-market principle and was growing wealthy from the sale of pastilles made from the local shamans' herbs and medicaments. The Porras brothers also supported Roldán. Most important of all was the position of the Church hierarchy, feudal lords, and representatives of the Banca San Giorgio.

Roldán delivered a speech that was nationalistic, predictable, and emotional. He spoke from a rough platform at the foot of the bell tower. He guaranteed the Indians' freedom (although with the "individual responsibility Christian doctrine entails"). He vowed a return to morality and propriety, implicitly condemning the Paradisiacal nudity and uninhibited eroticism that was never a problem in discreet whorehouses. He promised prompt and fair economic development. It was the first "Occidental and Christian" address in America.

That same afternoon they drew up a code creating the unstated slavery of the *encomiendas* and *repartimientos* which, by royal decree, were to award the colonists ownership of inhabitants along with land, as well as the right to take Indian women as concubines and household servants without distinction of class or rank.

By nightfall, the aggrieved Las Casas would write (Volume I, Chapter 160): "One has seen the dregs of Castile, ex-felons and convicts deported for murder, claim kings and lords as vassals for the lowest and most menial labor. Their wives, sisters, and daughters taken willingly or by force. They called these noblewomen their 'servants.'" Roldán's cynical admonition was: "Take everything you can get your hands on, because you never know how long this will last."

Juan Ponce de León, a melancholy and erotomaniacal nobleman, was favored with the daughter of the *cacique* Guaironex. Cristóbal de Sotomayor, a hawkish lord, received the sister of the *cacique* Agüeybana.

The chronicler Pietro Martire recorded that once he ended his harangue, Roldán had winked roguishly at the peasants who still had not decided whether to back the revolutionaries, and said: "Join us! Instead of a hoe, your hands will be filled with delicious tits. The Indians will do the work, while you take your rest." (*Décadas*, Volume V, Chapter 5)

Then everyone gathered at the site of the projected cathedral and there before the cross-gibbet intoned a stirring *Te Deum*, led by the reorganized choir of seminarians and novice priests.

Father Buil, standing to the right of La Diabla, who was dolled up like a veritable Evita, mounted the makeshift pulpit (which in time would be replaced by one the Mission Indians carved of *petiribi*, and "in modern times on exhibit in Santo Domingo") and sermonized:

"The fall from grace is our essence, and guilt is our sign. The sole purpose of our lives is the quest for salvation through the sacraments of the Holy Mother Church. Let no adventurers tell you that there is another Paradise. There is but one, the Heavenly Paradise that awaits us after death, after we have lived a life of obedience!" And he concluded: "And in the historic words of Colonel Roldán, 'We are free, but we must never forget the teaching of Saint Augustine: free will is the source of sin.' "

The Colóns, led by the governor Bartolomé Colón, had no heart for confrontation. They, too, were hoping for a swift resumption of *doing*.

They decided to send two emissaries to Cabo de Piedra to negotiate, without seeking authorization from or informing the admiral, who was still installed beneath the Tree of Life.

Roldán was drinking brandy in his hammock when his soldiers announced:

"Colonel, sir; two emissaries from the Colónists are outside."

"Shoot them," said Roldán, with the dour succinctness of a man establishing a tradition. Some time after the echoes of the shots had faded, Roldán, piqued by idle curiosity, summoned Sergeant Carrión and asked, "*Che*, what did those two want?"

The matter went no further. Bartolomé Colón lost two rather useless nephews. The next day he sent La Diabla, who had a notorious sweet tooth, a large platter of sugar-sprinkled *frittelle*. Padre Buil shaped the resultant status quo.

It was a true *coup d'état*. Roldán had to be content with being named mayor, although in fact he held the reins of power. He was the strongman: he had the keys to the arms and the gunpowder. This scandalous praetorian appropriation was to be the longest-continuing crime of *doing* in America.

The people were jubilant. Businesses remained open even at night. As proof of the restitution of Spanish theology in all its guises, Sunday afternoon at exactly five o'clock, a *corrida* was held with Joan Velmont's bull.

The matador was magnificent. He killed the charging bull with a single swordthrust.

The financiers' representatives and entrepreneurs set into motion the creative spirit that had been dulled by the delights of Paradise and the subsequent contentment simply to *be*.

Doing was revived, with demoniac furor. The beach was transformed into a frenetic beehive.

Roldán, who was known to have shares in the Gran Catalana Company (woolens, serges, prints), issued a regulation requiring every resident to be clothed within seventy-two hours.

Brief *naguas* were replaced by long skirts. All the native women, even the princesses, looked like nuns or maids.

A nefarious trade sprang up in "ladies' " undergarments, featuring whorish designs dictated by the frustrated fetishism of Iberians who had felt threatened by the natural nudity of the natives.

There was a true orgy of black bloomers with narrow red ribbons, elastic garters covered in shirred silk, *bustiers* with an infinity of ties and unpredictable buttonholes. There was a return to the delectable torture of anguished unbuttoning. During those days there was a heavy demand for and scarcity of first-quality European cloth. Someone even stole Padre Buil's cassock; it was found by police dogs on the beach, crumpled like a slain deer, and divested of every one of the 155 tiny buttons that had undoubtedly made their way to a clandestine workshop for fetishistic garments.

Act of nakedness and "indecent exposure" were harshly repressed, and condemned from the pulpit. La Diabla's whorehouse spawned two branches. La Italiana and the formidable Sword Swallower ascended to the rank of madam.

The princess Siboney rejected the absurdity of a gray pinafore and white muslin stockings. She appeared in the center of the Plaza de la Cathedral at twilight, totally naked, walking like a queen, her smile white as rice kernels.

She was arrested, ridiculed, and tried. In the archive of the Indies housed in Seville one can still find the record of the hearing: "Siboney and others/ nakedness in a public walkway and drug addiction." (Document number 5.885; shelf 72)

·

Even before instructions arrived from Spain, the clergy had already declared that the natives were not angels. Padre Buil, Padre Valverde, and others had held a Solomonic episcopal conference (even though the Vatican had yet to designate a bishop). The admiral was denounced. Landsknecht Swedenborg was accused of being mad, and internment was recommended.

It was proclaimed that the Indians were not angels or pre-Adamic inhabitants of a supposed Earthly Paradise where the fall and death were unknown. They were mortals. It must be determined whether they had a soul, and, in the affirmative case, in what measure. Meanwhile, the Spanish should treat them affectionately, like domestic pets.

In fairness, therefore, the religious code made the rape of Indian women a venial sin; it was recommended that confessing priests grant forgiveness after a penance of three Our Fathers and three Ave Marias (roughly the same punishment as for having confessed to masturbation motivated by the memory or the portrait of a Spanish woman).

Those ecclesiastical clarifications were indispensable in orienting the attitude of the business community at the moment of an economic boom.

Indians were selected to be sold as slaves in Seville. The first shipment was five hundred units. But the merchandise did not withstand the voyage well: they died of pneumonia or sorrow, not equipped with the indomitable solace of the African blacks, their music. An unfortunate venture.

The years of entrepreneurial frenzy began. There were more than enough hands for labor, and the Spanish began to learn how to utilize the local raw materials. For example, the rolled tobacco leaves the Indians used ritually were readily accepted in Europe. Dr. Nicot, based on the scientific report of Francesco Montani of Milan, universalized its use by demonstrating that in addition to giving pleasure, nicotine cured cancer. Value-adding manufacturing was prospering: leaves of tobacco began returning from Europe, often as contraband of Dutch pirates, in the form of snuff and pipe tobacco colorfully packaged in boxes with labels depicting hunting scenes.

But it is only fair to say that the prime motivating force for the economic development was provided by the textile industry. Man's earliest labor—from plucking a fig leaf to the sheepskin togas Jehovah contrived for the first pair of sinners before sending them out into the cruel world.

The number of Colóns in this category rapidly increased, in spite of their theoretical loyalty to the admiral. They had not forgotten their past of thread and scissor. Giovanni Colombo established the first clothing shop (in a cabaña that soon became the House of Fashion, with its own homosexual French couturier).

The first bolts of serge and tropical-weight cashmere arrived. The competition was merciless.

Caciques from the interior, with the serenity that comes only from wisdom and hereditary chieftainship, could be seen standing motionless under the blazing sun, subjecting themselves to the pawing of assistants hurriedly taking their measurements. "Shoulder, seventy-six. Armhole, twenty-seven. Length, ninety-five."

From this—compulsory—vogue for attire, the capitalistic fever spread like wildfire to other fields.

Detailed marketing studies were conducted. The result was that anyone who had been drinking *yerba mate*, like the Tupi-Guaranís, ended up drinking Ethiopian coffee from Talavera mugs (for the mayor and bishop, fine Limoges cups).

The native cocoa bean, the "delight of the gods," returned from across the Atlantic in bars of Swiss chocolate, manufactured according to the process invented by Herr Uhlich, an unsuccessful clockmaker.

In order to pay less and sell for more, currency became the standard exchange. The customs house of Seville fixed rates of exchange that some decades later would be regulated by private, not state, powers in the stock markets of Amsterdam, Novaya Gorod, or London. (Astuteness on the part of pirates gradually transformed into technocrats.)

An increasing number of entrepreneurs imported illumi-
nation for moonless nights, but soon the practice became a
widespread vice. Many trafficked in salvation, invented all
manner of physical and metaphysical diversions: horse races,
German philosophy, soccer, Lovaina theology.

The Spanish were generous; they educated the natives so
they too could enjoy the Europeans' well-being.

The first methods for conserving frost were imported.
This facilitated the concoction of cool coconut milk drinks
and rum and coke cocktails. Expensive orgeat and *chilate*
drinks. Everyone seemed caught up in the craze for coolness. (In the refrigeration industry, as in many other areas,
the Iberians were soon displaced by blond pirates who unloaded their products by night and then "unloaded" them
at unfair prices. William Westinghouse and Jan Philips,
great wholesalers in temperature control, were outstanding in
this trade.)

The Indian sandal was replaced by espadrilles. Beautiful
feathers were exported in huge quantities for the use of
chorus girls, diplomats, and European admirals. Spring water
was bottled, labeled with its medicinal properties, and sold
at the cost of gold. Dr. Chanca opened a private sanatorium
and pharmacy.

There was even an industry for group outings. (The
pirate Cook would replace the Iberians in this business as
well.) Gods, burial grounds, and pyramids were transformed
into items for museums or sites for excursions.

From the beginning, faith was a centerpiece of industry.
There was mass importation of altars, cassocks, and chasubles
from Gamerilli, censers, religious prints in color or black and

white, Bibles, crucifixes, and catechism manuals to suit every pocket. The essence of monotheism must be learned by heart. Any person who did not know perfectly "There is but one true God" and "You shall have no other god before me" would be flayed.

Bishop Landa, who burned nearly all the Maya codices, would synthesize the essence of those years of frenetic *doing* in the epilogue to his famous *Relación*: "The Indians have gained immeasurably with the arrival of the Spanish nation. They now have, and will have in increasing number, many things that with the passage of time they will by necessity learn to enjoy: horses, mules, dogs, asses (difficult to breed), hens, oranges, melons, figs, pomegranates, the use of money, and many other things which, although the Indians had not known and had managed without, will by the having of them cause them to live more like men. Above all else, those things that have been granted them without cost: Justice, Christianity, and Peace."

The plants, the great trees, the jaguars, were the first to discover the imposture of the false gods.

The families of monkeys, so nervous and lively in their reactions, realized, too, that the peasants and blacksmiths were using their scythes and hammers as instruments of destruction. It was absurd: they were cutting down the jungle along with the complex life it had contained since the beginnings of time. They were tearing out grasses and vines, burning foliage, until they had stripped a rectangular desert of bald earth. Then the white-faces labored day and night, sacrificing the happiness of their wives and children, and time for love and the gods, to the purpose of replanting. Their feeble mastic trees aroused the indignation of the ancient jungle.

They were "useful plants," in regimented rows, and their value was determined in the market.

The monkeys, almost simultaneously with Colonel Roldán, led the first American conspiracy. Although it was obvious they did not have the necessary forces, they surrounded the gigantic ceiba the humans called the Tree of Life. They howled without respite. They hurled excrement.

But the naked, rosy-fleshed man, the admiral, could not understand their language. With his customary vanity, he preferred to believe they were offering a kind of homage.

The monkeys then sought the aid of the jaguars and the Carib Indians (eternally bellicose and resentful because of their legendary ugliness). The cats clawed apart a family of Asturian settlers and badly wounded a Basque who was planting garlic and tobacco (already an agent for the gringo Dunhill). But without effect.

The happy palm trees were decimated. The pallid barbarians did not understand that palms are like simple and happy young girls at the seashore.

Two respected and sacred *vivarós* were hacked down to make the counter and benches for a tavern built by Domingo de Bermeo, who sold the surplus wood for a row of kneelers in the cathedral.

The great *vera*, the most important female tree in the region (plants tend toward a matriarchate), convinced them that it was a losing battle; these pale men were cursed with a bent for extermination. The intruders had forgotten their relation with the Great All-Being; they were traitors to the eternal brotherhood of life. Depraved, but joyless in their depravity. As for their leader, the admiral, the *vera* warned: "He is a dreamer. Do not trust him. He has lost sight of reality."

Where the white ones advanced, the natural order was shattered. They even diverted streams to water their vine-yards, not knowing that those delicate silver ribbons that run through the jungle are sacred: they are strands of life demanding the greatest respect, arteries of the great body of the world.

Mirrors of dead water severed from the Great Mother of Waters (she who maintains harmony between the heavens and the depths of the earth) appeared everywhere. They were mere puddles, stagnant pools that had lost their purity and pulsing and life. Soon they gave off a terrible stench, became breeding beds for toads, and caused epidemics of colitis among the Iberians.

The exodus of the big cats toward the wooded hills was pitiful to see. The colonies of monkeys trooped into exile in long night marches. "We shall return! Forward to victory!" But who could believe them?

So serious was the aggression that even the frivolous macaws and birds of paradise, weary of having their long feathers stolen to adorn the hats of Italian swashbucklers, flew off toward the interior, relinquishing forever the joy of falling to sleep to the sound of the sea in the dark night.

•

After the murder of Bimbú, repeated rapes, and epi-
sodes of transvestism and sadism, the conviction grew among
the chiefs that they had made a deplorable theological error
in regard to the bearded ones from across the sea.

The invasion was without doubt genocidal. The Spanish
were the new cannibals, capable of devouring the cannibals
themselves.

In Vega Real and Xaragua, the supposed gods demonstrated that they were in fact the feared *tzitzimins*.

From the day they had encountered Europe and the
bearded ones, that is, since October 12, 1492 (according to
the non-Venusian calendar of the pale ones), they had submitted docilely to the malodorous "divinities."

They had accepted slavery with resignation because the
Fourth Sun had expired and the cassocked covey had explained that "life is a vale of tears."

When brutal *encomenderos* lashed and cudgeled them,
they struggled to their feet in order to offer them the other
cheek and the unbeaten parts of their bodies, as they had
been advised by Padre Valverde.

They fulfilled the Christian teachings to the letter. After
they had been tortured (blinded and castrated to force them
to reveal the location of deposits of pearls and gold), they
picked up their clothing, bowed, and thanked the gods with
evangelical orthodoxy:

"I forgive you, great lord, for what you have done. Do
you wish to beat me again?"

The lords spit sunflower seeds, swallowed a sip of brandy,
and muttered:

"Fool! Get out of my sight!"

If one of their daughters was raped, with diligence and Franciscan abnegation they went to their cane huts to seek out their youngest, huddling in terror, and led them to the rapists, receiving nothing in return.

Their early stringent orthodoxy, however, began to erode as they discovered that they had trapped themselves in a gross error.

"If this is Christ, then Christ is criminal," was the thought of the elder *caciques*.

Anacaona and Siboney, more clever and worldly than others, learned to use to their own advantage the insatiable lust of the Iberians and a few of the Genoese. (Bartolomé Colón believed he had conquered his own forever in Vega Real.) But almost all the Indian women became slaves or servants.

Their dances, like the *areito* and the *naual*, so graceful and healthily erotic, degenerated into whorehouse rumbas and *milongas* (no one was interested in refined hand movements or how they used their eyes; only the unimaginative, uninterrupted trembling of naked buttocks was appreciated).

The murder of the beautiful Bimbú was a warning. Evidence of future horror was overt once the crier read Roldán's ordinance about "branding and earmarks for beasts of burden and natives." Husbands and fathers were to appear in the cathedral plaza with their women and children, even the youngest, to be branded. Human beings were marked with a G, probably derived from *guerra*, the word for war. An *encomendero* could add a personal mark if it had been previously registered in the Office of Patents and Trademarks.

This practice made traffic in concubines and servants more orderly, and averted disputes when the princesses were stakes in a card game. All transactions were to be business-like, and recorded by a scribe. This would help lend stability and security to the natives' lives.

The duty of guarding the huts where the workers slept was assigned to dogs, usually German shepherds. They were unrelenting in tracking runaways and quick to smell out any suspicious activity. They came to have such importance that some of these zealous guardians of Christian order were the subject of biographies. The chronicler Oviedo, for example, extolled the moral influence of one Becerillo in these words: "He was a ferocious canine defender of the Catholic faith and of sexual morality; he tore apart more than two hundred Indian idolators, sodomites, and other abominable offenders, having with the years become increasingly fond of human flesh."[3]

Cases of collective suicide are recorded in the "Hordancas para el Tratamiento de Indios" (Zaragoza, 1518).

Groups closed themselves in their huts and set fires of poisonous smoke. They tied stones around their necks and threw themselves into rivers, following the lead of the family patriarch. They hanged themselves from sacred trees.[4]

---

[3]Author's note: Fernández de Oviedo, *Historia General y Natural de Indias*, v. 10. Also deserving of biographies by Juan José Arrom, Herrera, Chalevoix, and others were Becerillo's son Leoncico, Bruto, Amadis, Calisto, and Amigo. Colonel Roldán organized a canine commission, guardian of public morality and censorship. In this, too, he was a precursor.

[4]Author's note: Please refer to statistics on p. 240.

But nothing was more scandalous than the conduct of Captain López de Ávila, one of Colonel Roldán's men, with the Princess Anaó.

In the course of suppressing an uprising, Anaó was taken prisoner. She had promised her husband, one of the warriors who had rebelled against the women-branders, that she would never allow herself to be possessed by another man.

This is what Friar Landa, who observed the events with Franciscan tolerance, wrote in Chapter XXXII of his *Relación*: "The native women were valued for their uprightness. And with reason, for before they knew our nation, Spain, they were without equal—according to the elders who lament their condition today. Of this I shall give one example; Captain Alonso López de Ávila, a brother-in-law of Montejo, captured a genteel and comely Indian woman. Fearing she might not be killed in war, she had promised her husband to know no man but him. The usual methods of persuasion were insufficient to prevent her from taking her own life rather than be sullied by another man. For which reason she was thrown to the dogs."

Landsknecht Todorov, who helplessly witnessed this atrocity, thought he would go mad. The philosopher Jean-Loup Vasselin, who had already sent his *Traité de la Modération* to the Royal Academy in France, seized the first opportunity and returned to his native land with a shipload of Brazilian timber destined for Cádiz.

Shortly after, Landa was appointed Bishop of Yucatán.

The *Tecuhtli* of Tlatelolco must be notified; he had sailed home with supreme pride at having corroborated the fulfillment of the prophecy: the return of Quetzalcoatl and his minor divinities.

The poets wrote the text of the message to be sent with the swiftest of their messengers:

It is ended.
The mother says, lifting up her
newborn child: "O little one! O my son!
You have come into this world to suffer;
To suffer and lament in silence!
From the East came the bearded ones,
the false messengers of the sign,
the foreigners,
the rosy-cheeked men.

Ay! We grieve because they have come,
because they have arrived, the great pilers
of stone, of roof poles for building,
with fire at the end of their arms.
We grieve because they have come!
Our gods shall return no more!
This "true god from the heavens"
will speak only of sin,
only of sin will be his teaching.
Inhumane are his soldiers,
cruel his fierce mastiffs.

Only for the time of madness,
only for the mad black-robed priests
were we made Christians.

It was the beginning of misery,
the beginning of tribute,
the beginning of beggary.

We are sure. We have lived the reality.
The era of Sun in Movement has begun,
which follows the ages of Air,
Fire, Water, and Earth. This is
the beginning of the last age; the kernel
of destruction and death has been
sown. The Sun in Movement; the Sun
on earth, that shall pass."

(*Book of the Ancestors* from
Chilam Balam de Chumayel)

The Taino emissary never reached the *tecuhtli*. The ferocious mastiffs tore him to bits before he sailed.

The text, recovered by Roldán's men, is to be found in the Vienna Museum of History, in the same case as the feather crown of the emperor Moctezuma.

•

Nothing altered the calm of the admiral, who was convinced that the disturbing events Padre Las Casas had recounted were merely temporary, the delayed response of people who after centuries of wickedness could not accept the blessings of Paradise. Though it was foundering, they still clung to the doomed ship of Evil.

"It will pass, it will pass. *Tutto finisce*," he murmured, absorbed in the fascinating intimate world, the stirrings and whispers, of the jungle.

"You hear that, Padre? You hear? That is the moan of the wild orchids."

Las Casas felt powerless; the admiral seemed not to believe the violence occuring on the coast:

"They are exporting angels! Yesterday they shipped off five hundred of them to be sold in Seville." But it was pointless to continue.

What's more, the admiral was not compatible with the future bishop. He felt that the bishop's rational ravings fell far short of his own imagination. When he spoke to him of theology, it seemed to him that it was as if the priest were trying to control and study the Ocean Sea by pouring it into empty mineral-water bottles.

Things were more complicated in this later stage. The admiral was curled up in time like a cat on a hearth. He was lounging in *being*, and little by little everything human was growing dim.

When he heard the news of Ulrich Nietz's expedition, Las Casas felt completely alone. The Landsknecht seemed freed of a terrible incubus. His head was in the clouds; he was chafing to march to the shore to communicate his awful knowledge.

He ventured a comment about Las Casas's unwavering faith:

"Can it be that this young saint has been here in the jungle and not heard that God is dead?"

Three attitudes of great significance were taking shape: the admiral in his contemplative state was, to put it in traditional terms, already saved; Landsknecht Nietz, risen from the abyss of madness, was eager to encourage man to take the place of the now defunct Ancient of Days; and Las Casas, the incorrigible Judeo-Christian, was less interested in living than in dying and seeing God.

Each of the three men was indifferent to the other two (Roldán and Buil could sleep in peace). The only thing that bound them together was the fact they were living beneath the same canopy, the Tree of Life.

People who had followed them at the beginning had now abandoned them. They wanted more excitement. The modest joys and frustrations of everyday life.

The little mute dogs remained faithful, nosing among the hammocks and lean-tos. What did they divine in these men from distant lands?

The Indians, disoriented by the lack of activity of these three gods from the sea, had passed from adoration to indifference. They had heard rumors of what was happening at the beach, and had watched the human exodus following the footsteps of the monkeys and jaguars (the beginnings of the physical and psychological retreat that has lasted five centuries).

From time to time the admiral emerged from the lethargy of the reunited and reluctantly talked with the other two.

"Have you noticed, Landsknecht Nietz? The days are growing longer. The net of time is unraveling. It makes little sense to speak of 'day,' 'night,' 'week,' 'year.' The words are mere illusions. Tricks to measure us, control us, subject us. What does 'youth' mean now? 'Old age'? 'Death'? What, for example, would you answer if I asked you how many days we have been here?"

"Four years!" Padre Las Casas replied impatiently.

"What, Padre, do you mean by 'four years'?"

"Four *years*."

"Four years?"

Las Casas did not know what to say. He could see that the admiral had, quite successfully, divorced himself from metrics, calendars, and the usual measurements of distance.

Colón continued:

"We are also losing harmful illusions about our supposed knowledge of space. . . . Is this the continuation of the world we knew? Can you add these thousands of leagues of unexplored land to the territory of Spain, say, or Andalusia? No! It would be like trying to add four hens and four guavas."

Las Casas listened helplessly. Colón concluded:

"We are in a different space. At last we are inside the world, *in* the world and not in reality, gaping for all eternity with our tailor's tape in our hand."

It was evident that the admiral had suffered a probably irreversible mutation. The rational consciousness characteristic of Occidental "men of reason" had forsaken him.

Unconsciously, whether as self-punishment or self-acclaim, he had been transformed into the first complete South American. Although he had not been born of carnal union between races, he was the first mestizo. A mestizo without an umbilicus. Like Adam.

Wise Taino elders and the *cacique* Guaironex analyzed the evolution—or involution—of that god from the sea who

behaved differently from the rest of his companions from
beyond the sea. They reasoned, correctly, that he would be
the first human to live in the new cycle of the Black Sun.

This new creature lived in a state of apathy, without
high expectations or explicit despair. Abandoned by Prometheus.

He surrendered completely to idle hours in his hammock. He ate what grew around him or fell from the trees,
without a trace of nostalgia for red meat—or, in his case,
pasta. What did he eat? Bananas, sweet potatos, salted ants,
quantities of coconut milk, mango juice.

His days were long and uneventful. Neither subsistence
nor existence pried him from his hammock. A few yawns
could occupy twenty minutes. By now he had lost all notion
of time as he had known it!

In his mind, where rational corridors and cables had
ceased to function, memory and reality, as in dreams, blended
into a single continuum, so that verb tenses—past, present,
and future—were lumped together in the oblivion of a gram-
matical museum.

The Taino shamans concluded that drugs were not indi-
cated; his internal capacity for the secretion of delirium was
perfect, perhaps of a level as high as that of the poet-king
Nezahualcoyotl. So in his case they omitted the *peyotl* and
ayahuasca usually so effective in counteracting the brutalizing
effect of reason.

The river of thought and dream flowing through the
admiral's mind had taken on an American coloration. The
black-and-white gothic landscapes of Castile illuminated by
the light of human bonfires had been replaced by gentler
images. When Anacaona appeared, the princess who with her

unfortunate husband Caonabó had been carried back to Spain, her image invariably fused (again, the mestizo) with that of the unforgettable vision of Simonetta Vespucci as Venus in the Botticelli painting commissioned by Lorenzo the Magnificent. But Anacaona's legs were like two bow shafts stretching toward a central fire, and Simonetta's hair, the color of old gold, like the autumn dusk above the Arno.

Isabel walked by in the clothes she had worn at the siege of Granada, but against a background of palm trees. Then La Beltraneja with her bay percherons. Far in the distance, as if in the depths of time, Beatriz Arana, seated on a keg of leeches, awaiting her executioners.

All these figures from memory had in common a certain indolence: they stretched, they drowsed, they gazed at geraniums. Everything merged into synthesis or symbol (as in dreams), the years of terror in Castile reduced to black mantilla-draped shadows of women on their way to seven-o'clock mass.

These are lethargic memories that lead neither to drama nor to historical grandeur. Even the fiery Beatriz Bobadilla appeared several times in the penumbra of the loveshrine, lying on her bed of snow-white fleece, but she is a blue-black panther with the green eyes that transfix her victim before she springs.

A new form of imagination is in gestation. The cinammon skin of Siboney, the black flowers along tropical trails. The alleged perfidy of Anacaona.

The admiral passes carefree hours beneath the branches of the Tree of Life.

*   *   *

Las Casas set out along the ascending path Ulrich Nietz had exhausted days before. He was borne along on the wind of faith: he was seeking God in His essential invisibility.

He found the marble gates and other irrefutable traces of the One God. Item: a waterfall crashing on rocks below, producing a deafening roar and generating a mist with the seven primordial colors of creation. Item: a beetle with golden dots on its back. Item: a serpent with a clearly drawn Christian cross just below its head. Item: no fewer than a dozen gigantic butterflies dusted with the Vatican colors, a delicate yellow and a white like powdered sugar.

He had no doubts. He had found sufficient proof. He had been trained to understand God from the aspect of absence. The presence of His great absence, to state it with the precision of the eminent men of the Church. He fell into a profound prayer of celebration and gratitude. On his knees in the mud, he endured a series of nocturnal downpours. A real drenching, but he was sustained by an inner warmth that kept his skin dry. The electric charge of faith.

In the depths of his soul he had heard the silence of God, grave and expressive.

He noticed that the sign of the petrified serpents was repeated in several stone ruins glimpsed through the lianas. Beyond shadow of doubt, this was the symbol of God's fury toward the instrument of temptation. He found an enormous anaconda head, similarly petrified.

He had his evidence of the language and designs of God. God's fingerprints were more prominent here in this abandoned Paradise than anywhere in his creation. Even the most incompetent investigator would find overwhelming proof of the unmistakable will of the All-Powerful.

He returned more sure than ever of his pastoral mission. Now, shoulder to the wheel!

He passed by the Tree of Life, stopping only long enough to retrieve his cassock, wrinkled and faded by the rains. He barely greeted Landsknecht Swedenborg. The admiral was sleeping.

•

Death descended. Everything changed in Castile. The bells of Salamanca, Arévalo, Segovia, and Madrid tolled dolefully. Clappers muted in black cloth. Gray peals.

There had been somber news in the course of recent years. The plague of the Indies, syphilis, was rampant. Brothels had lost their medieval gaiety. Shameful pustules and chancres. Lead salts (the same treatment François I would recommend to Carlos V) were imported from the Hanseatic cities. The long era of venereal peril began, the curse of the body that would endure slightly longer than the Inquisition itself (until the discovery of penicillin).

Multiple misfortunes befell Fernando and Isabel; their first daughter, the Queen of Portugal, died, and also their grandson *don* Miguel. Juana, hypersensitive, married to Felipe the Handsome, was in the throes of a severe crisis; she was blind with jealousy. Half naked, beneath stormy skies, she had perched above the iron gate of the castle of Medina del Campo and refused to come down.

Torquemada died, and with him the empire lost the machinery of collective guilt. He lived seventy-five years of untiring redemptive cruelty. One morning he was found in his bed, inanimate, cold, covered in a thick powder of sperm. Successive layers of dried semen on his thighs, like sheets of mica, had turned into an odorless powder as his body heat evaporated. The clinging odor of French pissoir that accompanied him throughout his life had dissipated. A number of Catholic chroniclers, misled by the absence of stench, ventured to record that "he died in an aroma of sanctity."

But their greatest sorrow, their major misfortune, was the death of Prince Juan, the favorite son, the newly married heir, only twenty years old. The delicate and marvelous Prince Juan, educated in *belles lettres*, in holy war, in elegance.

The physical debility and delicacy of that son who had not inherited his parents' angelical terribleness had always terrified Isabel, but she had never thought he would die as he had, of love. Incapable of sustaining his erotic obsession for the beautiful Margaret of Austria.

He had grown so weak in the abuse of the gods that in the last months he lost all defenses against worldly reality: the glimpse of a hunchback or an ugly spinster was enough to bring on a fever. During a banquet he had fainted when the tenor missed the high notes of a *romanza*.

As Isabel was traveling to Medina del Campo to try to dislodge her daughter from above the gate, Fernando was informed of the serious illness of the prince, and he raced toward Salamanca without stopping at posthouses.

When he arrived, he realized that the proximity of

death had reversed normal roles: the prince was the father of his father the king.

"Father," Juan said to him. "I have known nothing but happiness, love, and gifts. Let us accept the will of God with humility."

The king wept silently, almost with a peasant's fathomless grief. He kissed the delicate hands of his exhausted, defeated son. He told him:

"My beloved son, you must answer now that God calls you. For He is above any other king, and has for you kingdoms and dominions greater than those that were yours or to be yours."

That night Pietro Martire wrote: "With his demise were lost the hopes of all Spain."

Death, in all its might and power, struck the queen, never to leave her. Her world whirled around her. She had to fall back toward the palace of medieval metaphysics from which she had fled with Fernando during the creative years of the parabola of the Renaissance. Her passion for the Earthly Paradise, and her faith in her body and the fiesta of action were mortally wounded.

When Fernando informed her of the worst news she could hear, she merely murmured:

"The Lord giveth and the Lord taketh away. Amen."

The adventure of the terrible adolescents was abruptly terminated. Isabel's face sagged; she was struck by illness: an insatiable thirst. She turned her back to the world and set her gaze on the realms of the beyond. She would grope her way through icy mists, desolate, searching for the face of her most beloved son, Prince Juan, already in the world of the dead.

It was the end of the sect of the seekers of the Earthly Paradise.

King Fernando passed from grief to resentment, as if he had been cheated or deceived. Devastated by sorrow, he spent hours meditating on the "curse of America." The figure of the admiral was never far from the horizon of his wrath.

As a distraction, he devoted furious energy to matters of state.

In a black mood, he studied all communications from the Indies, and listened to the slander and envy circulating in the court. He was informed about the ordinances, the rebellion of Roldán, the concerns of the church hierarchy.

He had always considered Colón a mystic without temporal loyalties, an extremely dangerous species.

He brooded over the fact that because of him the New World was divinely interdicted, its arable lands covered by the cloak of God, a property owner who forbade use of his lands in his absence.

Worst of all, the admiral had had the gall to propose that the natives were angels. Not even slaves to be bought and sold. Fernando settled the matter: he declared that they were vassals, and capable of being converted to Christianity. That is, they were not divine property, nor chattel of the Spanish rabble that had confiscated them.

Then, with almost no delay, Fernando acted: he summoned Commander Francisco de Bobadilla and appointed him his plenipotentiary.

That same gray afternoon in Castile, amid the sound of muffled drums and the interminable litany from the chapel of ladies-in-waiting reciting the rosary with Isabel, he signed the order for the arrest of Colón and his men. It was March 21, 1499.

•

He surrendered peacefully. Any man who has passed the threshold of the Open is forever immune to the trivialities of the apparential world.

Colonel Roldán was clever enough to manipulate the temporary power of Commander Bobadilla (he yielded to his authority with the same tactical skill Hitler would employ centuries later with Marshal Hindenburg). He volunteered to command the party detached to the Tree of Life.

The admiral seemed unsurprised when he saw the party erupt from the jungle. They surrounded his hammock, kicking aside dozens of indifferent dogs that seemed accomplices to the lassitude of the gray-haired man who spent his days dozing beneath the Tree of Life.

"Your excellency, I arrest you under order of their majesties the king and queen." These were Bobadilla's only words.

His subordinates rushed forward. They clothed the admiral in a Franciscan robe, as if Colón's Arcadian nakedness were his most serious crime and constituted a criminal offense against public decency.

Rattle of chains and shackles. Quinteros and the cook Excobar had brought them in a box of irons. (Since the first days of the revolution, Padre Buil had generously placed at

Colonel Roldán's disposition all the instruments of inquisitorial procedures. Ever since, in America, repression would have the profound flavor of redemptive, pastoral, exorcising torture.)

The admiral, patiently seated in the hammock, observed as they hammered the heavy fetters around his ankles. He marveled that they erred only once.

The march toward the coast was slow and humiliating. The secretary, who had kept the required record of events, attempted to make conversation with the royal paymaster to mask the sound of irons rattling with every step.

Colón's brother Bartolomé, secular head of government, was arrested along with all the other Colóns: cheesemakers, tailors, and weavers who were making their mark in commerce and industry.

His weary eyes, grown accustomed to the filtered light of the jungle, were dazzled by the brilliant light of the coast.

There was one principal street (which in time would be called Colón Boulevard). It led to the plaza and the cathedral, still mainly of logs but beginning to be sheathed with carved stones taken from the native pyramids and temples.

All along this main street, the crowd hurled insults:

"Admiral of gnats!"

"Impostor! Jew swine!"

Captive to the vision of boundlessness, he could not judge them. He felt neither meekness nor anger. Not even scorn.

During the time he had lain beneath the Tree of Life, *doing* had obviously powerfully consolidated itself. The Hegelian "man of reason" had implacably gained the upper hand. Everyone, including his relatives, was busily sacking Paradise.

The angels, scourged, emaciated, had been apportioned among the *encomienda* owners. Decimated by suicides and labor deep in the mines. Victims of progress. Forever severed from the soul of the world in which they had lived as brother to papaya and puma.

The admiral was disconsolate.

"Man destroys what he says he loves most," he murmured.

During that humiliating procession, he had come to realize that his civilized fellows feared nothing so much as a return to primordial harmony. That they had been diabolically diverted to find their pleasure in sorrow. That like most readers of Dante, they preferred Hell to Heaven.

It was clear: after the brief shock of the Ordinances, they were once again comfortably engaged in exploitation, the ardors of happiness, and the effort to hold decency above the countless temptations of vileness. It was a game, or a vice, guaranteed by Roldán's immutable order.

Nostalgic, nevertheless, on Sundays they purified themselves of weekday evil. Squarcialuppi and the brand-new crew of Italian priests reminded them from the pulpit of the blessings of Paradise. Exhorted them to be unconditional supporters of Good.

The admiral observed that in addition to the cathedral, many other buildings were being constructed of masonry or adobe. He marveled at the profusion of signs: Santángel Bank & Hawkins Ltd., Bologna Beauty Salon, Palace of the Inquisition (Semper Veritas), Cook Travel Agency, United Fruit Company, Castile Hotel, Sagardúa Buffet.

*   *   *

Then came the day no one could have imagined, nor been militarily prepared to respond to: the amazing revolt of the dogs.

It was a silent invasion. More passive resistance than assault.

An army of the diminutive dogs of Paradise (nostalgic for Adam, the admiral and Landsknecht Swedenborg believed). Undersized, voiceless beasts so undoglike that the first Spanish chroniclers had even denied their genus, as Heidegger would say, their "essence of dogness." Some described them as a "species of edible rodents that do not bark but shriek if beaten." These chroniclers did not suspect that their souls, absorbed from dead or vanished masters, were guiding them toward the Great All-Being after the alarms of life. (The Toltecs had sanctified them and included them in the Calendar. Any dog might be a *nahual*, the repository of a suffering human soul.)

The settlers watched them swarm down the dunes toward the town, like a flowing mantle, unafraid of the fiercely barking mastiffs or the shouts and musket fire of guards unable to stem the canine tide.

They filled every corner of the town. They did not bite, not even the children. They did not howl. All they did was urinate wherever they could: walls, supplies, on any motionless vertical surface (including the boots of the blind Landsknecht Osberg de Ocampo, who never listened to what anyone was telling him).

Insignificant, always denigrated, now in numbers they formed a mammoth and formidable beast. Their enormous, peaceful, silent presence was terrifying.

La Diabla closed the doors of her establishment and gathered her pupils on the upper floors, in the Paris salon.

Shouts, cries, ringing swords. Young children galloping madly about, crazy with joy once they learned the dogs would not bite.

The dogs held the city in thrall for more than an hour.

By midafternoon they decided to retreat to the jungle. Since that day, and for all time, these standard-bearers of nostalgia have declared rebelliousness through lack of action. They did not fade into remote forests with the arrogance of the jaguars, or flee to high treetops like the quetzals and delicate orchids. Ever since, in silent packs, they have wandered field and town, from Mexico to Patagonia. Rarely, spurred by extreme hunger, they have attacked sheep and horses. (Stories of these episodic assaults abound in the viceregal history of Río de la Plata and Nueva Granada. Once, after the turn of the twentieth century, the dogs even surrounded and cut off a small military fort.)

They are ubiquitous, these irrelevant creatures no kennel club would register.

The small disciplinary party headed by Colonel Roldán finally reached the coast.

As the admiral stepped into the yawl that would ferry him to the caravel of his deportation to Spain, he saw on the beach great piles of the carved marbles of the Gate. A chain of forced laborers up to their waists in water were loading the blocks. He lifted a hand to the son of the *cacique* Guaironex, and to the bearded rebel Mordecai, who was paying dearly for his ideas on redemption.

The carved stones, numbered with carbon according to the plan of the specialists who had dismantled the *zócalo*, were being shipped at the request of the Catholic University of Brussels, where a section of "Amerindian Archaeology" had already been opened and the stones of the Indian temple square would be installed.

The admiral looked toward the decimated palm grove that once had murmured a whisper of welcome; he saw the forced laborers and the large mustaches and gunbelts of Roldán and his men. He realized that America would remain in the hands of tinhorn dictators and autocratic *corregidores*, like the palace of his childhood, seized by lackeys who had known how to steal the arms for themselves.

Invincible, he murmured:

"Purtroppo c'era il Paradiso."

TRANSLATOR'S NOTE

Translators inevitably call upon countless resources, both friends and the printed word, for information and terminology beyond their personal knowledge. In addition to those anonymous but greatly appreciated collaborators, I wish to acknowledge specific translations and studies that eased the passage of this novel into English:

The Voyages of Christopher Columbus, tr. Cecil Jane (London: The Argonaut Press, 1930)

The Journal of Christopher Columbus, tr. Cecil Jane (revised and annotated by L. A. Vigneras; London: The Hakluyt Society, 1960)

The Log of Christopher Columbus, tr. Robert H. Fuson (Camden, Me.: International Marine Publishing Company, 1987)

The Other Bible, ed. Willis Barnstone (San Francisco: Harper & Row, 1984)

Columbus' Ships, José María Martínez-Hidalgo, ed. Howard I. Chapelle (Barre, Ma., 1966)